I think back to Mount Rainier, where Miles and I camped. A national park means a lot of out-of-the-way places to hide, which is exactly what we need if Miles is going to wake.

If. That word is like a punch to my gut, and the misgivings I've dammed up for the past few hours flood in to drown me.

If. How can two little letters hold so much importance? Wield so much power? How is a single stunted syllable able to threaten a world of pain and simultaneously dangle a glimmering, flashing jewel of hope?

If Miles awakes, he will be a changed person. He will have the gift of life: free of disease and aging. *If* he doesn't, then the one person who matters most to me—outside my clan, of course—will be gone. Abruptly. And forever.

ALSO BY AMY PLUM

After the End

The Die for Me series

Novels
Die for Me
Until I Die
If I Should Die

Novellas
Die for Her
Die Once More
Inside the World of Die for Me

UNTIL
THE
BEGINNING

YA
FIC
Plum
2016

AMY PLUM

An Imprint of HarperCollinsPublishers

HarperTeen is an imprint of HarperCollins Publishers.

Library of Congress Cataloging-in-Publication Data

Plum, Amy.

Until the beginning / Amy Plum. — First edition.

    pages   cm

Sequel to: After the end.

Summary: "With the help of her friend Miles, Juneau continues her desperate search to find and rescue her clan, but the same forces that abducted her people are after her because, unbeknownst to Juneau, she is the answer to unraveling an ancient secret that could change the world"— Provided by publisher.

ISBN 978-0-06-222564-1

[1. Extrasensory perception—Fiction.   2. Nature—Fiction.   3. Love—Fiction.]   I. Title.

PZ7.P7287Up   2015   2014038504

[Fic]—dc23   CIP

                                                                       AC

Typography by Ray Shappell

16 17 18 19 20 PC/RRDH 10 9 8 7 6 5 4 3 2 1

First paperback edition, 2016

For Gretchen, for survival,
and for closing the book on our own Alaska

"I'M A SCIENTIST, NOT A THEOLOGIAN. I DON'T know if there is a God or not. Religion requires certainty. Revere and respect Gaia. Have trust in Gaia. But not faith."
—James Lovelock, author of the Gaia hypothesis

1

JUNEAU

MILES HAS BEEN DEAD FOR ONE HOUR. I DO NOT know if it is true death—if he died of blood loss after I dug the bullet out of him—or if this is the death-sleep that I summoned by giving him the Rite. There is only one way to find out, and that is to wait seven more hours and see if he starts breathing again.

I rise and leave my post at the door. Turning away from the blazing red of the sunbaked desert, I enter the cool darkness of the one-room shack. My vision swims as my eyes adjust, and it is a few seconds before I can see him. Not him. His shell.

The vacuum left by his spirit's departure pulls me across the room, and I stand over him, looking down at his naked body. He is a study in white and red: The little bit of skin that isn't smeared with clotted blood is the shade of curdled milk. Honey-colored curls brush his paste-white forehead. His lips are parted, his jaw loose. Blood is smudged across his cheek, but whether it is his or mine I don't know.

I hold up my palm and see that blood still oozes from where I cut myself with the ceremonial knife. The contents of my bag are strewn across the floor. I squat down, and from the pile of stones, dried herbs, and feathers, I pull a strip of cotton and wrap it tightly around my hand to bind my wound.

And with that small, final act of caring for myself, I am suddenly drained of my adrenaline-fueled vigilance. My defenses finally down, the full force of what I have done strikes me. I sit down on the floor, resting my head in my hands.

I may have killed this boy. I may have sent him away forever.

I performed a ritual on him—gave him a powerful drug—that has only been used on members of my clan. On people who were ready for it, whose spirits already embraced the Yara. Who looked to Gaia for strength.

And Miles . . . he is not strong. He wants to be. There is much in him that is good. But he hasn't even started thinking about his place on earth . . . his part in the superorganism that makes up Gaia.

Never mind spiritual strength; all of my previous Rite-travelers were in perfect physical condition when I led them into death-sleep. They weren't like Miles, barely conscious with a bullet freshly dug out of his side. He had lost a lot of blood. Was already dying.

What have I done?

Miles could be lost in death, unable to find his way back. Unable to recognize the signposts along his path. That is . . . if he is actually in death-sleep and didn't undergo true death before the Rite took effect.

I push myself to my feet. I can't lose hope. I must treat Miles as if he were any other Rite-traveler. He *did* take the vow. He agreed to become one with the Yara. To dedicate his life to the earth and the force that binds every living thing together. And to trade his short human life for one that could last hundreds of years, if not more.

He agreed to it all. But it was a spontaneous decision, made in a desperate moment. What would happen to him if it wasn't truly sincere?

"He chose it," I say to reassure myself. In the dead quiet my words sound hollow. Meaningless.

I walk across the room to him and begin humming the Song of the Path. And as I do, I am pulled back into the trancelike state that cocoons me when I perform the Rite. I leave my fear behind and immerse myself in what I am supposed to do. What I was taught to do.

The candles forming a halo around his head flicker their last, casting an eerie light on his marble face. I blow them out one by one as I walk in a circular path around his body. One candle for each turn.

My breath slows as the last candle goes dark and I begin singing the words, willing Miles to move toward death's gate. To approach it, to brush it with his fingertips, and then to turn and come back to land of the living. To me.

I untie the cloths binding the gold nuggets to the soles of his feet as the words drop from my lips. I replace the stones to their leather bag and stow them carefully in my backpack. And still I sing.

Like my clan members who I accompanied, I am Miles's companion in this Rite. Someone who knows him and cares about him. Who will ease his passage to the hinterlands of death and back to life—a different life—one without aging or disease.

I take his cold, bloody fingers and unwrap them from the moonstones they clasp. I tuck the gems into my bag, and continue working methodically, packing everything away: all of the herbs and minerals, the agate cup and blade, the leftover candles and matches. All the while, my words take Miles down the Stony Path toward the River.

When I'm done, I continue caring for Miles, peeling back the bandage I made by wrapping my shirt around his chest. Blood no longer flows from the bullet hole. I wonder if he will start bleeding again if I move him, and if he does, if it will make any difference.

I smooth back his hair, feeling his cold forehead under my fingertips. I brush his eyelids closed as I sing of what he will see on the Path, and touch his chin to shut his mouth. And then I do something I never did to my other Rite-travelers. I kiss him. I touch my warm mouth to his cold one and, closing my eyes, wish that I could transfer my life to him. That my spirit could slip out from between my lips and reignite his extinguished flame.

I have never known love—at least, nothing other than a child's love for her parents or the fierce love of friendship. So I don't know how to label what I feel for Miles. There is something there. An unopened bud. And I hope with all my heart that it won't die before it's able to start blooming. Before I can even tell what kind of flower it will be.

More emotion than I have let myself feel for a long time threatens to overwhelm me. For once, I allow it to come. My tears fall onto Miles's cheeks. Crying is a foreign thing to me, but I let it happen. Until finally, something shifts inside me and the tears stop. I feel empty but strong.

I take a deep breath and rise to my feet. It's time to go. I have to get him—us—away from here. I've done everything I can do to help him begin his path. I can continue the Song later.

I lean over the lifeless corpse of this boy who made me cry. And, though I know he can't hear me, I fold my arms across my chest and speak loudly and clearly. I speak to the Miles I know—the rebel, the boy who loves to break the rules. I dare him to take his wild, unfocused defiance and direct it toward the task he faces.

"Miles Blackwell," I challenge. "You better the hell live."

2

MILES

THE SCENE . . . IT KEEPS REPLAYING AS I SLEEP, over and over again like it's on loop.

It starts once again, as from the darkness I hear her voice. "Miles," she says, and it's like a pure musical note piercing through the thick fog enveloping me. "Miles, are you still here with me?"

My mouth is already open. All I have to do is push out the words, but it is like shoving a boulder up a hill to get them out. "I think so." I want to see her, but my eyes won't focus. She is an angel radiating a light so intense it has blurred her features.

"You have to swallow this," she says. I feel something warm touching my lips and a tangy paste being smeared onto my tongue, and then a flood of water cascading over my mouth, my face. I swallow automatically, and then choke and cough, spasms racking my body. She wipes my mouth with something soft.

The musical notes come again, penetrating the haze. "Miles Blackwell, do you hear me?"

"Yes," I hear myself respond.

She says something about the Yara. About my becoming one with it. About dedicating my life to the earth. I hear the words but they bounce off me, like I'm made of rubber. My words scratch against my throat. "Juneau, what the hell are you talking about?"

"Miles, do you agree to trade your life of eighty years for one of many hundred?" she continues.

And now my mind is clear enough that her words make sense. Juneau is giving me the Rite. She is giving me the drug that my father is so desperate for. She's trying to turn me immortal. I wrench my eyes back open, and there she is, shining like a supernova. "If I don't, do I die?" I ask.

"You might die anyway. But this is my best try," she confesses, and her eyes are tipped with flames. Flashing. Shining in the candlelight.

I fight to get the words out, but my voice is like dust. "Then I do, Juneau."

She moves around me and settles my head in her lap. She combs my hair with her fingers, and it feels like she's stroking my soul. Kneading it into a peaceful rest. I have been holding on so tightly that when I let go and breathe my last breath, it is a comfort. It is a relief.

Before the scene replays once again, there is a pause. It's long enough for me to formulate my thoughts into questions: Did this really happen? And if so, where am I now?

3

JUNEAU

ALTHOUGH WE'RE HIDDEN FROM THE MAIN ROAD, this deserted cabin a half hour outside Los Angeles won't hide us from our pursuers for long.

I breathe deeply until the hypnotic daze that floated me peacefully through the Rite evaporates and my mind is once again sharp and clear.

I assess Miles as I would a kill: height, weight, and shape of the animal needing to be shifted. Miles is probably six foot one and has an athletic build.

Even though I'm strong, he's close to a foot taller than me. It will be like transporting a yearling deer. *If I had my dogs and my leather puller, it wouldn't take more than a minute*, I think, and the husky-shaped hole in my chest threatens to reopen before I slap a bandage on it and resolve to think of them later.

I walk outside and cross the dusty yard to the car. The sun beats the desert around me into shimmering submission. Sweat beads on my forehead and under my arms as I drive the car as close as I can to the porch and dig a sleeping bag out of the trunk. Nothing moves in this punishing heat except a couple of lizards scuttling from one hole in the ground to another.

Once back in the cabin's dark coolness, I unzip the sleeping bag and spread it out next to Miles's body. And then, as carefully as I can, I roll him onto it, pull the loose side over him, and zip it up around him.

Grasping the top of the sleeping bag, I drag Miles out of the cabin onto the porch until he's next to the car, and open the back door. Wiping sweat from my eyes, I rummage through a box of tools in the trunk and find a length of thick, flat cord labeled TOW STRAP. Like a spider binds her victim, I wrap it up and down around Miles's sleeping-bag shroud. Then stringing the cord in through the backseat, and out the front seat, I anchor it to one of the posts holding up the shack's front porch roof. Using the same principle as my husky-puller dogsled technique, I drive the car forward a few feet, and Miles's body is shifted from the porch partway into the backseat. I'm able to wrangle him the rest of the way in.

Jogging back to the cabin, I grab my bag and give the empty room one last glance before closing the door. I don't want to leave any trace of our having been there, but seeing the pool of blood staining the floor, I realize the futility of that plan.

I toss my pack into the front seat and unzip the top of the

sleeping bag. Miles's mouth has fallen back open and his eyes stare blindly at the car's upholstered ceiling. I close them gently and hum a few more notes of the Song.

Before sliding into the driver's seat, I scan the horizon, and instantly my heart is in my throat. There is smoke—way off in the distance—in the direction we came from. I wonder what is burning. And then, suddenly and terrifyingly, I understand. It's a car, and it's heading directly toward us. It's still a long ways off, but I can see the flash of metal and the cloud of dirt kicked up by its wheels.

Immobilized by panic, I force myself to think. I need to hide us. In a split second I know what I have to do. I must Conjure the camouflage Whit used to hide our village from the outside world. Or, as he explained it to me back then, to protect us from the brigands when he Read they were coming. This was his most difficult Conjure—camouflaging the whole village and keeping it hidden until danger passed. But I need to reproduce it. I have camouflaged myself before, but have no idea if I can expand it outside myself to include the car and even the cabin if possible.

I try to remember what Whit did, and realize that the totem he used to Conjure the metamorphosis was the snowshoe hare feet. The one I tossed into a fire just days ago.

It doesn't matter, I remind myself. *You don't need Whit's material crutches to Conjure the Yara. You only need your faith in your link with it.* I think of the powerful connections I've experienced since I stopped using totems, and know I can do this. But I will need to push aside the fear and grief of the last few hours in order to concentrate.

I focus on slowing my racing heartbeat and spread my arms wide. I direct my mind to contact the Yara, and feel the lightning bolt of power when I connect with it. I call on the energy that flows through all things and imagine myself changing . . . transforming into the colors around me, which in this case is a uniform reddish dirt brown. I look down and see that not only my skin but my tank top and jeans have taken on the desert's brown. I blend in perfectly with my environment.

Now the car, I think, and imagine the Yara stretching out from me like a net and wrapping around the car. A dot of earthen red appears on one door, then spreads quickly to envelop the whole thing. Miles's car fades into the background and disappears.

My confidence is grounded. *I can do this.* I focus the Yara's energy on the cabin. I wait. Nothing happens, and the car is getting closer, maybe even close enough to see the cabin. And if they see it, they might stop to check it out and discover the pool of blood—evidence of how recently we were here.

My heart races, and I fight to maintain my calm. *Metamorphose!* I urge, and I feel a spark of electricity burning through my veins like flames. And as I watch, the shack disappears. We are now, for all practical purposes, invisible.

As the car approaches, I recognize the man riding in the passenger side. It is Murray Blackwell, head of Blackwell Pharmaceutical and father of the boy lying dead beside me. He must have mobilized this search party as soon as he discovered his son abducted me from his own house, where he was keeping me prisoner.

And all for a drug, I think. All because he wants to know the "formula" for the elixir—Amrit, as he called it—that I use to perform the Rite. He and whoever kidnapped my clan are desperate to get it. "Another example of violence spawned by capitalism," I can almost hear Dennis say—one of his favorite refrains in our Past Civilizations lessons. Now the infernal machine wants to suck *us* into its cogs and wheels, and I'm the only one left to fight it.

A burly man sits behind the wheel beside Mr. Blackwell, and the two security guards who kidnapped me from Salt Lake City are in the backseat, craning their heads to survey the barren landscape. The car moves so slowly that it seems like an hour before they pass us and are following the dirt road over the crest of a ridge.

I don't dare breathe. The Conjure weighs heavily on me. I'm pouring with sweat now, my clothes clammy against my skin. I flex my fingers and roll my head to both sides to avoid freezing up completely, and wait. In a couple of minutes, the car reappears at the top of the ridge. Its passengers scan the horizon, searching for what is right in front of them.

This time the car passes mere feet from me. Mr. Blackwell's eyes meet mine for just a second, and although he can't see me, panic scorches a jagged hole in the pit of my stomach. He looks away, and I can once again breathe. I wait until the car is out of sight, once more just a plume of dust on the horizon, before I let go of the Conjure. The car, the cabin, and I slowly infuse with our true colors. I lean back against the car, trembling from the effort and residual fear. *They were so close.*

But I had done it. I worked a major Conjure, and did it without a totem. A flash of hope bursts through me. I am capable of more than I imagined. My father's words come back to me, "You're a prodigy in the Yara, Juneau. Just like your mother was."

Whit kept so much from me, claiming that he was waiting until I was older. Until I had undergone the Rite myself. But I don't need his permission anymore. I don't need his questionable expertise, cobbled together from other belief systems and trial and error. I am ready to explore the Yara on my own terms.

My battle against my clan's kidnappers is just beginning. But instead of apprehension, I feel excitement. I've had a powerful weapon at my fingertips my whole life, and I'm finally learning to wield it. I feel unstoppable.

4

MILES

I AM BEING DRAGGED ALONG A CURRENT, FLOAT-
ing in a wide river with tall trees on either side. My body is pulled
under and pops back up as if I were nothing but a twig floating
on the surface of a stream. I am unafraid, my senses bathed by
the sound of the rushing water and the touch of the cool liquid.
Only the smell of the sparkling pure air in this dream world is
missing—absent because I do not breathe.

Someone is next to me. I can't turn my head, but I know it's
Juneau. She rides the river beside me. From somewhere far away
I hear music. Singing. An exotic tune, the words of which I can't
quite capture, but their purpose is clear. The song, like the silent
girl beside me, accompanies me. Wraps me in its security. Its confidence. Others have been here before, and the song accompanied
them, too.

A roaring noise grows louder every second—it is hollow, like the noise inside a seashell. The trees on either side of us disappear gradually, the riverbanks flattening out until finally I am thrust with great force out of the mouth of the river into an ocean so wide that no shore is visible. I can feel my body dissolving in the saltwater waves that toss me back and forth, and still Juneau is there. Staying close.

My body melts away until there is nothing left but a small white ball, feathers, beak, and a flash of light. And like that, I am sprung into the air. The words of the song grow clearer, and I sense another bird keeping pace with me, just outside my vision. I flap my wings, banking steeply as we climb together, high over the endless ocean. We catch the wind and soar.

5

JUNEAU

I SCRAMBLE INTO THE DRIVER'S SEAT, GRAB THE atlas off the floor, and open it to the map of California. On the way here, I was too busy concentrating on steering us through a car-chase shootout to keep track of directions. Now I have no clue where we are on the map. I scan the horizon through the dusty windshield. I have two choices: go out to the main road Mr. Blackwell and company just took, or follow the dirt road over the ridge to see where it leads.

I head for the ridge. Once on the other side, I stop the car and get out to look around. A desert vista spreads before me, ending at the foothills of green tufted mountains in the distance. *We could hide there,* I think. It's just a matter of crossing the flatlands before being swallowed by trees. But, not far along, the dirt road we're on narrows to little more than a path. *That must be why Mr.*

Blackwell and his men turned around, I think. And that's exactly why I'm going to follow it.

I get back in the car and check the clock on the dashboard. 3:24 p.m. Miles has been dead for almost two hours. Which means six hours to go. I need to get us somewhere safe before he awakes. *If he awakes.*

I put the car into drive and, without thinking, press my foot down hard. The wheels spin, throwing up a cloud of dust. I pick up my foot and let the forward motion of the car carry us a few yards before pressing down very lightly. The tires catch and the car moves smoothly ahead.

My first time driving was intimidating, especially since it involved stealing the car from under Miles's nose. But now I've figured out what most of the dials and buttons are for. In a way, I want to keep this car—the only one I've ever driven—for the security of its familiarity. It's everyone else's familiarity with it that's the problem.

Mr. Blackwell isn't the only one after us. I wonder what happened to Whit and his military thugs after they chased us through the desert and shot Miles as he drove. Even though I saw their jeep flip over, I didn't stick around to see how bad the damage was. They could have gotten their vehicle back on the road. And if they did, it won't be long before Whit tracks me down. Only weeks ago he was my mentor—and my clan's Sage. Not only is he skilled at Reading, but he knows me better than anyone besides my own father.

I drive toward the mountains for a half hour, seeing nobody.

Hawks circle slowly overhead. It's slow and hard-going driving this made-for-the-city rich-boy car across a desert. I try to steer across the flattest surfaces, but even so we jolt and bump along, every rock and crater I hit shaking the car violently.

Finally the path turns left and heads off away from the mountains. I decide to follow it instead of setting out off-road. Before long, my path turns into an actual dirt road and, soon after, becomes paved. And before I know it, we are driving past a lone gas station with a dozen or so motorcycles and a few cars parked behind.

My body stiffens as I look for any sign of Whit's green jeep or Mr. Blackwell's sleek black car. But the only person I spot is a man kneeling down next to one of the motorcycles with tools spread on the ground around him.

He stands as he hears my car coming. He's wearing a one-piece jumpsuit that probably started out white but is now a finger painting of rust and oil and dirt. Whipping his cap off, he uses the back of his arm to wipe his forehead. He strolls over when I stop.

I glance in the rearview mirror to make sure my sunglasses hide my eye's telltale starburst, and then reach back and pull the sleeping bag over Miles's face.

The man approaches the car, hands in his pockets. "You lost?" he says.

I hesitate. "Um, yes. I made a wrong turn a ways back, and have been trying to find my way to a main road."

He takes his cap back off and replaces it on his head. Squinting up at the sun for a moment, he looks back at me. "So where're you trying to go?"

"East," I say.

"Mmm-hmm." He nods and then spits a brown liquid out the side of his mouth. "She says she's going east," he says under his breath.

"I guess I could get some gas while I'm here," I say, and pulling past him, park the car up to the sole gas tank. The man follows, wiping his hands on his pants, and starts pumping the gas.

I watch him. The way he hides his hands in his pockets, the way he talks to himself, the way his posture seems to curl inward— he's as easy to read as a children's book. He is solitary, doesn't trust anyone but himself, and is probably involved in some shady business that has nothing to do with selling gas. He would betray me in a second if there was something in it for him. "Do you get much business here?" I ask finally.

"Rent out those dirt bikes," he says, nodding his head toward the motorcycles. "Got a few out today, but the season really picks up in June. High school and college kids, mainly. Like to ride around the desert." He clicks the nozzle of the gas hose and places it back in its rack. "That'll be sixty-two eighty five," he says. I pull my pouch out of my backpack and hand him a hundred dollar bill.

"I'll get you your change," he says, and turns to go back to the station.

I get out of the car to stretch my legs while I wait. "What are all the cars for?" I call after him.

He turns and waves toward a couple of new-looking cars, "Those belong to the kids who rented the bikes." He points at a row of three pickup trucks in various states of disrepair. "The trucks are mine."

I walk over to them and he follows me, hands in pockets. There's a black pickup that looks like it died a painful death years ago. Another, cherry red, is in better shape. The third is a dark forest green—a good color for camouflage. And although it's not new, it seems to be in good condition. I walk around it, inspecting it from every angle. CHEVROLET is spelled out in letters across the back. The truck bed is wide and spacious.

I walk back to where he pretends to watch something in the distance, as if I'm not there. "I'll trade my car for yours," I say finally.

He spits again and then laughs. "You're telling me you want to trade your brand-new Beamer for my Chevy?"

I don't know what that means, but I nod. "I'll give you my blue car for your green."

He squints at me suspiciously and asks, "You in some kind of trouble, missy?"

"Maybe I am. What's it to you?" I ask, straightening my back.

He scans my face like it's one of his broken motorcycles—trying to diagnose my problem. Then he sighs, his whole body sinking an inch as he exhales. "Well, hell, who am I to ask questions?" he says, and striding up to the green truck, opens the passenger side and pulls some papers out of the glove compartment.

I copy him and go to get all the papers I can find out of Miles's car. When I return, the man has spread a paper that reads "California Certificate of Title" on the hood of the pickup truck and is writing on it. "There you go, missy," he says. "I've put my name down and signed it. You can fill your part in yourself." He hands me the paper, and then watches as I unfold my own certificate and place it on the front of the pickup. I hesitate, and glance up at him.

"Just sign right there," he says, pointing to an empty spot on the page. "I'll take care of the rest." *I'm sure you will,* I think. From the crafty look on his face, I am convinced of what I suspected from the beginning: Miles's car is worth much more than this man's. But it's worth nothing to me if it's going to get us caught. So, as the man sticks his dirty hand forward and I reach out to shake it, I consider it a deal well made.

I press the button on Miles's keychain that opens the trunk of the car, and begin transferring the camping equipment to the pickup. The man helps me until I close the trunk and move toward the backseat. He sees the zipped-up sleeping bag and freezes. "Whaddya got there?" he asks, uneasily folding his arms across his chest.

I have no idea what to say, so I just stand there looking at it, and finally admit, "It's heavy."

"Is that right?" the man says, chewing slowly. "Well, I can't help you with that, but there's a dirt bike loader with an electric winch in the back of each of my trucks." He paces over to the green truck, lowers the tailgate, and pulling out a metal ramp, leans it between the truck bed and the ground. At the top of the ramp is a winch, much like the kind my clan used to move heavy objects. Except this one has a box and a button instead of a hand-turned crank.

He eyes the sleeping bag warily. "I'm just going to go get the change for your hundred, and by the time I get back that thing's going to have disappeared. Right?" And he turns and leaves.

I get back in the car, drive it a few feet from the truck, and open the back door. "I'm sorry, Miles," I whisper, and then grabbing the sleeping bag by the corners, yank hard until his body flops down onto the dusty parking lot like a bulky slab of meat. I use all my strength to drag Miles to the bottom of the ramp. Working quickly, I hoist him into the back of the pickup and stow the ramp and winch in their slots on the side of the truck bed.

I let myself into the truck and turn the key. It starts, and after fumbling a bit with the lever, trying to get it to point to D, and making the truck leap forward by pressing the pedal too hard, I stop in front of the shop.

The man comes out of the building and walks up to my window to hand me a few bills and coins. I give him Miles's keys, and he pockets them, satisfied. "Truck's tank is full of gas, so here's your change and we'll call it even. Sure has been a pleasure doing business with you," he says, pulling his cap off. He runs his fingers through his hair again and glances at the back of the truck. Spotting the sleeping bag, he pulls his cap back on. And without looking back, he returns to the bike he was working on and picks up a wrench.

I pull out of the station and head down the road until I see a sign. Finding my position on the map, I see that if I follow the road for a few miles, I can get onto a highway heading east.

And with Miles's dead body in a sleeping bag in the back, I put the truck in gear and head toward Arizona.

6

MILES

ONE SECOND THE BRIGHT SUN IS WARMING MY wings, and the next I am standing on two legs in total darkness. The far-off words of the song grow faint and then stop, and a voice—her voice—whispers. "This is where I leave you, Miles. I can't go any farther. Be brave."

"What do I do now?" I ask, but I'm alone.

A little ways ahead, at foot level, a line of light appears. I approach, groping through the void until I touch a hard surface. Sweeping with my fingertips, my right hand brushes something round and cold. A doorknob. I turn it, and walk into a room that I know better than any other. A room that has haunted my dreams for the past year.

I enter, leaving the door open behind me. I glance back at the darkness. It looks almost inviting now. Anything's better than what I'm about to see.

I scan the room. Everything is in place. The framed family photos on the dresser, the scattered chinks of light from the blown-glass chandelier, the mayhem of empty medicine bottles on the bedside table. I take another step, and grief pierces my heart like a knife blade. I know what I will find.

She's there. On the far side of the bed, curled up on the ground in a fetal position. She lies in a puddle of vomit. It's spread out around her head in a halo of foamy bile.

"Mom." My voice is muffled by the thick layers of sadness padding every square inch of the room. Only the rhythmic chattering of my mother's teeth indicates that she's alive.

This is the worst part—the part where I try to go to her, but can't. Where I am stopped by an invisible wall. Where I pound helplessly on it with my fists, screaming at her, screaming for help, but unable to go to her.

But this time is different. My bare feet continue across the thickly carpeted floor. The wall has disappeared. I approach her, crouching down to touch her sweat-drenched hair, and I know what has changed. Why I am allowed past the wall. My mother and I are in the same place: the still and quiet space between our world and the next. Standing on the edge of the precipice. We are both about to die.

7

JUNEAU

THE LANDSCAPE GROWS HARSHER AS WE APPROACH the Arizona border, and signs for Mojave National Preserve begin to appear along the highway. I think back to Mount Rainier, where Miles and I camped. A national park means a lot of out-of-the-way places to hide, which is exactly what we need if Miles is going to wake.

If. That word is like a punch to my gut, and the misgivings I've dammed up for the past few hours flood in to drown me.

If. How can two little letters hold so much importance? Wield so much power? How is a single stunted syllable able to threaten a world of pain and simultaneously dangle a glimmering, flashing jewel of hope?

If Miles awakes, he will be a changed person. He will have the gift of life: free of disease and aging. *If* he doesn't, then the one person who matters most to me—outside my clan, of course—will be gone. Abruptly. And forever.

I banish the thought from my mind. I glance automatically at the clock on the dashboard and register the fact that it is 5:30 p.m. This is the second time I've used a clock in one day, and I feel the shame of compromise. The sun, moon, and horizon are all I've needed in the past.

I'm in a new world now, I reason. I should use every modern tool I'm given. If I can add my own skills to the tools the outside world has developed, I will be in a position of strength, instead of handicapped by my lack of knowledge—like I was in the airplane or in Mr. Blackwell's office at the top of a skyscraper. I must master the rules of this new world. I'll need every possible advantage to face the unknown enemy who kidnapped my clan.

At the next national park sign I pull off the main road and begin traveling north, following arrows toward Mitchell Caverns. When I reach a fork in the road, I turn away from the tourist site and head east toward some unmarked rock formations. Dark red earth swoops down from one tall mesa and back up into another flat-topped mountain. Gray rocks are stacked around them like children's blocks. I drive around them and park in their shadows. No one can see us unless they go off-road like I did.

I climb out of the truck into what looks like the surface of another planet. The rock formations look alien, and although there is vegetation—clumps of sagebrush in gray, green, and parched yellow—it look like it's been tossed carelessly around instead of held to the ground by roots. The earth seems too dry to sustain life. I walk around the truck and open the tailgate. Climbing into the truck bed, I crouch beside the sleeping bag and unzip it.

My heart lurches when I see his face.

Miles's skin has taken on a sickly purple color. His eyes have begun to film over, white cloud spread over the lake green. This hasn't happened before. The Rite-travelers' bodies never deteriorated. Although I feel a stab of panic, I reassure myself that this case is different. It was hot in the back of the truck, and besides... my clan members were in perfect health. Miles was already dying. *This has to work.*

I close his eyelids, smooth back the honey-colored curls, and kiss him lightly on his mottled forehead. "Please come back, Miles," I urge, and continue unzipping the bag, exposing his overheated corpse to the cooler air in the shadow of the rocks.

He looks too vulnerable, lying there naked. I pull his blood-stained clothes out of my backpack and dress him, shuffling his limp body back and forth until I've got him in underwear and jeans. I stand back to look at my work, and something in my heart tugs. An unfamiliar ache that confirms just how much this boy means to me.

I pull myself away and begin setting up camp, pitching the tent between the truck and the rocks. Although we're hidden, my senses are on high alert. I realize that I'm reacting as I did in Alaska: on continual lookout for brigands. Ready to defend myself against survivors of an apocalypse that never happened. Even though my real-life enemies are nothing like the desperate marauders of my nightmares, they are more frightening because I don't know what to expect from them. They are unknown entities using unfamiliar methods.

Without thinking, I reach for my crossbow and then remember that it's gone. I dropped it during the scuffle with Whit's men in Salt Lake City. I can make myself another one if I find some suitable wood. In the absence of my preferred weapon, I get out my bowie knife and set it beside the fire. Its steel will be my security tonight.

I glance up at the sky. It's a couple of hours before sunset. Suddenly ravenous, I remember that I haven't eaten since morning. I am too exhausted to make a fire, so I end up eating beef stew straight out of the can, and finish it off with a small stack of crackers.

The disappearing sun fills the sky with reds, oranges, and pinks that are almost as stunning as a borealis back home. Scanning the horizon one last time for cars or wandering travelers, I unfurl a sheet inside the tent and lie down. Miles still has hours to go before he will awake (because he *will* awake) and I need to rest while I can. Minutes pass as I stare at the top of the tent, immune to sleep. Finally I give in to what I want, scoop up my covering, and return to the truck.

Spreading my blanket by the sleeping bag, I lie down next to Miles. I scoot back until I feel him behind me, then close my eyes and sleep.

* * *

I awaken with a start. A noise just came from somewhere nearby. A whisper. I sit up and scan the sky until I find the North Star and the moon. Their positions tell me that it's somewhere between ten and eleven. Miles should have awakened by now.

I place my hand over his mouth and nose. He's not breathing.

My heart swells painfully. Becomes the size of a balloon. Threatens to pop.

I know I did the Rite correctly, but what if he had lost too much blood before it took effect? Tears scrape the back of my eyes, and I lower my head to rest it on his chest. And I hear something. A heartbeat.

I sit back up, and watch as Miles's lips twitch and his mouth opens. He takes a sudden breath, filling his lungs with air before coughing it back out.

"Miles!" I yell.

"Juneau," he whispers. "I can't move." His words are ragged. Forced. His eyes remain closed.

"It's okay, Miles," I urge. I'm so overcome with emotion, I can barely speak. I wipe a tear away. "You just woke from death-sleep. You won't be able to move for a while."

"I can't see," he says, and I reach over and open his eyes. The white film, though still there, is clearing up.

"It's you," he breathes.

I lean over and kiss him lightly. "You're alive."

"Thanks to you and your New Age juju," he says through stiff lips. I laugh and flush with relief. Death has not changed Miles.

"You're part of that juju now," I respond. "You're one with the Yara, Miles. You're not going to die for a very long time."

He closes his eyes and is able to open them again. After a long moment he says, "I had dreams about that, while I was . . . dead or whatever."

I nod, and want to ask him about his Path. Every Rite-traveler comes back with different tales. The settings rarely vary, but their experiences on the Path are as different as the person traveling it. And with Miles's past . . . with his situation . . . I can't even imagine what he had to face. But I won't ask now. He needs time to understand what all of it means. To accept what has happened to him.

He scans the night sky. "The last time I was conscious we were in my buddies' old drinking shack outside L.A.," he says.

"We're a few hours away, in the Mojave, hiding from your dad and Whit."

His eyes meet mine. "Have you seen them?"

"Yes," I respond. "Your dad and his men drove past the cabin, but I camouflaged us. They didn't see a thing."

"Good party trick," he says, and that old teasing smile spreads across his lips. He's regaining control of his facial muscles. "What about Whit?" he asks.

"If he survived the crash and managed to get the jeep back on the road, he'll be after us, too. But we're well hidden, and you're going to want to sleep pretty much nonstop for the next few days."

Miles's eyes move left and right. "Where am I lying?" he asks.

"In the back of a Chevrolet pickup truck."

"Which you got by . . . ," he prompts.

". . . trading it for your car."

A bemused smile forms on Miles's mouth. "You traded my BMW for a Chevy pickup?"

"Is that a bad thing?"

"Let's just say that the other guy must be pretty damn happy."

"I'm sorry," I say. "I needed a car no one would recognize."

"It's okay," Miles says. "My Beamer didn't really suit you anyway. But this Chevy . . . yeah, I can see you driving one of these. I mean, if there are no available dogsleds."

I smile and throw my arms around him, pulling him up off the truck bed. "You wouldn't take advantage of a temporarily paralyzed guy, would you?" he asks, his voice muffled by my shoulder.

"Of course not!" I say, pulling away with mock horror.

"That wasn't a question," he says, his eyes shining with mischief. "It was a request."

I smile. And leaning forward, I kiss him.

8

MILES

I'M BACK. AT LEAST I THINK I AM. MAYBE THIS IS hippy-dippy New Age me, and as soon as I can move again I'll start craving tofu and Birkenstocks.

I'm just glad I'm here. Juneau saved me. Back there in the cabin I could literally feel my life flowing out of me. I know I passed out a couple of times, and each time I came to feeling less connected. Like I was becoming immune to gravity and might just float off into space.

And as I began to drift, one thought outweighed all the rest: I didn't want to die. Not just because I was afraid of death. But because what was previously a pretty empty existence for me has finally begun to take on some meaning. And it's all because of the girl lying next to me in the back of this pickup truck. Juneau.

I guess that means she's saved me twice: from death and from myself. I'm in her debt. But this is one debt I'm going to enjoy repaying.

9

JUNEAU

WITHIN MINUTES, MILES DRIFTS OFF TO SLEEP. I wish I could lie back down, press myself close to him, and shut off all of my worry and fatigue for a few short hours. But I have a lot to do before he recovers. And once he does, we must be ready to leave.

Recovery from death-sleep varies from person to person. Everyone awakens paralyzed, but since I've helped Whit perform the Rite, I have seen people walking in as few as three days and as many as six. Which means I have no idea how long Miles will be incapacitated.

Although it would be pretty much impossible for Mr. Blackwell to find us here, Whit might be able to Read and Conjure his way straight to us. So my first step is to find out where he is, and in order to do that I'm going to need a fire.

I scan the bone-dry landscape, and spot a few lone trees against the moonlit horizon. I can't tell how far away they are, and am hesitant to leave Miles here by himself. So I take him with me, driving a mile that would have been easy to walk. I make the ride as smooth as possible, even though I know I he won't awake.

I worried that my bowie knife wouldn't be sharp enough to cut through thick branches. But in the end, I don't have to hack limbs off—I find a couple of smallish trees lying dead on the ground. They are brittle enough to break apart with my hands. Once I gather enough wood, I load it into the back of the truck, propping the branches across the truck bed from Miles so that he won't get banged up in his sleep.

Back at the camp, I build a small fire—just big enough for my purpose. I sit down in front of it and slow my breathing, focusing on each heartbeat as I slip into the state I need to connect to the Yara.

My body actually shudders with the jolt of the connection, and energy fills me with what feels like a burning light. Now that I have stopped using totems to link to the Yara, my connections have been increasingly stronger. I try to ignore the power coursing through me and focus on the Reading. "Whittier Graves," I say, and stare at the tip of the flames, just above the blaze. And, after a second or two, I see him.

Whit lies in a bed in a white room, his head and arms wrapped thick in bandages. Next to him is a rolling tray with a pitcher of water on it.

Whit was injured in the wreck, and is being kept in some type of medical clinic or hospital. Which means he's not after me. For the moment.

My anger mounts as I watch him. He's a traitor. Using me and my clan as a "field test" so that he could sell the drug—the powerful mix of herbs, powdered minerals, and blood that we use in the Rite—to the outside world.

I wonder how much the other elders knew of what Whit was doing. I am more convinced than ever that the elixir was the reason they hid us all in the Alaskan wilderness. It was because of the Amrit that they made up the story they told us about an apocalypse. They didn't want us to leave. But why?

Maybe they wanted to hide the fact that they didn't age from the outside world. But that could have gone undetected for years. Having studied clan history, I know the date that they gave us for the onset of World War III, 1984, coincided with the birth of the first child to clan elders. Did they hide because they discovered Amrit caused a visible mutation in their offspring? That seemed a little more plausible. But even so, isn't it easier to hide a few children than entire families of well-connected scientists and theorists?

Maybe they needed the time to see how a second generation of Amrit users would fare. They wanted to make sure that the children's mutations were limited to the gold starburst in our eyes. As for Whit, he must have decided that if the elixir didn't prove to have more serious side effects, he would expose our secret . . . for a price.

I can't imagine that my parents were in on Whit's plans. I can't imagine them bringing me into this world as a field test.

My parents loved me. And they loved the rest of the clan. They would never do something that would expose our people to harm. Especially if it was just to make a profit in the commercial world that they shunned.

As my thoughts return to the here and now, I see that Whit's image has disappeared from the flames. I concentrate once more, picturing Miles's father in my head. "Mr. Blackwell," I say, and watch the flames. Nothing happens. I wonder if it only works with people I am close to. I never had to test this before—I knew all of my clan members as well as I knew myself.

I try my father, but only see the dark interior of an adobe hut. He must be asleep.

I try one more name. "Tallie," I say, and up from the fire rises the image of a woman with long curly hair the same color as the flames. She sits with a book in her one-room cabin, before her own blazing hearth. And just beside her, peering into the flames as if he himself could Read, is a black raven, as big as a cat.

Poe. I can't stop the smile that comes at the sight of him. I miss my huskies, Neruda and Beckett. They were such a fundamental part of my everyday life that I feel naked—exposed—without them. And although nothing can fill the hole that they left, I was a little less lonely the few days Poe was with me.

As I look closer, I notice something different about the room. A rectangle of white cloth hangs on the wall to the side of the kitchen, and in large letters across the top is written JUNEAU. Intrigued, I focus on the handwritten sign.

BEAUREGARD'S BONES SAID YOU'D BE CHECKING IN. BIRD

MISSES YOU. SO DO I. TAKE CARE. A wide smile stretches across my face. How like Tallie to write me a note after reading her possum bones. She feels like an adopted aunt. A slightly crazy one: the best kind. She misses me. And so does Poe.

I wish I could call him back to me right now. And as that thought crosses my mind, the bird in the fire flaps his wings and squawks. Tallie glances up from her book, and then looks around the room as if she senses I am there. Which is impossible, I know. But for a second our connection is so strong that I can almost feel the warmth of her fire and smell the freshly cut pine branches. "You take care, too," I whisper. I let my connection to the Yara fade until the image in the flames disappears and the night is silent once again.

The fire burns low before I finally rise to go to the tent. I lie down but can't sleep. I want to be in the back of the truck, next to Miles, but am afraid of waking him. He needs sleep. Opening his eyes and talking as quickly as he did is a good sign. He's already responding faster than most Rite-travelers. Although we need to get as far away from Whit, Mr. Blackwell, and their people as we can, Miles's recovery will be faster if his rest is uninterrupted.

My body is tired, but in my mind ideas are hopping and spitting like beads of water on a hot skillet. I leave the tent and add a few sticks to the fire, blowing on the embers until flames lick upward. Taking a thick branch I had set aside, I get out my knife and begin stripping the bark. I sing as I carve—a post-Rite song that the children sing around the yurt—and hope the words and melody will reach Miles and comfort him.

10

MILES

I AM BACK IN THE DREAM I HAD WHEN I SLEPT IN my car in the desert near Vegas. Juneau stands before me in a snowy landscape, dressed head to toe in skins and furs. Her long black hair cascades over her shoulders halfway down her back. The small box she holds out toward me spills golden light that bonds with my skin, starting with my feet and inching up my body as the molten metal burns its way to my bones. I can't move—I'm paralyzed.

"Juneau!" I cry, wanting her to close the box and turn off the lavalike liquid gold, but she just smiles at me. She is beautiful. Serene. "You are one with the Yara," she says as the gold reaches my neck and begins strangling the life out of me.

I ignite. I am a burning effigy of myself, and the snow around me melts from the heat I send off. Juneau, cheeks flaring pink in the heat of my flames, leans in slowly until her lips meet mine. I disperse into a million tiny sparks and fly upward to join my light with those of the stars.

That's where the dream ended last time. But now, the sparks stop and begin rushing back downward, fitting themselves together like a puzzle until I am standing there once again, whole, golden. And then the light fades and I regain my normal color and Juneau takes my hands and begins laughing. "You're like us now," she says. "Your life is the earth's, and earth will preserve you. You're Gaia's own child—protected from illness."

I look down at my hands—at my arms—and see the elements. I am made of water. Of earth and air and fire. I am no longer myself.

And upon that thought, I awake. I open my eyes and see a million stars scattered across the night sky above me. I try to lift my hand . . . to see if the dream was nightmare or reality . . . but can only move my fingers.

And then I remember. I died. And Juneau brought me back. I am struck by a wave of panic. What exactly have I become? Am I even human anymore? How do I know that Juneau's Rite had the same effect on me that it did on her clan? I'm not a hippy. I'm not an environmentalist. I haven't grown up talking to plants and seeing into the future.

It's Juneau, my heart reminds me. *The girl you gave up everything to run off with. The girl you . . . care for, more than you've ever cared for anyone else. If you can't trust her, who can you trust?*

And though I feel like I'm suffocating in fear and uncertainty, long fingers of sleep grab at me and begin pulling me under. I have one last thought before unconsciousness overtakes me. *I am no longer what I was before.*

11

JUNEAU

I AWAKE TO THE BUZZING OF BEES. SWATTING THE air around my head, I force open my sleepy eyes to a melon-colored sky. I sit up and see that it is dawn. The sun is barely visible behind the far-off horizon.

I have fallen asleep next to the now-cold fire. On the ground beside me is a pile of wood shavings and four smoothly carved pieces of wood, each gouged with a notch that will allow them to fit together to make two crossbows. They are almost as pretty as my last one, but have yet to be fitted with string, mirror, and spare parts carved out of bone, repair essentials that I always carry with me. I have a small arsenal of wooden bolts in my backpack. We won't be weaponless for long.

The buzzing sound is fading, but now it alternates with a mechanical puttering noise. Could it be a motorbike? Something like the desert-ready motorcycles owned by the man who traded cars with me? I turn in a circle, scanning the horizon. And then I see it. A small airplane heading north. Although too far to have spotted us, it's close enough for me to see the symbol painted on its tail: a black circle enclosing the letters *BP,* and between them a stick with a serpent wrapped around it. Ice flows through my veins as I recognize the logo of Blackwell Pharmaceutical—the same one that marked the airplane I was kidnapped in, the car I was driven in, and the building I was brought to against my will.

I prop myself up to see over the side of the truck. Miles is asleep under the blanket I draped over him last night. I shake him gently. "Miles?" I ask.

His eyelids flutter and open. He rolls his head toward me, and his groggy expression turns to one of alarm when he sees my face. "What's wrong?" he asks.

"We need to move," I say. "A Blackwell Pharmaceutical plane just flew past. They were headed northward. But if they're combing the park for us, they'll be back soon, and might spot us this time."

Miles clenches his hands into fists and strains as he lifts his head slightly off the truck bed. He holds the position for a second and then, groaning, eases his head back down. "I still can't move," he says.

"I could camouflage us," I say, "but if they're focusing on this area, I'll have to either keep it up for hours or turn it off and on every time we hear them coming. And what we really need is to get out of here."

"Can't you just cover me with a blanket and hide in the tent next time they fly by?" Miles asks.

"The plane is flying low enough that they might notice a suspiciously person-shaped lump covered with a blanket in the back of a pickup truck." I shake my head. "I'll have to use the dirt bike loader to get you down."

Decision made, I spring into action. Unhitching the back of the pickup, I pull it open and hop up into the bed. Miles presses his eyes shut as I shuffle him away from where the metal ramp is attached. I take it firmly in my hands to lift it off its supports, and . . . nothing. I yank it again. It doesn't budge.

I wiggle it around, trying to get it unstuck, but it only becomes more firmly attached. I lean over to see that one of the pins the ramp hangs on is bent out of shape. I'll need a hammer or some kind of wedge to bend it outward before the ramp will come free.

Far away, it sounds like the aircraft is turning. As the buzzing gradually becomes louder, my heart thuds hard against my rib cage. I feel my hands tremble and realize that I'm afraid. The close shave with the helicopters that kidnapped my clan, and my own traumatic experience in Mr. Blackwell's private plane have shaken me. I break out in a cold sweat. Even if I tried to camouflage us now, I'm not sure I could reach the Yara in my current state of anxiety.

I jostle the ramp again and run through my inventory in my mind: There are some tools in my repair kit that might work. I'll need to run back to the tent to get my pack. But the buzz of the plane is getting louder, and panic grabs me by the throat and squeezes hard.

I force myself to move, running for the tent. I eye my pack, but know there's not enough time to use tools now. Instead, I grab the pillows and covers and, sprinting back to the truck, I spread them on the ground beneath the tailgate.

I roll Miles to the edge, and lying down on top of him, press my chest to his and wrap my arms and legs around his body. His eyes are wide with alarm. "Juneau, what are you trying to—" he begins, but I interrupt.

"Just shut up and try to relax any muscles that are working," I say. And with all of my strength, I use my right arm and leg to wrench Miles's body up from the truck bed, and roll us off the back of the tailgate. For a split second we are falling, and then we land hard, Miles on top of me.

The cushion I made from the pillow and blankets breaks the worst of the landing, but my breath is completely knocked out, and it takes all of my strength to push Miles off me and sit up. Five heartbeats go by and then I am gulping in air.

The plane is closing in—the sound is coming directly toward us. I scramble to haul Miles beneath the truck. His feet leave furrows in the dry earth. Scoot and pull. Scoot and pull. The truck sits high up on big wheels, giving me enough room to sit crouched over underneath it as I drag his body.

My mouth is full of dust as I grasp Miles under his arms and give one last pull, then I clamber forward to hide my legs and feet under the cover of the truck. The airplane is on top of us: Its insect whine fills my ears as it passes overhead and continues on southward.

I lie for a moment, my chest rising and falling as I try to catch my breath. I cough, and my mouth tastes like dirt. I roll my head sideways to look at Miles, and there he is, inches away, his body turned slightly toward mine, arms limp by his side. His face is covered with sand, and there's a large scratch on his forehead. He watches me with that wide-eyed look and then licks his dry lips. "Are you okay?" he asks.

"Yeah, are you?" I ask, panting.

"Of course I'm okay," he says. "I landed with my full weight on top of you. I'm surprised you weren't crushed."

I can't talk, so I just shake my head as I close my eyes and press my chest hard with my palms. We are silent as the sound of the plane becomes distant and disappears.

My breathing slows to normal, and my heart no longer feels like it's going to explode. A sliver of pain shoots up the back of my neck, blooming poppy red behind my eyes. I'm going to be very sore tonight.

"Juneau?" I hear Miles say.

"Yes," I respond, turning toward him.

"You're amazing," he says, with an awestruck expression. "Trust me when I say you are, hands down, the toughest girl I've ever met. And I mean that as a compliment—in my most heartfelt please-don't-hurt-me-anymore kind of way." His teasing smile has returned, and this time it fills me with a happiness that makes me forget my aching back and mouthful of desert dust. This feels like complicity. Like we're a team. Like we're together.

I smile and reach over to touch his hair. "I promise not to hurt you if you promise never to get shot again."

"Deal," he whispers, and closes his eyes.

12

MILES

WHEN I WAKE UP, I AM IN THE FRONT SEAT OF THE pickup, held upright by a very tight seat belt.

Juneau stares intently ahead as she drives, and the gold of the starburst in her right eye flashes in the desert sun. Her finger-length hair is dusted with dirt, and stands up on end. Reddish clay caked on her arms has dried into a crinkled pattern. Right now she would fit perfectly into the postapocalyptic world she believed existed until a few weeks ago. Like Mad Max's extremely dirty sidekick.

I look down and see that I am shirtless, dressed only in my blood-spattered jeans and tennis shoes. I assume my shirt is too blood drenched to ever use again. I focus on my Converses and try to wiggle my feet. No go.

"Where are we?" I ask, and Juneau jumps. My voice sounds

like gravel, and I clear my throat and ask again.

"We've been driving parallel to the Colorado River, and are about to cross over it into Arizona."

We pass a sign that says NEEDLES FWY and then onto a bridge crossing high over a wide aqua-green river. "How did I get in the car?" I ask.

"I got the motorcycle ramp unstuck and used the winch to pull you in," she says, keeping her eyes on the road.

I watch as she expertly handles a pickup truck after teaching herself to drive barely a week ago. "Is there anything you can't do?" I ask, only halfway joking.

She considers. "There are plenty of things I've never done. Fly a plane. Speak Chinese. But nothing I can think of that I couldn't either learn or find a way around."

"Like lifting a hundred-seventy-five-pound man into the front seat of a truck," I say.

"For example." She glances over and smiles before focusing back on the road.

Just. Wow. This girl is so confident. Capable. Self-reliant. And generally kick-ass. I wonder what she could ever see in me. "Maybe, once I'm unparalyzed, I could impress you with my mad video game skills," I offer.

She laughs. "You've got to be good at something besides that."

"What," I ask, "besides dazzling chicks with my keen wit and striking good looks?" And I give her the smile that I used to use to charm people, which now seems more than a little ridiculous. Juneau rolls her eyes and I laugh. "Okay . . . skills . . . I can lift one eyebrow, put my entire fist in my mouth, and say 'cheers' in twenty-three languages."

Juneau looks over at me in disbelief and then bursts out laughing.

"Okay . . . if I have to toot my own horn, I used to be really good at lacrosse. In fact, I was the junior varsity captain." I clarify: "That means head of the team."

"Lacrosse was in the EB," she says, and digs into her literally encyclopedic memory. "Competitive sport, modern version of the North American Indian game of baggataway, in which two teams of players use long-handled, racket-like implements (crosses) to catch, carry, or throw a ball down the field or into the opponents' goal."

"Do you have a photographic memory?" I can't help but ask.

"No. As I said, we didn't have much to read," she responds. "And the *Encyclopaedia Britannica* was our only window on the world."

She glances down to check the atlas sitting open on the seat between us. Clicking on the turn signal, she pulls off the bridge and into a picnic area on the edge of the river. A couple of cars are parked nearby, and out in the water a speedboat pulls some shouting kids on an inner tube.

Juneau rolls down the windows, cuts the motor, and turns toward me.

"You played lacrosse. So you must have good reflexes. And if you were captain you must have leadership skills."

"The operative word here is 'were.' I kind of lost the taste for lacrosse when Mom's mental health started getting patchy. Kind of lost the taste for everything else, too."

I turn away from the pity in Juneau's eyes and lean my head back against the seat. I remember the abyss that opened up inside me after Mom left. The things I enjoyed before—my interests, my passions, everything else that I loved—were sucked right down into it. It was easier to feel nothing. The only activities that interested me were the ones that helped me forget the pain. Temporarily, of course. It always came back with a vengeance.

I wonder where the pain is now, and poke around inside myself like I'm hunting out a bruise. It's still there, but it seems smaller. More manageable. I wonder if that's because of Juneau. Or because, for once, I feel like I have a purpose. Or maybe it has something to do with the dream.

"What are you thinking of?" Juneau asks.

I start to say something funny—comedy being my favorite defense mechanism—but decide I don't need to do that with her. Not anymore. "I'm remembering... thinking about Mom. What it was like when she was sick, and then when she left," I respond truthfully.

"Want to talk about it?" she offers.

I shake my head. "Not yet." Without thinking, I raise a hand to rub my forehead. My eyes shoot open. "Hey, I can move my hand. And arm!" I exclaim.

"Not bad," Juneau says, offering me a happy smile. She knows full well I'm changing the subject, but gamely plays along. "Can you use your legs?"

I focus again on my feet, but only succeed in wiggling my toes inside my shoes. "No."

"I hope you don't mind, then, if I leave you here in the truck." She runs a hand through her hair, releasing a mini–dirt cloud. "I could use a swim." Opening her door, she steps out of the cab and goes around to the back of the truck to get some clothes and a towel out of her backpack. Then, walking onto the beach, she kicks off her shoes, strips off her tank top and jeans and dives into the water wearing only her bra and panties. They're blue. Not sky blue—a darker blue, like the ocean.

I don't know why I'm so surprised to see her strip. Juneau's underwear has more material than most of the bikinis you see in L.A. Maybe it's just the fact that she's wearing lingerie at all. Maybe I was expecting her to go commando, being raised by hippies and all. Or maybe I expected her to be super-modest. Then again, she's not only seen me naked, but dressed me while I was unconscious. Kind of a strange situation for two people who have only kissed. Okay, rolled around on the ground in a mad passionate kiss, but whatever.

I try to erase all thoughts of Juneau and her soft mouth and our steamy make-out session. We're not only on a mission—we're fugitives. Even if both of us wanted to, there won't be much time for rolling around anywhere in the near future. I lean my head out the window for some fresh air to cool me down.

Juneau splashes around for a moment, rubbing her hands over her hair and up and down her arms, washing off the dirt. Then she turns and swims toward the river's far bank, using broad strokes as her body glides through the water. In ten minutes she's across a river that would have taken me twice that time to swim. Without taking a break, she turns and heads back.

I lay my head back against the seat and finally let myself think about what has happened to me. I died. And then came back to life. So I'm basically undead. I'm a zombie.

An immortal zombie, I remind myself. One that doesn't smell like rotting flesh or have limbs falling off. I congratulate myself for looking on the positive side of things, but still can't help feeling like a freak.

I watch Juneau's head bob up and down as she executes a perfect crawl. *She saved your life,* I think, and feel torn. Part of me is just happy to be alive. To have survived a fatal gunshot wound. But another part is pretty freaked out. I'm something else now. Something that even Juneau isn't, since she isn't supposed to undergo the Rite until she turns twenty.

I've taken a drug that my dad would give his left arm to have, and it's changed me forever. I don't even know what it means. Do I have magical powers? Does this slowed-aging thing make me immortal? Awe and fear fuse inside me and rise like lava, scalding my chest and my throat.

I close my eyes and breathe out deeply, then inhale another lungful of air and blow it out as slowly as I can. I'm okay. I'm alive. And I'm with a girl I'm falling for. Okay, let's be honest, have fallen for. Past tense.

Opening my eyes, I watch as Juneau strides out of the water, dripping wet as she reaches for her towel. She rubs it over her head, wipes down her body, and then does a trick where she wraps the towel around herself, takes off the wet clothes and puts on dry ones without showing skin. Finally, she's walking toward the pickup wearing black jeans and a red tank top. Her cheeks are flushed from the swim.

She spreads out the towel and wet clothes in the back, combs her hair down so it's pixie instead of punk, and climbs into the driver's seat, leaning back on her door to face me. "I'd unstrap your seat belt if I didn't think you'd fall over," she says with a ghost of a smile.

"How long will I be paralyzed?" I ask.

"Are you hungry? Thirsty?"

"No."

"Then you've got a while to go," she says. "You won't need food while you're still under the influence of the death-sleep. Most of my clan members stay in the medicine hut for four days, sleeping the whole time with two or three short awakenings. You're awake for long stretches, talking and making sense. It's like the fact that you were already on death's door has given you superpowers." Juneau says it jokingly, but spots the look on my face and pauses. "What?" she asks.

"Sorry," I say. "It's kind of frightening to hear that I'm an anomaly: no longer a 'normal' human, but not like the rest of your clan. I don't even understand what my 'new and improved' body can do." My joke falls flat. I shake my head. "Okay. What this means is I'm eighteen years old and I'm never going to get older. I won't grow another inch, won't develop past where I am right now. Right?"

She nods. "Pretty much. But you're alive. And *I* happen to like you the way you are right now." She leans over and wraps her arms around me, and I rest my head on hers.

We sit there for a full minute, her soft hair cushioning my cheek. Finally she pulls back, enough so that our faces are mere inches apart. She closes her eyes and leans in to give me a warm, soft kiss, and then stays close, running her fingers through my hair. I breathe in her breath and it calms me. Centers me.

"I promise to tell you everything I know about the Rite I gave you," she says. "I'll tell you everything the elders taught me about the Yara—the truth along with the lies.

"Then you can do what I'm doing now . . . figure out what makes sense to you. Which parts you believe—which parts make a difference to who you are. Who you can become."

I don't know what to say. I'm so tired all of a sudden, I don't know if it's the conversation, the death-sleep, or both. It all seems too big for me. I lean back against the headrest and run my hand through Juneau's hair. Pull her to me and close my eyes. I feel unconsciousness grip me and sleep tug me under.

Juneau's words come from outside the warm, still place I'm sinking into: "Old Miles, new-and-improved Miles, it doesn't make a difference—I'm just glad you're here."

13

JUNEAU

AS I EXPLAINED TO MILES, MY CLANSPEOPLE barely wake during their death-sleep. So when he reenters his death-sleep, it isn't like he's merely nodding off. It's more like he's sucked into a vortex of unconsciousness. This reassures me. He's not as much an anomaly as he fears—the other Rite-travelers were never on the run during their transition. That must explain the different reaction.

Miles doesn't even budge when I get out to fill the tank and use the gas station restroom. I wear my sunglasses to hide my starburst, but the woman behind the counter is watching TV and doesn't even notice me.

Back in the truck, I dig through our supplies for any remaining food, and am forced to throw out several bars of melted chocolate and some cheese that went bad in the swelter of the desert sun. I move the bottles of water behind the seat to keep them as cool as possible, and put what remains beside me: two apples and a pack of chocolate fudge Pop-Tarts. Not the most nutritious meal I've ever eaten, but all the gas station had was candy and I don't have time to hunt.

I slip a Pop-Tart out of its package and munch on it as I reassess our situation. There are two things that concern me: how fast Whit will get out of the hospital, and how far Blackwell's men will chase us.

I sift through the facts. Whit can track me by Reading. But he doesn't trust his guards. In Salt Lake City, he slipped the fragment of the New Mexico map to me without them seeing. And his shocked reaction when one of them shot Miles is another indication that he's not completely in charge. Although Whit knows I'm heading for New Mexico, his guards don't. And if he doesn't trust them, I don't think he'd set them loose on me if he's not there. Until he's out of the hospital, they are not a factor I need to consider.

As for Mr. Blackwell, if he was so upset about Whit disappearing before they could make a deal, he must not know about the kidnappers. He wouldn't be aware of where my clan is being held. Therefore he has no idea which direction I'm heading. The farther Miles and I get from L.A., the wider his search will become and the safer we will be.

Which all means one thing: I've got to continue driving as far and as fast as I can, and avoid anywhere someone could recognize us: hotels, gas stations, roadside shops. Blackwell might have alerted the police that his son was missing. I wonder how long it will be before he finds Miles's car and discovers that I swapped it for this truck. The dirt bike guy obviously knew our exchange was fishy, and he has plenty of other cars to drive. Maybe he's hidden it away for a while. I can only hope.

I crumple up the Pop-Tart package, glance over at Miles's sleeping form, and press my foot to the gas pedal.

14

MILES

I AWAKE TO THE SOUND OF FLOWING WATER AND the smell of grilled meat. My eyes scan the tree cover above me. Beyond the branches the stars are so bright they look fake—like I fell asleep in a planetarium. I brush back the blanket spread over me, lift my hand to rub the sleep from my eyes, and sit up to look around. And then it clicks: I'm moving. I'm no longer paralyzed!

Juneau sits a few yards away, studying the atlas next to a fire over which a line of dead animals are strung on a spit. And this time, I don't even care about the carnage. I'm so hungry I'd eat whatever it is raw. I test my legs, drawing them up to my chest and laugh from sheer joy when they actually work.

Juneau glances over at me, and then does a double take. "You're awake . . . and you're moving!" she exclaims, and leaving the fire, jogs over to me. "Do you think you can stand?"

"Only one way to find out," I say, and taking her hand, let her haul me up to my feet.

"After only two and a half days of death-sleep and you're standing!" she says, and then as I slump back to the ground remarks, "make that *were* standing."

"My legs are on fire!" I gasp, rubbing my burning thighs.

"That's normal," she says smiling as she expertly kneads my stinging calf muscles. "You've got poor circulation from not moving for so long. You'll be fine in a few minutes. Hungry?"

"I could eat a horse," I say, and then glance cautiously at the mystery meat over the fire. "Um, I don't mean that literally."

Juneau looks back at the spit and laughs. "They're doves. Enough for both of us. Well, if you're hungry, then your death-sleep is definitely over. Welcome back to the world of the living."

I look down and touch the bullet hole in my side. It's already healed. All that's left is an angry red scar. Juneau had abandoned her masseuse duties to tend the fire. "I sure am glad to be back. It's thanks to you," I say.

She picks up the spit, turns it, and positions it back over the flames. "You wouldn't have actually gotten shot in the first place if you hadn't met me," she remarks, avoiding my gaze.

"That's true," I say, and she looks quickly up at me. "You're a very dangerous person to be around, Juneau Newhaven. But do you see me running away?" I grin and wait for her to return my smile before changing the subject. I point to a brand-new crossbow lying on the ground next to the fire. "Did you just make that?" I ask.

"Yes," she says proudly, and hands it to me so that I can admire it. "I started it while we were back in the Mojave. Finished it and strung it once we got here. These doves are its first kills."

I nod, trying to block out the word "kill" and the image it brings to mind of Juneau as a kind of teenage warrior.

"Do you like it?" she asks.

"It's awesome," I say, turning it over to inspect her handiwork: The wood is finely carved and a shard of mirror carefully inset in one side of the bow.

"Good. Because it's yours. Mine's in the tent."

My jaw drops. "You made *me* a crossbow?" I ask.

She smiles. "Yes. Don't worry, I won't ask you to hunt for food. But since everyone we've come up against so far has been armed, I figure we might as well even the odds. Target practice starts tomorrow."

I still don't know what to say. I hate weapons. I really do. But this seems different. Juneau made it herself. For me. I run my fingers across the surface of the wood. It's perfectly smooth. "It's beautiful," I say.

For the first time since I've known her, Juneau actually blushes. But before I can point out this historic moment, she grabs something from inside her pack and tosses it to me.

"Got this for you, too. Picked it up at the gas station this morning." She looks at my chest appreciatively and grins. "Not that I mind you walking around half naked. But I don't want you to be cold."

I hold it up: a black Arizona Cardinals T-shirt. "I didn't know you were a football fan!" I say, grinning, and throw it over my head.

"I've never seen a football game," she admits. "But it was the design with the smallest letters. There were no plain ones. I can't imagine paying money to wear an advertisement for someone."

"It's not that weird, once you've gotten used to it," I say, wondering how long it'll take Juneau to get used to the modern world . . . if she'll ever take things like this for granted like I do. And, I have to admit, I sincerely hope she won't.

I push myself up once again, and this time succeed in standing. I pigeon-march in a circle past the truck, behind the tent, and back to the fire. Then I jump up and down a bit, and it feels so great to be able to move that I run a few laps around the clearing before flopping down next to Juneau.

"I'm back from the grave," I proclaim. Stretching my arms straight out in front of me, I groan, "It's alive!"

"And that would be a reference to . . . ," Juneau asks, amused.

"It's what Dr. Frankenstein yells when his monster walks," I say, dropping my arms in disappointment. "Haven't you ever seen it?"

She hands me one of the spits, and blows on her own, then picks a little piece of meat off with her fingers and pops it in her mouth. "We had the book. Mary Shelley. Read it but haven't seen it. I've never been to a movie." She frowns at me, like I should have known that.

My hand stops halfway to my mouth. "You . . . have *never* seen a movie?" I don't know why this throws me off. I knew she and her clan were off the grid out there in the tundra, but for some reason this strikes me as more extreme than her other deprivations. A life without movies? I can't imagine it.

"The elders talked about them," she says. "They would sometimes tell us their stories around the feast fire. My favorite was when Nome's dad would tell us Star Wars. He knows those films by heart."

"That would be episodes four, five, and six," I say. "They did the prequels around fifteen years ago." Juneau's eyes light up. I shake my head. "Don't get too excited. You're not missing much. The originals are far better."

I pop a piece of dove into my mouth—Juneau's cut the head and tail off so it looks like a miniature chicken, which is fine with me—and my stomach rumbles loudly as I chew. It's been two days since I've eaten. "Oh my God, this is so good," I say.

Juneau smiles. "So you're a movie expert?" she asks.

"Now that you mention it," I say, "I should have named that earlier as one of my skills. I've put in hundreds, maybe thousands, of hours watching movies. Besides video games, which is my hands-down forte, my film trivia knowledge is excellent, if I do say so myself. Go ahead ask me anything."

"I wouldn't know where to start," Juneau says, and then changes her mind. "Wait. Best line from Star Wars. Not to prove that you've seen it. But to convince me of whether or not I should trust your taste."

"How would you know what the best line from Star Wars is?" I challenge.

"Nome's dad was constantly quoting them."

"That question's too easy," I counter. "I don't even have to think about it. There's one all-time jaw-dropper of a line in those films, and nothing else can top it."

"Let's see if we agree. On the count of three, we both say it." Juneau counts to three, and we both say in our deepest Darth Vader voices, "I am your father."

"Woo-hoo!" Juneau waves her dove around like a victory flag. "I knew there must be a reason I liked you!" she teases.

I point at her with my spike. "Tell you what. As soon as we save your clan, we're doing a movie marathon. All six Star Wars films in chronological order."

At the mention of her clan, Juneau loses her bubbliness, but not her smile. And cocking her head to one side, looks at me thoughtfully. "You got yourself a deal," she says.

Before the mood can drop any further, I change the subject. "So where are we?" I ask.

"In New Mexico. I drove over eight hours while you slept. We're about two hours south of Albuquerque, and according to the National Wildlife Refuge sign back there"—Juneau is all business now, pointing off into the distance—"we are camping in a bosque." She pauses and, when I don't say anything, she continues, "You want to know what a bosque is, don't you?"

"I figured you were going to tell me whether or not I asked, so go ahead," I say, relishing her impatience.

She holds her spiked bird up like a teacher's pointer. "It's an oasis-like ribbon of green vegetation, often canopied, that only exists near rivers, streams, or other water courses."

"What else did you memorize off the sign?" I ask.

"That our particular bosque borders the Rio Grande, which ties for the fourth largest river in the United States," she says, flourishing her dove.

"So we're camping out illegally again," I say.

She nods, unbothered, and takes another bite of meat. "It was the only place I saw to hide. For as far as you can see all around us it's just treeless, dry land."

She leans back onto her elbows and peers at the moon, and I can tell from her expression that she's calculated our location, the time, and God knows what else. I follow her gaze and see . . . an almost-full moon. That's it. I need a crash course in just about everything that exists farther than a mile outside city limits.

"The fact is," she says, sticking her spike into the ground and reaching for the open atlas, "I'm not quite sure where to go next. We're three hours from Roswell. And the spot that Whit marked on the map is a little bit northwest of it." She puts her finger on the lower-right-hand section of the state.

"Can't you ask the Yara? Read, or whatever?" I ask, feeling awkward, like I'm speaking a language I haven't yet learned.

"Well, I have fire-Read it a few times, so I know what the place looks like. And I tried to Read the wind, but that . . ." She pauses. "Do you want me to explain how the Yara works?" she asks, raising an eyebrow.

"Yes," I say tentatively. "I mean, I'm going to be doing those kind of things, right?"

Juneau bites her lip. "I think so. But probably not right away. I'm guessing it's going to come with time—that it will arise in you gradually, now that you've chosen to be one with the Yara."

"So it's not automatic?" I'm surprised by the pang of disappointment I feel. I guess I was looking forward to the superpower perks of my "condition."

Juneau clears her throat, and I can tell she's deciding how to explain things, since she doesn't seem too sure of herself. "If you had asked me two months ago if the Rite and being one with the Yara and hyper-long life were all one thing, I would have said yes. But now that I know that Whit was going to sell Amrit to the outside world as a 'cure for aging,' I've started to question the other 'benefits' I thought were connected to the Rite.

"I'm wondering if being one with the Yara, and the capacity to Read, isn't a completely separate thing," she continues. "I mean, the children in our clan can Read, and they haven't taken the elixir. Maybe it's because we were raised to believe in Gaian principles—to be close to the Yara until the day we choose to be one with it—the day of our Rite."

"Or, it could be because you've already got Amrit flowing through your veins. You're born with the starbursts in your eyes, and didn't you say the children are better than the elders at Reading? Couldn't it be from the Amrit your parents took, and not based on beliefs?"

Juneau considers what I said, then shakes her head. "You saw what happened when I started doubting the Yara. I began to lose my gifts."

"So maybe it's a mix of drugs and belief," I say.

Juneau crosses her arms. "I just don't know." She doesn't look convinced. "What seems most likely to me is that you, having taken the Amrit, will now age at an imperceptible rate. You won't ever get sick again. No illness . . . no disease. But that's it. If you want to be one with the Yara—if you want to Read—then it will take a change of heart. A change of perception. A sensitivity toward the earth and the superorganism that we're a part of."

As Juneau talks, my thoughts are spinning. I'm trying to remember everything she's told me in the past, which isn't easy since I thought she was talking utter crap up to a few days ago. I nod, and feel vaguely uncomfortable. It's not nice to be the guinea pig. The one case that tests the variables in this life-and-death experiment. I've passed the lethal part of the test . . . now I have to find out what it means in real terms.

It's time to change the subject. "So how are you going to use the Yara to find your clan?" I ask.

From the half smile on Juneau's lips, I can tell she's happy to leave the existential crisis behind. Picking the last piece of meat off her spike, she reaches over for a bottle of water, takes a sip, and hands it to me.

"I can fire-Read to see where people are right now. Sometimes I see through the person's eyes, and others it's just an image taken from something outside them. I can Read the ground to know what people are feeling. Reading trees and rocks can help me know what the weather's going to be like in the future or any important events that happened near them in the past. Water's our best bet—it's what Whit used to see if brigands were coming . . . I mean, people from the outside world. It isn't focused on one person and their immediate surroundings."

"So we need water. Didn't you say we're near the Rio Grande?" I ask.

"It's just a couple minutes that way," Juneau says, pointing into the trees. "But it's dark now. I wouldn't be able to see much. We'll try that tomorrow morning."

"Is that the only option?" I ask.

Juneau shifts uncomfortably. "I'm sure there are a lot of things I don't know. Either intentionally or out of his own lack of knowledge, Whit's kept me . . . kept all of us . . . in the dark about the limits of the Yara. Now that I'm sure he was mistaken about the totems, I wonder what else he was wrong about. What else he didn't know. I'm just learning what I'm capable of. The possibilities could be endless . . ."

I nod and take a swig from the bottle.

"There is, of course, one option for Reading that I haven't mentioned," she says slowly. "An oracle."

I choke on my mouthful of water.

"But I won't ask you to do that again," she adds quickly, raising her hands in a gesture of surrender.

I feel the blood drain from my face. "Please don't," I squeak, and then hit myself on the chest to get the water out of my windpipe. When I can once again breathe, I reach over and put my hand on Juneau's. "I'm sorry. I want to help. But I really, really don't want to do that again. Spouting out prophecy while you've got me in a trance. I just . . . I can't."

"I know," she says, and pulls her hand away from mine. "That's okay."

"Juneau—" I begin.

She interrupts me. "I was wrong to do it like that the last time—without your consent. My manipulating you—"

"Drugging me," I interject.

"Yes—drugging you—made it a traumatic experience instead of something that can be beautifully mystical. That was totally my fault."

"Well, thank you for the belated apology," I say with a smile. "But I already forgave you."

"I know." She stares at the fire.

"But that doesn't mean I want to do it again."

"I know," she repeats, pushing her foot over to rest against mine.

We sit in silence. The only sound is the rippling of nearby water and some very loud bugs chirping away in the dark.

"Juneau," I say finally.

"Yes?"

"Want to show me how to put bullets in my new rabbit killer?"

Juneau laughs, and the heaviness lifts. "They're called bolts," she says. "And I think we can come up with a better name for your crossbow than that."

"What? Not Rabbit Killer?"

"Lame," Juneau says, grabbing her backpack and unzipping the top.

"Bunny Slayer?" I offer.

"Lamer," she replies, hiding her grin as she pulls out a handful of sharp wooden pegs.

"Well, what's yours called?" I ask, taking a bolt from her and rolling it around in my fingers.

"My last one was Windspeed. I'm not sure about this one, but I was thinking maybe Ravenflight." She looks at me, gauging my reaction.

"You're naming your crossbow after Poe?" I'm incredulous.

"What's wrong with that?" she asks defensively.

"Well, 'deadly' isn't exactly the word that comes to mind when I think of that bird. 'Bumbling,' maybe. 'Annoying,' definitely."

Juneau's jaw drops in feigned shock. "How dare you?" she says. "Poe is my noble messenger. My faithful companion. Besides, I think you're jealous of him."

"How faithful can he be if he's off playing house-raven with that mountain woman?" I ignore the jealous jab.

"Poe *is* noble," she insists. "And Ravenflight it is."

"Just to spite me," I challenge.

"Yes."

"Fine. If we're using avian nomenclature, I'm calling mine the Hoot of Hedwig."

Juneau is baffled. "What in the world is that supposed to mean?"

"It's a reference that pretty much everyone would recognize."

"Besides me," Juneau says slowly.

"Exactly," I respond. "Annoying, isn't it?"

"Not in the least," she says, lifting her chin and glancing off into the night with an air of supreme disinterest. She sighs and, taking a bolt, fits it into a groove on the top of my crossbow.

"Literary reference?" she asks, still concentrating on the weapon.

"Oh, wouldn't you love to know . . . crow lover," I reply.

She bursts out laughing. And the look of pure happiness in her eyes makes everything that has happened, and everything that we are still facing, unquestionably worth it.

15

JUNEAU

ALTHOUGH MILES SAYS HE'S AFRAID HE WON'T BE able to sleep, he starts nodding off right after a short but successful round of target practice. I send him to the tent, but remain by the fire so I can Read it as it burns itself out.

This time, I go through my entire list of names. Everyone of interest. When I Read for Dad, I see inside the same adobe hut, where he lies on a cot staring at the ceiling, a candle flickering on the floor next to his palette.

It is dark in Tallie's cabin, the windows softly illuminated by the glow of moonlight.

Miles's dad is sitting in front of a computer screen in his office at the top of the Blackwell building. The lights of L.A. twinkle through the glass walls surrounding him.

Whit is out of the hospital. There's a thick white bandage

around his head. He's sitting, writing, at a desk in what looks like a hotel room. *On his way to hunt me down,* I think. But if he plans on sleeping tonight then, by Gaia, so will I. We both know where I'm heading. Now it's just a question of avoiding him while I figure out how to free my clan. A faceoff is inevitable. I just want to delay it for as long as possible.

I check in with my friend Nome and see her sitting outside under the stars, talking to Kenai. "I'm coming," I whisper, and wish they could hear me. I could see them as early as tomorrow, if Miles and I get lucky. My heart is sore with missing them—the pain is even more acute now that they're within reach.

I look away from the dying flames and feel suddenly and completely overwhelmed. As if in allowing one small hole for my loneliness to trickle through, I've knocked down a dam and my feelings are flooding out. I don't let myself cry, though. I'm afraid that if I start, I won't be able to stop.

I wrap my arms tightly around myself as I remember life in the clan. How I was never alone unless I really wanted to be. Unlike now. It's me against the world . . . against the bad guys, and unless I win, I might never see my clan again.

I think of the heavily armed guards with Whit, and it occurs to me that I might die. I remind myself that I'm the one everyone seems so concerned about catching. They all want something from me. So maybe I'm too valuable for them to kill. I can only hope that this is enough to protect me.

I glance over at the tent, and remember that I'm not alone. Miles is with me. He chose to come with me, although neither of us understood at the time what that would involve. He cares enough about me to go against his father. To leave his home.

I scatter the embers with a stick and make my way to the tent. Looking inside, I see Miles's outstretched form. He's sleeping in his T-shirt and boxers, his bloody jeans folded up in the corner. His face is peaceful, like he doesn't have a care in the world. Like he's just any eighteen-year-old on a road trip.

I long for that kind of freedom. To be a regular person. Not someone on whom the lives of forty people depend. Not someone who is being hunted across the country because I carry a secret other people will kill to get. I feel the weight of my burden, heavier than ever. I wish I could sleep and never wake up. But that isn't my fate. That's not why I was given my gifts.

Crouching, I climb into the tent and zip the door closed behind me. I sit down next to Miles and stroke his light brown curls with my fingertips. I want to tell him how I feel. To explain the responsibility I've always felt toward my father and my clan. To have someone to share the burden with.

"Miles?" I ask, and his eyelids flutter open.

"Juneau," he says, waiting.

"I . . . I can't . . ." is as far as I get. I have spent too long keeping those feelings to myself. Hiding my emotions from even my friends. The words disappear on my lips.

Miles sits up. His eyes brush my face, reading the set of my mouth, the pain in my eyes. "You're worried," he whispers, and I nod. If it were only that simple. He wraps his arms around me and draws me in to him, hugging me and stroking my hair until I push him softly away.

"I don't want comfort," I explain. "I want to erase everything. To chase reality away. I want . . . I need to escape. Just for a moment." The words are spilling out—unplanned, unfocused—but their meaning doesn't matter. Miles understands.

I lean toward him, and he meets me halfway. His lips brush mine and set off a firestorm of sensations inside me—feelings so powerful that I have no doubt that more is involved than just a boy and a girl kissing. It's the Yara, whipping around us like a wind. Sweeping us into its current and filling us with its fire.

Miles pulls me to him until my chest presses tightly against his, but I want to be closer. I run my hands under his shirt, and he lets go of me for as long as it takes him to rip it off. My fingertips crackle with invisible sparks as I run my hands over his bare skin.

His eyes widen with surprise: The fireworks set off by the touch of our skin are obviously something new to him. I pull him back down so he lies beside me. We watch each other from inches apart, weaving our arms and legs and bodies together into a tangle of us. And then I kiss him and the world falls away.

We are two tiny dots on the surface of the planet, so close that we look like one. One with each other. One with the earth. Joined together, we are both set free.

16

MILES

I WAKE UP NAKED IN AN EMPTY TENT. I GROPE around until I find my clothes, and pull on underwear, jeans, and the T-shirt Juneau bought me. Running my hands through my hair I try to pat down my bedhead before unzipping the door and stepping out into the oasis of trees where Juneau pitched our camp.

Flashes of sunlight bounce off the surface of rapidly moving water just yards away, and I catch a glimpse of Juneau's red tank top from where she crouches next to the river. An enormous smile hijacks my face as I think of last night, and hope to God that things won't be awkward between us. I push my way through thick bushes to the river's edge.

She turns and, seeing me, puts her hands on her hips. Her expression is one that's new for me—an intimate but teasing smile acknowledging that last night actually happened and wasn't just the best dream I've ever had. "So . . . did you sleep well?" she asks.

"I think I could call last night *Death-Sleep 2: The Sequel*," I admit, and not knowing whether or not I should go up and kiss her, I stick my hands in my pockets and wait for a sign from her.

She looks like she wants to laugh, and extends a hand to me. Deciding to do what's natural, I take her hand and pull her in for a hug. She feels like pure joy in my arms. I wonder if that's how I feel to her. "Are you still worried?" I ask.

She leans back and looks at me, amused. She shakes her head. "No, somehow I got distracted last night. And this morning I poured all my worry into coming up with a plan."

Pulling away from me, she squats down next to the water. The moment I could have kissed her has passed—she's reverted back to all-business Juneau and doesn't seem the kissy type—and I'm left with a stab of regret. Mainly over the fact that I wish I could take her back to the tent and see if the magical effects were a figment of my extremely happy imagination or if the sparks and fireworks and electrical shocks were actually real. Although last night wasn't my first, it was definitely the only time sex had been a pyrotechnic extravaganza.

And then it occurs to me: This could be part of the earth magic. The Yara. Juneau and I hadn't been alone. "The force that binds all living things," or however the hell Juneau describes it, had been in the tent with us. And though it's a freakily bizarre idea, it's also kind of hot. Juneau interrupts this enticing train of thought by pointing to something in the river.

"Can you see the picture on the water?" she asks, and points to a flat stretch of water cascading off a rock and reflecting the morning sun. I focus on it, and it's like finding shapes in clouds: I can see colors reflected in it, forms moving around, but nothing precise. *There's nothing there,* I tell myself. I shake my head.

"It's okay," she says. "I wasn't expecting you to. Just wanted to be sure. What I see is the area where my clan is." She gestures toward the patch of still water. "Far from their group of huts— but I can't tell exactly how far—there's a huge mansion-like house. And in front of it are some camouflaged guards, like the ones who were with Whit."

She peers intently at the water, her forehead creasing in concern. "But this is the weird part. In another area of the fenced-in space it looks like there are wild animals roaming around." She turns to me. "Do they have lions in New Mexico?"

"They probably have coyotes like we do in California and maybe cougars. But lions . . . I doubt it."

Juneau purses her lips and looks back at the water. "No, I definitely see a couple of lions. And a zebra."

"A zebra? Are you sure the water's showing you New Mexico?" I ask, trying not to sound skeptical.

"Positive," she replies, and turns back to me. "It's all part of a huge fenced-in area that encloses the desertlike land where my clan is, stretching all of the way up into faraway hills with sparse trees, where the animals are."

"Okay," I concede. "So what's the plan?"

Juneau weaves her fingers through mine and I try to ignore the current running between us and concentrate on what she's saying as she leads me away from the water, back toward the camp. "There are armed guards driving around in jeeps," she explains, as we edge by a bush of prickly leaves that sting me through my jeans. "So we can't just scale the fence and wander through. But we could follow the fence around the perimeter until we find my clan. Their huts are definitely visible from the fence—I've seen it behind them in all of my Readings. We need to get there first, though, and see it for ourselves before we plan our strategy."

I stop and rub my stinging leg. "You're saying 'we' as if I'm going to be a part of the strategizing," I point out. "After all of the stupid things I've done, you're going to trust me to help you come up with a plan?" Okay, I know I'm digging for compliments, but maybe after all we've been through I need a bit of encouragement.

Juneau lifts an eyebrow. "You've learned to make a fire, pitch a tent, and cook since I met you. And you didn't do too badly at target practice yesterday. At this point I'm considering you an asset."

"Why, thank you," I reply, satisfied now that I've gotten the back pat I needed.

"Plus, I'll bet you're good for more than that," she adds. "I saw metal boxes at several places along the top of the fences. With lights on them. Do you know what they do?"

"That probably means the fences are electrified," I say.

"As in, if you touch it, it shocks you?" she asks.

"Exactly."

Juneau brushes a branch out of her way and turns to me. "See. You're a definite asset. Yes, we're going to be creeping around in the wilderness, which is my domain. But we're doing it in a modern world that I still haven't gotten close to understanding. Your domain. Like my Seattle oracle so prophetically put it, I need you just as much as you need me." And she gives me a smile that fills up all the empty places inside me.

We emerge from the trees into our clearing, and Juneau kneels down next to the atlas. "Here's where the point on Whit's map was," she says, tracing a barren-looking area with her finger, and then moving it to the left where some green appears on the map. "It's not far from where this tree line starts. That's got to be it. At least, that general area. My clan can't be too far away. Maybe a three-hour drive."

Juneau crosses her arms, staring at the map. "Are you okay?" I ask.

She nods. "I'm fine. But from what I saw, my clan is being guarded by men who are well armed and well organized. We can't take them head-on. We'll have to come up with a plan to whisk my people out from under their noses. We can strategize while we drive." She sits down and begins pulling food out of the grocery bags.

"Breakfast, then we go?" I ask.

Juneau closes her eyes. Her worry is almost palpable. I want to take it from her—to see her in one of the rare moments where she forgets her "mission" and seems almost carefree.

She exhales, and then raises her face toward mine. "How about kiss me first, and then breakfast, and then we go."

"Gladly," I respond. I take her face in my hands and kiss her softly. "How did you know what I was thinking?" I murmur.

"You're easy to read," she replies, and then asks, "So why didn't you kiss me when you wanted to . . . by the river? You were trying to be sensitive, right? Or polite?"

"Gentlemanly," I add to her list.

"That's nice," she says with a bemused smile, "but you forget I was raised in the wilderness. No gentlemen for miles around. Only wild men. And savages."

"So are you saying you'd rather I just grab you and kiss you whenever I feel like it, regardless of the seriousness of the moment or the level of danger we're in?"

She crosses her arms and cocks her head to one side. "That depends. Can I assume that, as it would in my world, what happened in the tent last night signifies something?"

"What, exactly, would it signify in your world?" I ask, supremely enjoying the direction this conversation has taken.

"Oh, I don't know. Maybe that we're together?" Juneau suggests.

I rub my chin, pensively. "Together?" I ask, looking confused.

"A couple," Juneau clarifies, a dangerous sparkle in her eye.

"Hmm, yes. I think that in my society, one could assume from what happened in the tent last night that we are, indeed, a couple," I say.

"Then, yes, you are allowed to grab and kiss me whenever you wish," she concludes, daring me.

As Juneau knows by now, I never turn down a dare.

17

JUNEAU

MILES WANTS TO DRIVE, SO I LET HIM TAKE OVER while I trace our progress on the map. As we leave the bosque and head east, the strip of lush green land bordering the Rio Grande turns abruptly brown. The kind of barren brown that I had always imagined the earth looked like outside our hidden Alaskan paradise. An apocalyptic brown that suggests nothing's ever going to grow here again.

"We need to stop for gas," Miles says, and like magic a sign for a gas station appears ahead. We pull into the gravel courtyard of Pump-n-Shop, and Miles starts filling the tank.

We ate the last of the food this morning, and since I don't know how long it will take to run surveillance on my people's captors before we can act, I decide to stock up on supplies. I work my way through the grocery section, picking out milk, cereal, and bread, as well as packaged cinnamon rolls and canned soups and beans.

"What, no Pop-Tarts?" Miles remarks as he joins me in front of the cash register, where an old man is typing in the prices of my items.

"Didn't have them," I say. "But I think this should make up for it." I hold up a six-pack of Snickers.

"I'm not sure how environmentally correct your elders would consider this stash." Miles gestures to the pile of groceries and gives me a wry smile.

This grin, which used to make me want to slap him, now fills me full of bubbles—I feel ready to burst. In just ten days he's swapped the antagonistic jabs for affectionate teasing. It's not hard to choose which I prefer.

"Look at the selection," I say, gesturing toward the sparsely populated shelves. "If we could stay in one place for a little while, I'd have a garden up and growing in no time. But since we're on the run, I'll take what I can get."

Miles smiles broadly. There's something jubilant in his expression . . . like now that it's established that we're together, he's supremely proud to be with me. He winks and then leans forward on the counter and asks the man, "Is there a zoo somewhere nearby?"

"A zoo?" the old man asks, confused.

"If we wanted to see something like, I don't know, lions and zebras, is there anything like that around?" Miles asks.

"There's a zoo back in Albuquerque," the man says, lifting up his cowboy hat and scratching the fuzz of hair that's squished down underneath. "No zoo around here, though."

Miles nods. "Thanks," he says, and picks up the bags as I count out the cash for the gas and groceries.

"Although, if you wanted to shoot yourself some zebras, there's a crazy Texan who runs a hunting range over southeast of Vaughn," the man continues. "Don't know who he's paying off to look the other way, but he's got all sorts of wild animals over there. Fancy-pants businessmen fly in and pay top dollar just to shoot themselves some antelope or some such bullshit."

Miles lifts an eyebrow and peers at me out the side of his eye.

"You say he's south of Vaughn?" I confirm, my heart racing.

The man pulls an area map out of a rack next to the cash register, and unfolds it on the counter. He picks up a pen, then hesitates. "You gonna buy this?" he asks, looking up from the map.

I nod.

"Okay, then," he says. "Here's us." He draws a star on the east-west road we're on and, then moving the pen southwest to an area that looks completely bare besides a patch of green in one corner, he outlines a large rectangle.

"He's got himself this huge tract of land stretching from the desert south of Vaughn up into the foothills of the Sacramento Mountains here," he explains, pointing to the green part. It's in the same general area that I had guessed at in our atlas.

He shoves the map toward me. "That'll be five bucks," he says, and I add another bill to the money on the counter.

"Says he's able to reproduce the animals' 'natural habitat,'" the man continues, wiggling his fingers in the air like quotation marks. "Natural habitat, my ass," he mutters to himself, handing me my change and slamming the cash register drawer closed with a jingle of coins.

"Thanks so much," I say, slipping the change into my pocket.

"If you're not on one of his safaris, you won't be able to get anywhere near enough to see the animals, though," the man says, as Miles and I make our way to the door. "Crazy bastard's got the whole place electrified. Even has his own security guys guarding the place. Thinks he's running his own private army. Bunch of thugs, all of them. Not the type you want to get mixed up with, that's for damn sure."

Miles hesitates at the door. "What's the name of the guy who owns the place?"

"Avery. 'Hunt' Avery," he says, using his fingers again to punctuate. "Craziest bastard I ever did meet. Comes through here once in a blue moon. Richer than God. Thinks he *is* God." The man shakes his head, and turns to organize the cigarette packs.

Miles holds the door for me, and once we're outside I drop my bag and fling my arms around him, squeezing him with everything I've got. He stands there holding the grocery bags and looking amazed. "This could be it, Juneau. A man like that—filthy rich, own private army, huge tracts of land—that's the kind of guy who could kidnap a whole group of people."

I let go of him, scoop up my bag, and almost skip to the truck. "This is it, I can feel it," I say excitedly, as I climb into the cab. "We've found my clan."

The only thing to see on the two-hour drive to Vaughn is a flat expanse of dry grass stretching all the way to the horizon. In the distance to the south, a mountain range is barely visible, just a smudge of purple against the powder-blue sky.

The road is bordered by wood or metal fences, and a couple of times we pass vast herds of cattle. Miles plays with the radio dials, listening to one song until the reception turns static, and then pressing buttons until he finds another that works. We switch between country-and-western, Spanish-language stations, and what Miles calls "oldies." I find it all fascinating. The only music we had in the clan was the kind we made ourselves.

"You've never heard of the Beatles?" he says at one point when I ask about the song he knows all the words to.

"Of course I've heard of the Beatles," I say. "Marge, Kenai's mom and head cook, knew their songs by heart—and she sang on baking days. Plus, the Beatles had a whole paragraph in the EB."

"Ah yes, the 1983 *Encyclopaedia Britannica*, font of all knowledge," Miles jokes.

I cross my arms in challenge. "Do you know what a pangolin is?"

"Some kind of antique guitar?" Miles ventures.

"It's an African armadillo," I respond. "Some call it a scaly anteater. EB volume fifteen, Pachyderm to Primates. Don't knock the EB."

"Now that's exactly the type of information I wish I had at my fingertips," Miles says. "And in fact, I *would* have at my fingertips if you hadn't fried my iPhone five minutes after I met you."

I smile. "Frankie was right about that, too," I muse. "What if I hadn't broken your phone? You would have called your dad before we had even left Seattle."

"True, true," Miles says, thoughtfully stroking an invisible beard. "But only a week later, I saved you from him. Freed you right from under his nose."

"After which *I* saved *you*," I say.

"It's a good thing we're not keeping score." Miles laughs. "Because I'm not sure I could top your bringing me back from the dead."

He moves one hand from the steering wheel, and raises my fingers to his lips. "Rescued by my valiant lady," he says.

The kiss sends tingles through me, and Miles can tell. "Hmm, Juneau likes hand kisses," he says, and presses his lips to the soft skin beneath my knuckles.

I shiver. "You have to say the 'valiant lady' bit with it to score top points," I insist.

Miles bursts out laughing. "I'm glad you're telling me what you like," he says. "Because every time I think I know you, you pull the rug out and take me completely by surprise."

"Wouldn't want you to get bored," I respond.

"Not much risk of that," Miles murmurs, shaking his head.

I grab his hand back off the steering wheel and hold it in mine. "I wonder if your dad's still looking for us," I say finally.

"I'm sure he is," Miles replies. "But we've gone so far that there's no way he'll find us now. I can imagine him calling in the California state troopers to look for us on some trumped-up runaway story, but we're two states away and I doubt he'd put out a nationwide alert."

"Now all we have to worry about is the crazy Texan billionaire with the private army," I say. "Those had to be his men with Whit."

"The map Whit gave you pointed to the same area we're headed to—south of Vaughn—right?"

"Right."

"And this morning when you Read the river, you saw lions and zebras in the same compound as your clan, right?"

"Right again."

"And the guy who owns the wild-animal shooting range also keeps a private army, according to gas station man." Miles shoots me a look like *and two plus two equals . . .*

"It all adds up," I agree. "I saw those two military-looking guys with Whit in Alaska the day my clan was kidnapped. And there were more of them at the port in Anchorage looking for me. How many people have their own private army? It's got to be this Hunt Avery guy. But how in the world would Whit have a connection to someone like that?"

"He was probably offering Avery the same thing he was offering my dad. I'll bet if we looked into his business interests, he'd be the owner of a pharmaceutical company. Probably one of my dad's competitors."

"That would make sense," I say, and my heart sinks another inch. Why is there still a tiny part of me that hopes Whit is innocent? That this is all a mix-up and that he's somehow being manipulated? What did he mean when he said, "Things aren't as they seem," in the note he sent with Poe?

A squat patch of earth-colored buildings huddles on the horizon, growing gradually bigger and turning into a town. We pass a sign that says VAUGHN, POPULATION 737.

The first building looks abandoned. The next two, with signs reading AUTO REPAIR and GINGER'S GIFTS AND OFFICE SUPPLIES, are empty as well.

"It looks like a ghost town," says Miles. He takes a right at the main crossroad, and up ahead we see a neon sign lit up with STEVE'S BAR.

"We could stop here and ask about the ranch," I suggest.

"Or not," Miles says as two brawny men in a very familiar-looking camouflage uniform walk out of the bar. As we pass, one of them pulls a cigarette pack out of his jacket and offers it to the other.

I look in the side mirror and see them glance our way. "Go, Miles!" I urge.

Miles peers into the rearview mirror. "Right now they're not paying attention to us," he says. "But if we speed off, they'll be after us in a second."

The truck jerks and slams as we cross over train tracks. I'm so tense, my head feels like it'll explode. "It's definitely them," I say. "I saw them in Alaska. The guy who was smoking is the one who was sitting outside of the boat, checking all of the passengers when I left Anchorage."

"They've got the same uniforms as the two who were with Whit," Miles agrees.

"No question now," I say. "We're in the right place."

"Well, that's reassuring." Miles eases the truck over another set of train tracks. We leave town and head into the desert. "We located the right group of steroid-fueled weapon-toting giants. Now all we have to do is rescue a few dozen people they're keeping captive right from under their noses. Easy peasy. Right?"

He tries to make his tone light, but I can see that he finally understands the danger we're getting into. Miles is scared. And frankly, so am I.

18

MILES

AS WE LEAVE VAUGHN AND HEAD SOUTH, WE drive over a small ridge to find ourselves facing a road that continues straight ahead until it gets so tiny that it disappears on the horizon. The land around us is flat and brown. Off in the distance on one side is a faraway mountain range. The green trees on its slopes make it stand out like an oasis in the middle of sand dunes.

I pull off the road and put the truck in park. "There's no way we can hide in the middle of this wasteland," I point out. "They'll see us coming from miles away."

Besides getting that wild glint in her eye when she told me to speed away from the bar back in Vaughn, Juneau seems completely unafraid. She's in leader mode again, 100 percent practical. No room for emotion.

She unfolds the map and points to where we are, a couple inches northwest of the penned-in rectangle. "It looks like the guy's ranch is mostly desert," she says, "but over here"—she puts her finger on the green—"it extends to include some of those mountains up ahead."

"Should we head for those, then?" I ask.

Juneau studies the horizon, and then says, "Let's think about this like a hunter would."

"You think like a hunter. I'll think from a military tactics point of view," I say. Juneau shoots me a skeptical look. "Remember my skill set? Video games and movies: best tactical training you could ask for!" I wink and Juneau rewards me with a smile.

Then, pressing her lips together, she considers things for a full minute before speaking. "Say that Avery and I are both predators and my clan is our common prey. Avery's already captured them, but he wants to trap me too. If Whit is working with him and gave me the map, he knows I'm coming. He's using his catch to lure me in. Daring me to steal it so he can trap me, too. We have to swipe Avery's prize from under his nose while he waits for us to do it."

She pauses and looks at me.

"Okay, then," I say, translating what she's just said into the storyline of one of the war games I'm so good at. "I can think of two ways to do that: stealth or strength. With the stealth option, we'll have to somehow trick them or distract their sentries so that we can help your clan escape while they're not looking. Strength option means that we fight Avery's army head-on, which would involve surprise, speed, and heavy weaponry."

"Plan A's looking kind of good right now," says Juneau.

I nod. "Either would require a good knowledge on our part of where everything is and what we are up against."

Juneau nods at me, a glimmer of respect in her eye. "You're pretty good at this," she says.

"Well, it's not quite as impressive as sticking my entire fist in my mouth," I say.

"False modesty," Juneau lobs back.

"Oh, sorry. I am AWESOME!" I say, striking a muscle-man pose.

"Better," she says, grinning. She looks back down at the map. "Now, my first reaction would be to want to drive straight across the desert, and then once we're near the gate, leave the truck and go the rest of the way on foot, hiding along the way. To get to my clan as quickly as possible."

"Won't they spot the truck?" I ask.

"Even if Avery has a few dozen men, this is a huge area to guard," Juneau says, tapping her finger on the rectangular area, "But, yes—if someone is patrolling the perimeter, like I saw in the Reading, they will at some point see the truck."

I frown at Juneau, skeptical. "You said that's your first reaction. What's your second?"

"To use restraint. Head for the mountains and take more time scouting the area from the outside before breaking in. We could take this road," she says, pointing to a tiny black line on the map. "It's a little farther and will take us longer, but we avoid the ranch and stay hidden. We could drive the truck as far as possible into the trees, and then hike till we hit the corner of the perimeter fence that extends into the woods."

"I vote for the creeping-around-in-the-woods option over the barging-in-like-gangbusters one," I say without hesitation.

Juneau nods. "Normally in a situation like this I would ask for a sign from the Yara. But seeing the future would require an oracle—" she begins. I put my hand up in a hold-everything gesture, and she continues, "But we're not going there."

There is an uncomfortable silence, which she finally breaks. "I want to go straight for my clan. To get this over with. But I've learned in the past that my emotions aren't always an indicator of the best possible plan. I have to go deeper, to my instincts. And those tell me that the best thing to do is to set up a base camp in the woods, do surveillance of the ranch, and assess what advantages nature offers us before we act."

"Then it's decided," I say, and putting the truck in gear, I head toward the mountains. I keep an eye out for any vehicles heading our way, but our car is the only thing moving for miles around.

We ride in silence for a few minutes before I say, "Can I ask you something about your religion?"

"I don't have a religion," Juneau says, looking curious. "Oh— do you mean my clan's relationship with the Yara?"

I nod.

"That's more metaphysical than spiritual. We don't worship anyone or anything. It's more a way of thinking about our position in relation to the rest of nature and the way we fit in with everything else."

"But I've heard you mention Gaia before. Isn't that the Greek earth goddess?"

"The Gaia Movement used the term to mean everything in earth's superorganism—living things, rocks, oceans, air—they're all mixed into one being called Gaia. Gaia exists in the past, back to the origins of life, and in the future as long as life exists. That's why we can ask the Yara—the force that runs through Gaia—to see in the past and the future.

"Time is relative. The past and the future have both happened—we've just figured out how to access those past and future 'memories' by Reading."

"Okay, this is where I screw my head off, shake it out, and screw it back on again," I say.

Juneau gets this sardonic smile on her lips and says, "Posturing."

"Huh?" I say.

"You keep doing this false modesty thing. Acting like you're no one special. Or that you don't understand what I'm saying because it's complicated. When in fact you're probably as smart as I am—"

"Ha!" I can't help from blurting out.

"What?" Juneau asks, confused.

"Try not to be too modest," I jibe.

Juneau just looks at me for a moment, and then says, "Why

would I try to be modest? I'm super-smart, with potential for genius, from what the educators in our clan say. And from what I can tell, so are you. So why try to hide it? Why imply that you aren't?"

I just keep driving with my mouth hanging open. I might have made some sort of gurgling noise, but am otherwise speechless.

Juneau continues to push me on it. "Is it some kind of cultural thing, this false modesty about your capacities? If this had been a week ago, I would have thought you were misleading me about your intelligence to put yourself at some sort of advantage. But now it just pisses me off because you're not being honest. With *me*!"

I finally get my voice back. "Stop! Holy crap, Juneau, ixnay with the inquisition! I'm not trying to pull anything over on you. It's cultural . . . definitely cultural. But I've never really thought about it before. Just give me a second."

I try to formulate my thoughts into something she will accept. "You . . . I mean, people . . . in society . . ." How do I even say this? "You're not supposed to act like you know you're smart because it's considered rude," I say finally.

Juneau starts laughing. "That's the stupidest thing I've ever heard. When you're in a group, you offer your skills for the use and survival of the group. You don't pretend you don't have them. It's not only disingenuous, it's withholding your donation to the common good."

"Is everyone in your clan like this, or are you the only one who hasn't been socially conditioned to act like a normal person?"

"That depends on your definition of normal," she shoots back, and then bites her lip. "I suppose a bit of both. Everyone knows one another's strengths and weaknesses because they're vital to our survival. But also, since I was five, I was expected to lead the clan. To be the clan Sage. So everyone expected me to be capable. False modesty would have been ridiculous."

I like the fact that Juneau listened to me, so I try to understand what she's explaining. To understand the role she had . . . that she still does. It's the reason she's like she is. And it's the reason we're here: because of this heavy burden she's always carried.

Her clan would expect her to try to save them. So that's exactly what she's going to do.

And in order for her to fully trust me, I'm going to have to sacrifice some of my own habits. Number one being my defense mechanisms. I've already sworn to myself not to hide my feelings behind jokes. Now she wants me to be completely honest with her about myself. Which means being vulnerable to getting hurt. Again.

What can be worse than your own mother abandoning you? I think, my gut twisting as the thought barges in from where it hides in my subconscious. And the answer comes with a double blow to my solar plexus: *the girl you've fallen for doing the same damn thing.*

19

JUNEAU

WE DRIVE THE REST OF THE WAY IN SILENCE. I'M trying to process what Miles told me about how people in the "outside world" behave. It sheds a whole new light on him, and the way he acts . . . the way he's been acting, ever since he went through the Rite.

He admits that he hides things. He covers himself up. He shows the version of himself that he wants others to see. Which means that there could be a whole sea of thoughts, emotions . . . fears hiding behind his blasé charm.

A voice in my head tells me that even though I criticized him for not being honest, I'm worse than he is. I let my duty toward my clan override who I am and what I want for myself. And I haven't only been pretending to my clan about it . . . I've been lying to myself.

As soon as that thought bursts its way into my consciousness, I push it back out and lock the door.

It takes us another tense half hour of driving on the main road as we watch for any vehicles approaching, either from Vaughn or from the direction of the ranch. When we pull off onto the one-lane road leading to the mountains, we both breathe a sigh of relief. Another half hour and we're driving up into the foothills, where scattered yucca plants grow like spiky green porcupines.

The road finally ends in a dirt path that stops abruptly at the base of a butte. We go off-road for the last bit, and do our best to hide the truck behind a rocky outcrop. There is nothing in sight—no houses, no cars, no phone, no electricity lines. It's only us and nature. Just the way I like it.

I step out of the car and the desert heat slams me in the face. We're just a few hours south of where we camped last night, but the temperature is noticeably hotter. I strip back down to my tank top, then pull a pair of jeans out of my pack. Taking my bowie knife, I cut off the legs, halfway up the thigh, and then roll the hem up twice to keep it from fraying. Unzipping the pair of jeans I'm wearing, I start changing into my new shorts. Miles sees and abruptly turns around, supposedly to give me privacy.

"Miles. You've seen me naked," I remind him.

"Although technically true, we were in the tent and it was unfortunately very dark," he responds, but keeps his back toward me.

"I went swimming in my underwear just yesterday, and my

semi-nudity didn't seem to bother you then," I say with a smile.

"You were treating it like a bathing suit," he says. "You're changing clothes now, and when it's under your clothes, it counts as lingerie."

I laugh. "You're a prude, Miles Blackwell."

"I most definitely am not a prude," he insists, and forces himself to turn around. But by this time I've got my new shorts on, so there's nothing to see. "I would describe most of my friends as letches," Miles continues. "I, on the other hand, have always prided myself on being a gentleman. And unless you are intentionally undressing for my benefit, I'd prefer not to take the experience for granted."

"All just pretty words," I say, but catch myself blushing.

Miles notices, and crows, "See, you do prefer gentlemen to wild men! Admit it!"

Ignoring his taunt, I clear my throat, picking up the knife, and gesture to his jeans. "Do you want me to make yours into shorts, too?"

"Gentlemen don't wear cutoffs," he says, crossing his arms defensively.

"So you're basing your choice on fashion, and not the fact that it's about ninety degrees out?" I ask.

"Of course not," Miles says. He nods up toward the mountaintop. "I was just thinking of how it'll probably get cold up there at night, and I'd rather be too hot now than cold later."

"Right . . . ," I say skeptically.

"Juneau, there is no way on this earth that you will persuade me to wear cutoff jeans." Miles laughs and walks away. Discussion over.

"Your choice." I shrug and, unable to hide the smile on my lips, slip the knife back into its leather sheath.

I stow most of our supplies in my backpack, and Miles picks up the tent and a bag of food, and we're off. Even though we'll be taking the time we need for surveillance instead of rushing right in, I don't want to lose any time.

We climb directly to the top of the first hill. My hiking boots provide traction, which would have made the trek a quick one, if Miles didn't keep slipping with his smooth-soled tennis shoes. It's funny—the star on the side makes them look like sports shoes, but he might as well be wearing ballet slippers for all the good it's doing him on the rocky slopes.

We crest the hill after a half hour and stop to drink some water. The sun is high above now; it must be noon or just after. "Are you hungry?" I ask. Miles shakes his head, but doesn't speak. I'm not sure if he's able—his face is all red and he's breathing heavily.

I remind myself that he just went through the Rite. Plus, the pure oxygen of the mountains must be hitting him like a brick wall. I have breathed the air in Los Angeles, and considering the difference between that and this nature-filtered mountain air, Miles might as well be on another planet.

I hand him the water bottle, and he takes a long swig. He bends over and puts his hands on his knees, still breathing heavy. "You know, it's funny," he says with his wry smile. "I'm in perfect shape. It's probably just the altitude that's getting to me."

"You just came back from the dead," I remind him.

"Oh yeah, that. It's definitely due to my recent resurrection," he says. "And if I asked you to take it a bit slower?"

"With my clan on the other side of that mountain?" I say, pointing to the tree-lined peak before us. I give him a wicked smile. "Sorry, but no chance."

Miles stands back up and pounds on his chest with his fists. "Okay, I'm ready for anything," he says. "Don't pay any attention to my shortness of breath, red face, or sweat-soaked clothes. It's all a ruse so that I can really pour on the speed at the end and impress you."

"Posturing," I say.

"Exactly," Miles replies.

I walk over and brush his fiery cheek with my fingertips. "If we keep up our pace, we'll probably reach the peak in just over an hour. And, if it would make you feel better, once we get there I'll fix lunch while you recover."

Miles nods, still gasping, and manages to wheeze, "Sounds good."

"First one to the top gets a Snickers bar!" I say, and skip out of his way as he tries to grab me.

20

MILES

I'M USELESS. TRULY. IT'S BECOMING MORE AND more obvious that Juneau would be better off doing this rescue without me. While I barely made it up the mountain, Juneau scaled the side like Spider-Man, not even having to look where she put her feet.

Once we get to the top, I sit down and put my head between my knees while Juneau scouts the ridge for a lookout point. "Come up here, Miles!" she shouts from the other side of a patch of pine trees.

"Can't move. Paralyzed. Think I'm having death-sleep flashback," I yell, gasping for breath as I hold my pounding head in my hands.

"Just walk over to me—I'm not even thirty feet away—and then you'll have my permission to pass out," she calls.

"Permission?" I grumble as I push myself to my feet and weave my way toward her. I give her a choppy salute. "Yes, sir, whatever you say, sir."

"Come have a look," she says. There's an excited gleam in her eyes. I look in the direction she's pointing and see it: an enormous wire fence, twenty feet tall, running toward the mountain through the desert, and then straight up the side, trailing halfway up one of the peaks before cutting horizontally across and disappearing in the distance.

"That's gotta be it!" I say, feeling strange. After weeks of Juneau talking about her clan being kidnapped, here is the material proof. We're within walking distance of the fence—the only thing separating Juneau from her clan. Besides several thousand volts of electricity and an army of bodybuilders with automatic weapons, that is. But still . . . we're here at last.

I glance back at Juneau, and she is practically crackling with excitement. She looks like she's about to burst out of her skin, and I know it's taking everything she's got not to rush the fence and go directly to her people.

"Okay, here's the plan," she says. "We're going to set up camp on the other side of the ridge so that if someone's patrolling the perimeter fence, they won't see us."

"I'm camp setter-upper," I say. "Just give me five minutes to remember how to breathe."

"I know I offered to fix us lunch," she says, picking up her backpack. She starts back the way we came, and even though all I want to do is throw myself spread eagle on the ground, I follow her. "But I'm so excited I'm not even hungry," she continues. "I want to start following the fence to see where it leads."

"Don't worry about lunch," I say, "but do you think it's safe?"

"I promise to stay out of view and not do anything rash," she responds.

"You want me to go with you?" I ask, praying she'll say no. I silently wonder if eighteen is too young to have a climbing-induced heart attack.

"No," she says quickly, and then turns to me. "I mean . . . it would be great if you could set up camp for us. That way you could recover from the climb and eat."

Perfect, I think. *We're on the same page.*

We walk a few yards down the other side of the mountain. Once we hit a small clearing, Juneau dumps her backpack and I let my bags fall to the ground. I watch as she fills a canteen from a water bottle and then rifles through her bag for her crossbow. She strings the canteen around her neck and hangs the crossbow on a leather strap over one shoulder.

I dig into the grocery bag and hand her a Snickers bar. "You won it. Plus, all that wholesome natural goodness should help sustain you till you get back."

She grins. "I'll just be gone an hour or two," she says, and turns to leave. Then, hesitating, she runs back to me, grabs my face in her hands, and kisses me quickly on the lips. She laughs at my surprise at this very un-Juneau-like display, and then is off. Now that I'm not weighing her down, she moves twice as fast, leaping atop a boulder and disappearing over the top of the mountain.

I stretch out and lay on the ground for a good ten minutes, until my breathing returns to normal and I stop my profuse sweating. Opening one of the water bottles, I pour the entire thing over my head and feel a lot better.

I pitch the tent in minutes flat, and put all of the cooking supplies in a pile, before hanging the bag of food from a tree branch like I've seen Juneau do. After gathering enough wood from the surrounding forest for a decent-sized campfire, I look around the clearing with pride. No way would I have known how to set up camp a month ago.

And look at me now—living off the land! *Okay, not quite, but close enough,* I think, as I make myself a peanut butter and jelly sandwich and grab a bag of chips and bottle of water and hike back up to the lookout point to eat my lunch.

I try to look at the landscape before me like Juneau would. How did she put it? "Figure out which advantages nature gives us," or something like that. I spot a little stream running down the mountainside a ways away, before the fence starts. I make a mental note to refill the water bottles from it. There's the ridge I'm on—the perfect lookout. It's surrounded by trees, so not obvious like some of the cliff tops down the mountain from me. That's two advantages. Juneau probably wouldn't even list those. She probably absorbed it all at first glance. For her, a landscape like this is like my living room is to me: She knows her way around it with her eyes shut.

I see something moving far off in the mountains, inside the gated area. It looks like an enormous reindeer, but since I sincerely doubt there are reindeer in New Mexico, I figure it must be something like an elk. Although, when I imagine it strung with bells and red reins, it does look *just* like the reindeers in all the Christmas movies. Elk. Reindeer. Maybe they're just two names for the same animal. *How clueless am I?* I think, feeling a pang of despair.

Don't give up just because you can't identify the first wild animal you see. I think of what Juneau said about being one with nature, and decide to try an experiment. I do like she does and calm my breathing, trying to slow my heartbeat. I close my eyes for a minute, and then opening them, try to see inside the landscape instead of just looking at the surface. And as I become still, I grow aware of things moving around me.

To my right, my peripheral vision catches a squirrel scampering down the side of a tree, grabbing a nut off the ground, shoving it in his mouth, and running back up to his perch. Far off in the desert, inside the gates, I see horses ... no—zebras. A whole herd of zebras walking through the desert toward the mountain foothills. Some kind of big bird—a falcon?—soars overhead, motionless as it floats on an air current.

I wish I had paid more attention in biology. Or at least watched more Animal Planet. The zebras and the squirrel are the only animals I'm actually able to identify. At least I know the elk-beast is some type of deer.

I close my eyes again, and feel the heat from the rock I'm sitting on baking the palms of my hands. I think of Juneau and wonder how she feels, being this close to her people. I wonder what she'll want to do once she's reunited with them. I mean once they're free, course. I hope that whatever it is, she'll want me to come along. And, without knowing that I already made the decision, I realize I'm ready to go with her. To follow wherever she wants to go. It seems like a huge, momentous choice, but really, it's one of the easiest ones I've ever made.

I focus on the picture of Juneau in my mind, and imagine her following the fence as far as she can without being seen, scouting the surrounding area for anything she can use in her quest. A tingling sensation travels up my fingers to my arms, and suddenly I'm experiencing an overwhelming feeling of excitement, mixed with sharp jabs of anxiety. It's something I've never felt before, not in this intensity. And it dawns on me that it's because these aren't *my* emotions. They're Juneau's. *I'm channeling her feelings.*

I scramble to my feet, and stare at my hands and then down at the rock. Was I . . . I couldn't have been. Did I just Read the Yara? I rifle through my memory for the explanation Juneau gave this morning about what kind of Readings produce what effects. Is ground for feelings? I can't remember. I seem to recall that Juneau touches the ground and thinks of the person whose emotions she wants to feel. At least that's what I just did, but unintentionally.

"No way!" I yell, and do this crazed dance around the top of the cliff. I did it! I connected to the Yara! I didn't think it was possible.

Wait. Reality check: *Juneau* didn't think it was possible. She said the Yara stuff only comes with a life change. By living in tune with nature, or whatever. How can I be close to nature if I can't even identify a freaking reindeer? It's the Amrit; I'm sure of it. Along with the advantages of antiaging and disease immunity, it must have a side effect of messing with people's brains. And then it hits me. The Amrit messed with my brain. I'm not just immortal. I'm magic.

My glee disappears and fear takes its place, slithering up my chest like a snake, and wrapping around my throat. *It's okay,* I tell myself. *It's a good thing.*

I know I should be excited. This makes me closer to Juneau. I'll be able to understand everything she talks about that, until now, has been only an abstract concept.

But what if this *isn't* the Yara. It shouldn't be this easy. Juneau said it would take a long time. Dedication to the earth, and all that. What if, because I'm not like Juneau's clan members, the drug that saved my life is making me go insane, and hallucinations are just the first symptom? *Don't be paranoid,* I think, but now that it's me doing the magic and not Juneau, I am truly freaking out.

I stumble back down the mountain to our campsite, overwhelmed by the warring thoughts pinballing through my mind: On one side this is one of the most exciting things that has ever happened to me; on the other it's the scariest.

When I get to the clearing, I am suddenly so exhausted that I crawl into the tent and flop down on the ground. It feels like residual death-sleep—the kind of fatigue that knocks you over the head and renders you unconscious.

As I drift off I focus once more on what happened on the cliff. Did I really connect to the Yara without even trying, or am I going crazy because I took a drug that wasn't meant for me? I can't know unless it happens again. Until then, I won't say anything to Juneau. No need to scare her, too.

21

JUNEAU

WHEN I GET BACK TO CAMP, MILES IS NOWHERE to be seen. But he's organized everything so well that I can't believe this is the same guy who sat in the car while I had to set up the tent, make the fire, and cook just over a week ago.

I unstrap my canteen and crossbow and lay them on the ground. Taking a piece of bread from the bag Miles hung from a nearby tree, I munch on it as I use a piece of kindling to draw a map in the dirt. Quickly, before I can forget anything, I sketch a facsimile of the section of fence leading along the mountain through the forest and down to the desert. I mark everything I saw along it: groves of trees, underbrush thick enough to hide in, several streams and the places they spill into ponds. I mark the animals I saw, on both sides of the fence, and the half-dozen metal boxes I spotted hung high up on some of the fence posts.

When I'm done I glance back around the clearing, wondering just where Miles has ventured on his own. And then I notice that the tent flap is zipped shut.

I walk over to investigate, unzipping it in one quick movement. And Miles, who was sleeping, leaps up with an expression so terror struck that I yell and jump back. "Holy crap, you scared the shit out of me!" he says, and pushes his way out the tent.

"*You* scared *me*!" I say, pressing my hand to my heart, which is hammering like a woodpecker. "What are you doing taking a nap in the middle of the day?"

Miles gets this guilty look on his face and says, "I was tired. That's all."

"Okay," I say, and walk away to sit next to my map while I wait for my pulse to slow to normal. When I look back at him, he's just standing there, staring at me in a weird way. "What's wrong with you?" I ask.

"Nothing!" he blurts out. "Nothing's wrong with me. Whatsoever. I'm totally normal . . . I mean, fine."

"Okay." I turn away from him and scribble a few more details onto the map. If he doesn't want to talk, I'm not going to force him to. But he's definitely bothered about something.

"What are you drawing?" Miles says, changing the subject. He stands next to me and inspects my map.

"I surveyed the fence, all of the way from where it enters the woods on one side to where it exits into the desert at the other," I say, pointing it out on the map.

"Did you find anything helpful?" he says, avoiding my eyes.

"Just a general idea of what is there," I say. "I wanted to see how far the enclosure goes. It's enormous, Miles. Two hours, and I just saw a small section of it. But we can definitely move undetected along the entire length of the barrier within the mountain area. I imagine this is where Avery brings his visitors to hunt"—I point out the water sources—"because that's where the animals are going to be. Where's the map?"

"In the tent," he says, and retrieves it. I spread it out so we can inspect the penned-in area.

"It's hard to know how accurate the gas station guy was with this box he drew. But saying it's generally right, it doesn't look like there are many water sources in the ranch. Just our mountain area and then these two rivers coming in from the east on the far side. Most of this is dry land."

"So what's that tell you?" Miles says, and his voice once again sounds normal. Whatever spooked him before has passed.

"I didn't spot any buildings near the foothills. So I'm guessing that Avery's house is near the rivers. Probably the adobe huts my clan is staying in, too, or else he'd have to bring them daily supplies of water. That means that the area we're looking for is probably over here." I trace from where we are on the western edge of the rectangle to the far eastern side where two blue lines branch out.

Miles whistles low. "That's a long ways away."

"Probably a whole day of hiking," I say, and scribble some numbers in the dirt. "Yesterday the sun rose around six and set at eight. That's a fourteen-hour day." I hold the pen against the map's scale and then up to measure the length of the rectangle. "If we left at dawn we might be there by nightfall."

I look up to see Miles's face. He looks like he's thinking about it. "Or," he says, running his finger along the bottom of the line, "we can drive there using a round-about route so we're not spotted, get there a lot faster, and have the truck for whatever escape plan you're cooking up."

"Good point," I say, pointing the pen at Miles. "I'm not used to counting motor vehicles as part of my assets. As for escape plans . . . I haven't even thought about that. In my mind, we need to locate Avery, my clan, and wherever the guards are staying before we do anything else."

Miles nods. "Well, since we decided on Plan A—the stealth strategy—that will probably involve stealing several cars and driving them out. As you said, we will have to know where the guards are located, as well as their vehicles, and any entrances or exits to the perimeter fence."

I can't help but smiling. Miles is actually allowing himself to show what he's got—his ability to strategize. He trusts me enough to lower his guard. Finally.

"What?" he asks, seeing my expression.

"Nothing. Go on," I urge.

"Of course, if we went with Plan B—the strength strategy— and fought them head-on, then *if* we win"—Miles pauses for emphasis—"we would seize their vehicles and drive on out of there. Which is pretty hard to imagine, seeing what we have to work with."

"Which is . . . ," I prod.

"Assuming that your clan has no weapons, since they're being kept captive, we can count on two crossbows, a bowie knife, and a pickup truck."

I laugh. "It's a good thing we chose Plan A, then. But if it comes to fighting, we can count on the strength of my entire clan," I say. "Oh, and hopefully some help from Tallie."

"Tallie?" Miles asks, looking completely thrown.

"Yes, the mountain woman Poe is playing house-raven with," I remind him.

"But . . . how is she going to help us from Utah?"

"Well, hopefully she's not in Utah anymore. I called her from Arizona and asked her to come to New Mexico."

"Wait. How?" Miles stammers. "I thought she didn't have a phone or electricity."

"She doesn't," I respond. "Before I left, she gave me the phone number of the general store that she hikes to every few days. I gave them a message for her, asking her to go to Roswell and wait for word. Hopefully she's gotten it by now, was able to borrow a truck, and is on her way. Which means one more person on the outside, plus another vehicle."

Miles just gapes at me. "And you'll be communicating with her . . . how?"

"While I was down near the fence, I used the Yara to try to contact Poe. The way Whit called him when he freaked out in the back of your car. If it works—hopefully—he'll come."

"Wow," Miles says. "Okay, then. I'll add Tallie and the bird to our list of potential assets." He looks back down at my map. "So should we leave tonight? Drive to the other end of the reserve, hide the truck, and scout? We could split up and run along the fence—I could go north while you go south until we hit the corners, and then both follow the fence west. If we split up we could cover more distance, and do it under cover of night."

I shake my head. "We have to stick together."

"Why?" he asks.

"Let's say there are guards patrolling the perimeter, as we suspect. If they make their rounds at night, all they'll need is a pair of headlights scanning that wide-open desert land, and they'll find us in minutes."

"And what would that change if we stuck together?" Miles asks.

"I can hide myself with Conjuring. I could even hide both of us, like I did from your dad and his men while you were in the death-sleep. But if you're on the other side of the ranch, I won't be able to protect you."

Miles pauses. "It's too bad I can't camouflage myself," he says, and looks strangely uncomfortable.

"That's Conjuring," I say softly. "You don't even know how to Read. Like I said, it's not like it comes automatically once you've gone through the Rite. It's a part of a way of thinking. Of living."

"I don't know," he says slowly. "I just thought I felt something while you were gone. It probably wasn't anything."

My silence speaks my opinion on that. Miles shrugs and tries to look nonchalant. "Okay," he says, and thrusting his fists into his pockets, walks away toward the ridge. I follow him to the top of the ridge, where he stops and looks out over the desert. I put an arm around his back and lean my head lightly against his arm.

"You're bothered about the is-Yara-religion-or-is-it-magic issue, aren't you? About how it's going to affect you."

Miles doesn't answer.

"Do you wish I hadn't given you the Rite?" I ask.

He looks up and watches a hawk fly in slow, looping circles as it searches the ground for prey. "I'm glad I'm not dead," he answers.

"You don't have to be like us, Miles," I say. "You can go back to California and live an extremely long life, aging imperceptibly for eons—as long as you don't get in the way of any speeding cars or bullets." I keep my eyes on the hawk. Sometimes it's easier to say something you don't like when you don't have to watch the listener's reaction.

"No, I can't, Juneau," he says, touching my arm and turning me to look at him. There's pain in his eyes, but along with it is a defensiveness I haven't seen for a while. "And even if I wanted to, I would have to move on a regular basis. People would notice after a while when I don't age. I would have to live like a nomad: setting up my life in one place, and being forced to leave once things looked suspicious . . . like every ten or twenty years. What kind of life would that be?"

"Some would think it was pretty amazing. Think of how many different lives you could live. How many places you'd see and professions you could have." But I know as I speak that he's not going to accept it. He hasn't had enough time to think things through. To get used to the repercussions of what he is. For me, it was always an inevitable part of life in my clan: a state I wanted to enter.

I see Miles's jaw clench as he deflects my words, refusing to let them sink in. There's nothing I can say to make him feel better right now. But there *is* something I can do to distract him. I squeeze his hand. "Feel like joining me for another round of target practice?"

"Now?" he asks, inching out of his dark mood. "Shouldn't we be getting ready to leave?"

"No, I think we should stay here tonight and leave in the morning. I want to try to get a message to my father before we get any closer. And you could use another night of rest to recover from your death-sleep. Plus, it would make me feel better if you get some more practice in before you have to actually use your weapon. If we're going up against a man with an army," I continue, "we better be able to defend ourselves."

The corners of Miles's lips barely move, but the pain in his eyes has disappeared. "As long as we stick with targets that aren't cute and furry," he says.

"Inanimate objects only—at least for you," I promise, and loop my arm through his as we turn and walk back to camp.

22

MILES

"MILES, I SHOWED YOU THIS YESTERDAY. TWICE. You were doing just fine then." Juneau looks at me, confused.

"I know, but I just like hearing you explain things. It's that bossy tone you get when you tell me what to do that just... drives me wild."

She grins and rolls her eyes. "Use the pull cord to cock back the bowstring," she says, showing me once again how to stretch the braided string back until it is tight.

I don't want to admit that I wasn't listening the first two times because of the way she was standing, her chest pressed closely to my back as she showed me how to hold the weapon.

"That's right," she says. "You loop it around this peg, the nut, which holds it in place."

I try not to get distracted again by her being basically wrapped around me, one hand holding the crossbow under mine and the other around my shoulder as I kneel with one leg on the ground. I can't imagine target practice has been this sexy. For anyone. Ever.

"Now you fit the bolt in," she continues, handing me one of her super-sharp carved wooden arrows.

I turn my head to glance back at her, and her cheek is an inch from my own. My face grows warm as electricity pings between us.

Juneau lowers her arms and stands up from her crouching position. She puts her fists on her hips and says, "You're not concentrating. This is important. Even if it's just for defense, since we won't be 'barging in like gangbusters to mow them down,' as you put it."

"Got it. I understand," I say. "Now can you take that position again? I don't think I can fit this bolt in on my own."

"Ha!" Juneau says, but with a twinkle in her eye she wraps her arms back around me and helps me fit the arrow into the track carved into the wood.

"Hold the crossbow up, in front of your face, high enough so that you're looking at your target just over the top of the tiller." I do as she says, and squint over the weapon toward my target tree, which stands about thirty feet away.

"Now with two fingers, you're going to pull the trigger, which releases the nut," Juneau says, and brushes her finger along a long piece of bone that runs along the bottom side of the crossbow.

"You're so sexy when you speak crossbow to me," I murmur,

and then squeeze the bone lever like she's showing me, and the crossbow recoils against my shoulder as the arrow goes flying across the clearing . . . and right past the tree.

"You did that on purpose," Juneau says, standing up from her crouch. "Your aim was good the first time we tried this."

"Why don't you shoot?" I ask, rising to my feet. "That way I can watch your technique."

"Okay," she says, and taking the crossbow from me, uses one smooth motion to cock the bowstring and slip a bolt into the track. She raises it to face level and aims, and the movement is so natural that the crossbow looks like an extension of her body. Like she's a part of the forest she carved her weapon from. She's a puzzle piece that fits perfectly in its place.

Watching her shoot is just one more example of why Juneau was so uncomfortable in Seattle, all nervous and jumpy, like a fish out of water. She belongs in nature, and it belongs to her.

Her fingers squeeze the bone trigger and the bolt goes flying across the clearing, so fast I don't even see it until it's embedded into the exact center of the target tree. Juneau smiles and holds the crossbow out to me. "Your turn," she says.

I take my time cocking the string. "How long have you been doing this?" I ask.

"Since I was seven," she answers.

"That makes me feel a little bit better," I say, fumbling as I slip the bolt into the track.

"What have *you* been doing since you were seven?" Juneau asks.

"Like I said, playing video games," I respond.

"Well, I'm sure you'd beat me at that," she says.

"I somehow doubt it," I say, and look over to where she stands, hand resting casually on hip. She's so small and reedy it would be easy for someone who didn't know her to assume she was weak. Which she'd definitely use to her advantage. She could probably take on a whole squad of those guards herself . . . if they didn't have the advantages of Kevlar and automatic weapons.

I raise the crossbow to shoulder level and hold it the way she had, my left hand supporting the weapon from underneath, and the fingers of my right hand under the trigger. I fire. The bolt embeds itself firmly into the tree, directly to the right of her bolt. Juneau exhales and pats my shoulder. "That's okay," she jibes. "We can't both be perfect."

"Oh yeah?" I exclaim, and swing her off her feet into an off-ground hug that sends her squirming for terra firma.

"One more time," she yells. "You might come close but you can't beat me. Let's see what you can do from a shorter range."

We move forward ten feet, and Juneau pulls her big bowie knife out of a kind of holster she's slung around her waist. "My knife against your crossbow," she says, and pulling her elbow straight up so that the knife is positioned behind her shoulder, steps forward and flings it toward the tree. I see a flash of silver as a stray sunbeam reflects off the metal, and in less than a second, the blade sticks firmly into the tree next to her bolt.

"Remind me never to make you mad," I say in awe. Before she can respond, I raise the crossbow again and shoot, this time lodging my bolt into the bark a hairsbreadth away from the knife.

"Not bad!" Juneau says admiringly, and runs to gather the knife and bolts from the tree. She comes back and hands me the arrows and we spend the next half hour trying to beat each other. I haven't had this much fun in years.

Finally Juneau takes the crossbow from me, loads a bolt, and says, "What should we hunt for dinner?"

"If I have to choose from fuzzy woodland creatures, then that rabbit the first night was pretty good," I say, still feeling squeamish about shooting my dinner. Although it's nothing like my nausea when I saw Juneau with the dead rabbit on Mount Rainier.

"Okay," she says. "Follow me." Juneau shows me how to walk silently, avoiding small branches and anything else that makes noise. We pass squirrels, birds, even a snake slithering its way across the leaf-lined ground, and none of them notice us. Finally she stops and nods toward a large brown rabbit. She raises the crossbow, squeezes the trigger, and the rabbit is instantly lying motionless on its side. She runs over and pulls the bolt out. I hear her murmur a few words to the animal as I walk up behind her.

"What did you say to it?" I ask.

"I thanked it for giving its life to feed us," she responds simply. "It's a part of the cycle of life. Energy from the earth passes from it to us as we consume it."

"Do you thank the plants you eat?" I ask.

"No, silly," she says. "Plants can't hear."

"And dead rabbits can," I counter. But she just smiles, like it's something I'll understand one day, and as usual, I can't help smiling back. Juneau kills one more rabbit, and like the first, hands it to me to carry. I hold the soft corpses by the scruff of the neck as we make our way back to the camp, careful not to look at them so Juneau doesn't see how uncomfortable I am. Of course, I'm a total hypocrite, eating meat without thinking about where it comes from since I was a kid. But even knowing this, I can't bring myself to watch as Juneau takes the bowie knife and skins and skewers them, and busy myself with building the fire instead.

After dinner, we sit silently in the light of the fire. Dusk has just begun to fall, the air darkening into that indigo haze that my mom always used to call "blue o'clock," when all of a sudden Juneau sits upright, her face shifting from relaxed to alert. "Don't move," she whispers as she reaches for the crossbow.

I don't see or hear anything. And then—from the woods in front of us—a twig snaps, and a dark silhouette materializes through the trees.

"I don't have a weapon," a voice calls.

"Well, I do, and I won't hesitate to use it," says Juneau, peering along the top of her loaded crossbow.

A man steps into the clearing, his face flickering orange in the firelight. He holds his hands up in an I'm-unarmed gesture.

"You," Juneau spits, her face as hard as stone.

"Juneau," Whit says. "Finally. I'm so glad you're here."

23

JUNEAU

"WHAT DO YOU WANT FROM ME?" I ASK, CROSSBOW glued to my shoulder.

"I just want to talk," Whit says. "No one knows I'm here. I haven't told anyone you're here either." I wait, motionless, until he shuffles forward uncomfortably. "May I sit down?" he asks.

"Do what you want," I say, keeping my fingers on the trigger as he lowers his hands and walks carefully to sit across the fire from me. Wincing, he eases himself into a sitting position.

He is wearing new clothes: a pair of jeans and a short-sleeved collared shirt. There are bandages on his arms, and now that he's closer, I see a long cut across his forehead, sewn up with at least a dozen stitches.

"Juneau, I'm not going to hurt you," he says.

"You already have," I say, and there's so much hatred in my

voice I can practically see my words take form in a violent red cloud.

Whit nods, like he agrees with me, then glances over at Miles. "I'd rather we talk alone," he says.

"Miles isn't going anywhere," I respond. "Whatever you have to say, you can say in front of him."

"Why? Because you've already told him about us? It seems I'm not the only one who has shared our secrets with the outside world," Whit says, looking wry.

"Our secrets aren't the only thing I've shared," I say. "Your *friend* almost killed Miles—would have killed him, if I hadn't given him the Rite."

"You gave . . . ?" The color drains from Whit's face, and for a second he loses his carefully guarded control and gapes at Miles. "That makes Miles the first person outside of our clan to take . . . the Rite."

"You mean Amrit," I say.

"Yes," Whit concedes, still gaping at Miles in shock. "But that was just three days ago. He's already recovered enough to walk around? Have you seen any other unfamiliar results or side effects?"

"You've had a whole clan to use as guinea pigs," I say. "Now get to the point."

Whit frowns and crosses his arms. "I'm only interested in him for his own sake."

"Bullshit," I say. "Hands by your sides." Whit puts his hands back on the ground.

"Take this," I say, passing the crossbow to Miles, "and shoot him if he moves."

"Is that really necessary?" Whit looks amused, like he thinks this whole thing is a joke.

"Completely," I respond, as Miles faces Whit and props the loaded crossbow on his knee. "Now talk."

Whit looks up toward the moon as if looking for inspiration, and then begins. "I know what this looks like. That you think I'm responsible for the attack upon our clan. And in a way, I am."

I watch him, using the same techniques of perception that he taught me to judge the truthfulness of his words. He is careful and keeps his face a blank page.

"It is true that I left Alaska to contact potential buyers of our Amrit, as I'm sure this boy's father told you." Whit watches me as carefully as I watch him back. He is trying to figure out how much I already know. I stare, unflinching.

"I went with the elders' approval," he says, and seeing my eyes narrow, he holds a hand up and backtracks. "Not their approval to spread word of the drug. That was my own doing. But I left our territory on occasion in order to get a reading on the outside world . . . on what events had occurred, so that we could stay informed of anything we needed to know."

"I figured that out when I saw the modern books you brought back," I say.

"It was important for us to keep abreast of developments in society," Whit explains.

"Why?" I ask.

"We needed to remain hidden, so it was important to know that we were staying off the radar of the outside world."

"You could have done that by going to Anchorage and reading a newspaper," I say. "Why the science books?"

Whit sighs. "Some of us never stopped pursuing our areas of research. It was essential that we stayed abreast of environmental and scientific breakthroughs."

"As essential as it was for you to betray us and sell our secrets to the highest bidder?"

Whit exhales and looks disappointed. Like he had been hoping I would see things from his point of view. He glances at Miles again. "Really, I would prefer that this boy not be pointing a dangerous weapon in my direction when he obviously doesn't know what he's doing with it."

Miles says, "Hey!"

"You can put it down," I say to him, and turn back to Whit. "You've been watching us."

"Of course I have. I wanted you to arrive here in one piece. Safely," Whit says. "And, as an aside, I didn't mean for Jake to shoot the boy."

"Well, that makes everything better," Miles says with a scowl, and places the crossbow on the ground beside him.

Whit ignores him. "Juneau, none of this has turned out as I wanted. I love the clan as much as you do—"

"I sincerely doubt that," I interject.

"You don't have to believe me," he says. "But everything I've done has been for the good of the clan." I can't help the look of disgust on my face, but stay silent. I want to hear what he has to say. "Just how much did Blackwell tell you?" he asks.

"Start from the beginning," I command.

"It was your mother, father, and I who came up with the formula for Amrit," Whit says. "We had a sort of think tank within the Gaia Movement, composed of the people you know as the elders. We were discussing solutions to restoring ecosystems, and one of the emphases was preserving endangered species—specifically those native to the United States. The zoologists in the group posited the theory that if the life expectancy of animals was extended, it would allow more breeding cycles, and thus more offspring—a giant step toward species preservation.

"At that point your mother came forward with a story she had heard as a child—a local legend, as I remember it—from her homeland of Mongolia."

"Mongolia!" I exclaim. "My mother was Chinese."

Whit looks uncomfortable. "Apparently her line originated in southern Mongolia. Surely your father would have told you about . . ."

I ignore that twist of the knife. Yes, it hurt—profoundly—that I was hearing this first from the man who betrayed my clan instead of my own father. But getting upset wasn't going to help anything. I quash the feelings for now, and decide to let them out in target practice later. "Keep talking," I insist.

"The story involved giving a wounded she-wolf a magical elixir that not only healed the wolf, but allowed it to live for several human-generations, spawning many litters of wolf cubs.

"Your mother began researching the origins of the legend, and the ingredients that could have been involved. I found similar stories in ancient Hindu texts, which called it Amrita. Since he is a chemist, your father began working with some of the plants and minerals mentioned in both your mother's legend and the texts I had found. Finally, we developed what we thought could be a workable formula. Our target test group was to be Mexican gray wolves, red wolves, and other wild canid species. We tested it first on laboratory mice, and then on a small trial group of dogs. It immediately became clear that animals given the Amrit became immune to disease.

"But before announcing it to the scientific community, we decided to put the elixir to the ultimate test, and took it ourselves. And when we saw that we survived without any noticeable side effects, we decided to expand the trial group to our entire circle. All survived without incident, besides, of course, going through what you know as the death-sleep.

"Thus began a discussion on whether or not it was a moral obligation to reveal our discovery to the world. Some, including me, were for—how could you not share such a groundbreaking discovery with humanity?—but the majority were against. The reasoning was that we should consider the life of the planet—Gaia—over the well-being of its animal species. If Amrit became available to all, it would lead to global overpopulation, and eventually to the destruction of Gaia. That was their hypothesis, at least.

"Around then your father noticed that some of the test animals weren't aging. And then Emily gave birth to Penelope, who was born with the ocular starburst mutation. We decided to go into hiding—at least until we learned what long-term effects the drug would have. And you know the rest of the story."

"So you gave up on your goal to solve the endangered species problem?" I ask.

"Your huskies' mother, Austen?" he says, lifting an eyebrow. I nod, wondering what he's getting at. "She was actually their great-great-grandmother. If we hadn't neutered most of the dogs, we would have had hundreds. Thousands, even."

My thoughts are reeling. The elders never stopped their research. We weren't the only test studies—our dogs had been treated and monitored for three decades.

Whit pauses to let this sink in, and then continues. "I never lost my conviction that Amrit should be made available to the outside world. I believe that its distribution could be made selective enough that population growth could be controlled. And the money that we could make would guarantee the clan financial stability. If the secret were out, we wouldn't have to hide anymore. But, if members did prefer their isolationist secession from society, they could buy themselves their own island and equip it with modern conveniences. The ancient elixir of life would be made available to those who could buy it, and our beloved in the clan would be safe and comfortable."

"The clan *was* safe and comfortable," I say. "Now they're imprisoned, thanks to you."

Whit holds up a hand. "Let me finish my story, Juneau. I

shopped the elixir to two institutions with which I had old contacts and felt I could trust: Blackwell Pharmaceutical, which based its business decades ago on a search for life-extenders. And Hunt Avery, who, since I met him in the sixties, has spent a fortune on cryogenics and disease eradication. Both, I knew, could provide the financial motivation I was hoping to present to the clan. But I wanted to dig further to establish if either would follow through with my plan for an ethical distribution of the elixir, not only making it available to the richest clients, but also ensuring that a quantity of the elixir went to countries with no money and rampant disease."

There is something not right in his face when he says this last part, but he's not telling me an outright lie. And then I realize: He's lying to himself. He used this humanitarian idea as self-justification.

"You see, Juneau," he continues. "I'm not evil. I care for the clan. I would never have sold them out."

"Then why are they living behind an electric fence?" I ask.

Whit clears his throat. "Yes, well, it seems that when Hunt Avery discovered that he was not the only interested party, he made a rather desperate move. He did something he felt would persuade me to give the elixir only to him."

"Kidnapping your clan," Miles says.

"He calls it *courting* the clan," Whit clarifies. "Winning them over to his point of view."

I shake my head. "He's holding them hostage, Whit. But for what? He's got you. He's got the clan. I'm guessing you must have given him the formula. So why hunt me down?"

"I made your capture a condition of my cooperation," Whit says. "I couldn't just leave you behind, alone in Alaska. Avery sent his guards with me to find you and bring you back to be with your father. Your clan."

I watch him for a moment. His face gives nothing away. "Why didn't you explain this to me before?" I ask finally. "In the first note you sent via bird?"

"Because I suspected you wouldn't believe me. I figured you had Read me and would find it questionable that I was traveling alone with two guards when the rest of the clan was imprisoned."

"You were damned right about that."

"It's why I gave you the map. I knew you wouldn't come willingly with us. But I also knew you were looking for your clan and I wanted to help you find them. I needed us all to be here together in order to ensure everyone's safety as we finalize the deal with Avery."

"You mean he's kidnapped our clan and you're still doing business with him?" I ask.

Whit just watches me.

"You're sicker than I thought," I say.

"Come with me," he says. "I'll take you to our people. I'll negotiate our release and ensure that we are safely taken to wherever we decide to go after this. You can trust me, Juneau. You're like a daughter to me. I only want the best for you and the clan."

I tuck my head down into my arms and try to think. He's not telling me the whole truth. That's clear. But a lot of what he said made sense. Although he acted behind the backs of the elders, he believed he was doing it for the good of the clan.

I look back up at Whit, and he gives me that smile. His Juneau smile, the one he's been giving me since I was five years old, the one that tells me how important I am to him. And I know that I can't make this decision alone. I can't trust myself to be level-headed when it comes to Whit.

"Miles," I say. "Do you think I should go with Whit?"

Miles meets my eyes. "Absolutely," he says, and looks from me to Whit, ". . . not."

24

MILES

WHIT MAKES AN UNHAPPY HARRUMPHING NOISE, but I keep my eyes on Juneau.

"There's no way you should go with this guy," I insist. "He's lying."

"When did you start taking advice from teenage boys—" Whit begins, but I cut him off.

"I overheard my dad saying that you were the key to the drug, Juneau. That there would be no deal without you. I don't understand why, but I don't think Whit was just trying to make sure you weren't left behind. I think he needs you."

Juneau looks at Whit, and I spot sweat gathering along his hairline. "Juneau," he says, "this can all be over tonight. I can conclude the deal with Avery and get your clan out of there by morning. Just come with me."

Your clan? I think. I glance at Juneau to see if she heard it, too.

She sits, watching him, as he gets more and more nervous. "You got what you wanted, Whit. I'm here now. You know I'm safe. I'll wait here while you do your deal with Avery. Once the clan is released, you can come back and get me. I promise not to budge."

"I can't just leave you here," says Whit, looking fiercely uncomfortable now.

"Yes you can," says Juneau. She stands up, and reaches down to pick up the crossbow. She holds it loosely by her side as she indicates with a gesture that Whit should stand. And I know that this is a rare moment. That there has been a sea change. Juneau is no longer his student. She just took her last step out from under his control, and is now wholly and completely on her own. She heard Whit out and decided not to side with him. This is huge.

"You just go on ahead," Juneau urges when she sees he's not leaving without her.

"I understand your decision," Whit says finally, shoulders slumped in defeat. "But if you change your mind, just come on down to the ranch. I'll make sure the guards know you are to be shown safely to me."

"I thought they didn't know I was here," Juneau says.

"They don't," Whit responds quickly. "But I'll tell them that if you happen to show up, you are to be brought to me unharmed."

"Well, that's sure generous of you," Juneau says, and her face is devoid of expression, sarcastic or otherwise, as she raises the crossbow to eye level, aiming it straight at him. "Go," she commands.

Whit's shocked expression says it all: He sees he's lost her. He turns to leave the clearing. Juneau waits, holding her pose, until he disappears into the trees. She lowers the crossbow to her side and with a look of emptiness holds out her hand to me.

"Don't you think he'll come back with guards?" I ask. "If they're not already surrounding us, waiting for a sign from him." I take her hand and pull her closer.

She shakes her head. "No, if he wanted to take us by force, he would have sent guards to seize us instead of coming himself. I don't know why, but he wants me to come willingly—to cooperate."

"So you believe him about just wanting to protect you?" I ask incredulously.

"Honestly, Miles, I don't know what to believe anymore. Part of what Whit said rang true. And then other parts he's talked himself into believing are true, even if they aren't."

"And then there are the flat-out lies," I add.

Juneau nods worriedly and slings the crossbow over her shoulder. "Let's go."

"Where?" I ask.

"We're leaving the fire and setting up camp further on," she says.

"I thought you said Whit wouldn't send guards after us."

"No, but someone could have followed him," she says. "Or, if they suspect he met with me, they could easily track his footprints back here. It would be foolish for us to stay."

In five minutes we have the tent rolled up and most of the supplies packed into Juneau's backpack. I follow her as she does her silent walk through the pitch-dark woods, trying to place my feet where she has stepped. What seems like an hour later we finally stop, and she looks around.

We're in a little clearing where the lack of tree cover allows the moonlight to illuminate the ground. "Here's good," she says. "We can see enough to set up camp."

We pitch the tent in silence, and I can tell that Juneau's not just being quiet to avoid detection. She's mulling over every word that came out of Whit's mouth. Going over it again and again, trying to weed out the lies from the truth.

I'm focusing on hammering tent pins into the ground when I hear a flutter of wings and a loud squawk. I look up to see a large black bird, the size of a cat, swoop down from the darkness and land on the ground nearby.

"Poe!" Juneau yells. I can tell she's using every ounce of restraint she possesses not to throw herself on the raven. Instead, she squats and holds out her hand toward him. He waddles over and lets her pet him and coo over him and I can't help but roll my eyes. But when she looks over at me, her eyes shining with excitement, I have to admit I'm glad to see the bird, too.

"So after selling us out to Whit back in Utah, you decide to fly back and grace us with your birdy presence?" I call to him.

Poe looks at me and cocks his head to one side, as if he were actually listening. "Hey, look!" I say. "The bird finally acknowledges my presence."

"Maybe he missed you, too," Juneau jokes, and scoops Poe into her lap.

"Look at this fancy harness Tallie made you," she says, and opens a little leather pouch attached to his back. She pulls a paper from inside.

"Can you hand me a flashlight?" she asks. I take one from the bag, crouch down behind her, and shine it on the paper as she unfolds it. She begins reading the large, loopy writing out loud as I follow along, peering over her shoulder.

Got your message, borrowed Mikey's truck, and left immediately. I had just checked into a hotel in Roswell when Poe started acting all crazy like he wanted to get out. I figure you called him and am letting him go. I'm at the Days Inn, just up the road from the UFO Museum. If you're near, come find me. If not, send a note by return raven. You and Mr. Take-You-Far better be careful. Beauregard's bones see trouble ahead. Tallie

Juneau sets Poe down and turns to me with a huge smile. "She's here. Add Tallie and her truck to our list of assets."

"Plus her bone-reading," I say. "The possum sees trouble ahead. I guess that means Avery's not just going to hand your people over and let us go."

She nods. "Yeah, I wish she was more specific. The fact that trouble's coming is kind of a given."

"So what do we do? Send a return message asking her to meet us on the other side of the reserve?" I ask.

Juneau shakes her head. "No, you and I need to scout more first. Once we know what we're dealing with, we'll figure out how she can help." She gets up and grabs the notebook and pencil out of the bag. "Plus, Poe has a more important mission to carry out first. I need to get word to my dad that we're here."

Juneau scribbles a note explaining that she and "a friend" are positioned on one end of Avery's reserve. That we're coming to free them. To be ready. And then she asks him to give her an indication of where they are located, if they are guarded, and what their situation is. She puts it in the envelope in Poe's harness and sends him off into the night.

The note is typical Juneau. Factual. Efficient. Non-emotional. And, instead of signing off with "love" or some other affectionate term, she simply writes, "So many questions." Fair enough. He's lied to her, betrayed her, and withheld information about her own mother's background.

So many questions. I hope, for Juneau's sake, that her father will answer them. And that the answers will somehow make her feel better. She's had enough bad news in the last few weeks to last her a lifetime.

25

JUNEAU

AFTER POE LEAVES, ALL I CAN THINK ABOUT IS the note he'll bring back. What will Dad say? No doubt he and the rest of the clan have Read that I was coming. Hopefully he can give me some indication of where they are. That is, if they've been allowed to move outside of their immediate area. The only images I've gotten of them show them near the adobe huts.

I wonder if they've even seen Whit or know of his betrayal. I suppose that they Read him, too, and probably saw images of him with the guards. From that, I'm sure the elders could hypothesize as to his part in this story.

Miles builds the fire in silence as I take the rabbits from the cloth I hurriedly wrapped them in and prepare them for roasting. I am grateful that he leaves me with my thoughts instead of asking worried questions about how I am doing (like Kenai would) or drilling me for every single thought I had about the encounter with Whit (like Nome would).

Miles gets me. I mean, he didn't at first. But he knows what I've gone through in the last few weeks. He was there. And he finally understands—as well as he can—what I come from.

He knows I need to be left alone right now. And I love him for that.

I noticed some spinach-like greens growing nearby, and picked some to go with our meal. Once enough fat has dripped off the rabbits into the pan, I add the greens and stir until they have wilted. All the while I am thinking. Hashing over what Whit told me in my mind. Picking it apart. Trying to sort what I know to be truth from what I suspect to be lies. Weighing everyone's motivation: my mother and father's, Whit's, the other elders'.

When the rabbits are done, I come out of my daze and see Miles sitting across the fire from me. He gives me a sympathetic smile. "I found the perfect spot for dinner," he says. "If you'd like to take the rabbits, I'll take"—he looks down at the pan—"whatever that is, and we're on our way."

I wrap one of the rabbits in cloth—it will be our meal tomorrow—and taking the other, follow Miles to the top of the hill and out onto a rocky outcropping. One of our blankets is spread on the ground, with camping plates, knives, and forks laid out on it beside paper napkins. In the center is a small mountain of wildflowers, arranged in an impromptu bouquet. "When did you do all this?" I ask, unable to hide my surprise at this un-Miles-like gesture.

"You were off in la-la land for a good half hour. I was just trying to be useful." Miles plays it off like it's nothing, but I reach over and take his hand, and we sit for a minute looking at the vista that he planned for us: an unimpeded view of the hunting reserve. Spaced at even intervals, the fence's red lights flash slowly . . . eerily . . . like ghoulish beacons declaring humankind's dominion over nature.

But then I look up and see the night sky practically spilling over with twinkling stars, backlit by the glowing haze of the Milky Way, and humanity's feeble attempt at supremacy seems laughable. *All this will end,* I think, looking back down at Avery's electrified barrier, *but nature will go on forever.*

We eat in silence, and afterward lie back on the blanket, watching the celestial display as if it were entertainment for our pleasure alone. I reach over and feel for Miles, and he grasps my hand in his.

"Tell me about your dream," I say, and even though we've been quiet for so long, it feels like we've been communicating the whole time. Like my out-of-the-blue request was a continuation of a conversation we were already having.

"Which one?" Miles asks, turning his head to look at me.

"The one from your death-sleep," I respond. "I wanted to ask you before, but thought you might need time."

"I had a few dreams in the death-sleep," he says, and a haunted look drifts across his features.

I hesitate. "You don't have to . . ."

"No," Miles says, turning his head back to the stars. "I want to tell you."

"You probably had dreams on your way down the Path and on your way back. But the most important one . . . the defining one . . . is what you see when you reach death, touch it, and turn to come back."

Miles knows which one I'm talking about. He nods, and then closes his eyes. "It's a dream I've had before. It's one that's based in reality, but happened differently in the dream."

He sighs and squeezes my hand more firmly, like he's using it for support. "I told you my mom was depressed. That she left us last year and is living with her sister in New Jersey. Well, she did that after a suicide attempt—tried to kill herself with an overdose of sleeping pills. It was Mrs. Kirby, our house cleaner, who found her and called nine-one-one. I was at school. I didn't see it happen. But in my dreams, I'm the one who finds Mom. And it's so clear, so detailed—the way she lies curled up on the floor by her bed, the fact that she's been sick . . . vomited, the chattering of her teeth being the only indication she's alive—that when I awake, I can't believe it didn't really happen that way. That I wasn't really there."

"Miles," I whisper. I can feel the horror of the scene through the tremor in his voice, and my heart aches for him.

He squeezes my hand and goes on. "Each time I dreamed it, there was an invisible wall that kept me from going to her. But this time—in the death-sleep dream—the wall wasn't solid. I could feel it, like curtains brushing past me, as I walked through it. I was able to go right over to her, pick her up, and sit down on the bed, cradling her in my arms.

"I sat there with her for a long time, and the longer I stayed the less I wanted to leave. I felt this overwhelming urge to lie down on the bed next to my mom, close my eyes, and go to sleep. I felt so tired. Tired of trying. Tired of living. Sleep was so tempting. So inviting.

"It took every ounce of strength I had to stand up, my mother in my arms, and walk back through the invisible barrier and leave the room. I walked outside into the sunlight and laid her down in the grass. She opened her eyes and saw me and smiled. The sun became so bright it was blinding, and then it was over."

I exhale. "You chose life over death. You protected your mother even though she didn't protect you. You became the parent and chose to be strong enough to care for her as well as yourself." Miles sighs and looks back toward the stars.

"Things aren't supposed to be like this," I say. "We shouldn't have to be stronger than our parents—it's not the natural order. Somehow along the way everything got all messed up, and now we're the ones to inherit it. We're left to clean up the mess."

Miles is silent.

"I dream about my mom a lot," I say. "I wish I had known her for longer. I wish she could see me now. I have a feeling that everything I do is for her. So that she'll be proud of me. So that I can live up to the example she set: a leader with powerful gifts.

I've never even asked myself if that's what I really wanted. If carrying the burden of my clan's welfare is the role I want to have."

"You shouldn't have to live up to anything," Miles says. "You shouldn't have to live your life in response to your mother." He thinks for a moment. "Although, who am I to talk? Since Mom left, all I think about is how I must be a bad person if she didn't even love me enough to stay. That's the role I've taken."

"No, Miles—" I start to say, but he holds up a hand to stop me.

"So I've let myself be someone I'm not. But I'm done with that now. I've walked through the invisible wall in more ways than one."

He looks over at me. "You make me want to be a good person, Juneau. I see how you are and it makes me want to be strong." He sees my expression and stops. "What?"

I wipe a tear away. And then I roll onto my stomach and scoot over until our faces are a whisper's distance apart. And I kiss him.

The stars come down from the sky, so low that they surround us. They land like sizzling embers on our skin, and stick, glowing, to our bodies as we lose ourselves in each other.

26

MILES

JUNEAU LIES BESIDE ME, EYES CLOSED AND THE ghost of a smile on her lips, as I trace circles on the petal-soft skin of her lower back. A flapping of wings invades our blanket-padded island of tranquility. And although Juneau opens her eyes, she takes her time sitting up.

She doesn't even bother to cover herself as she reaches out to greet Poe. *Juneau, queen of nature,* I think, and have to brace myself against the surge of emotion that accompanies that image.

Poe lands smoothly on Juneau's wrist, like they've been practicing it for months. She sets him down on the blanket between us, and opens the pouch on his back. She pulls out the same piece of paper that she sent, and turns it over, holding it up in the moonlight to read what's written on the back. And then she hands it to me.

Juneau. Do not come. You are the bargaining chip. Without you, Whit can't have what he needs, and in the end will have to let us go. Besides, we can't escape. We tried to—once. After that, Avery took Badger, and is keeping him as insurance that no one will try to leave. I reiterate—do not come. They can't keep us forever. Go as far away as you can, hide yourself from Whit, and wait until they release us.

I wait to see what Juneau will say, but she's silent. "Is Badger a pet?" I ask finally.

"He's one of the clan children. Three years old."

"I thought the kids were named for towns in Alaska," I say, realizing that I'm going off topic, but too curious to let it slide.

"They are," she says. "Badger is a town in Alaska. You don't have to know geography to get into Yale?" She gives me a teasing push with her elbow and then stands and stretches. She is glorious.

I exhale and try to ignore my instincts, which are to pull her back down to the blanket and start over again. I focus on our banter and push more enticing thoughts from my mind. "Alaskan geography doesn't count," I say, rising to my feet. "Nothing ever happens there. Obviously, if forty people can hide there for three decades and no one notices."

Juneau smiles, seemingly grateful for the levity as we gather the plates, blanket, and scattered clothes. I slip on my boxers and jeans before making my way down the path, but Juneau strides ahead, naked and regal. Poe scavenges a rabbit bone and flies ahead of us to the clearing.

We do a water-bottle washing of dishes and put everything away while the fire dies down. "So are you going to listen to your dad?" I ask.

"Of course not," Juneau replies. She's put her panties and tank top back on and is sitting in front of the dwindling flames, jotting something in her notebook. She tears off the page and makes a clicking noise to call Poe. He drops the bone he's pecking at and goes to her, letting her tuck the note into his pouch. Following her whispered directions, he flies off into the night.

"A note to Tallie," she explains. "Asking her to find a computer and look some things up for us."

"Like what?" I ask.

"Anything she can find about the hunting reserve, especially a map if one exists. Details about Hunt Avery. And the old Hindu story about Amrita—I want to double-check what Whit told me."

I nod. "When are we leaving?"

Juneau stares at the fire and gets that focused look she does when she Reads. After a second, she says, "Whit's in a bedroom by himself, reading. He's obviously not coming back for us tonight." She looks up at me. "How about first thing in the morning?"

"Let's sleep, then," I suggest. I shake out the blanket we used for our picnic, and spread it out inside the tent on top of the other one, making one bed for the two of us instead of the usual one blanket roll each.

Juneau crawls into the tent with her crossbow, and lies down on her side facing it. I zip the door up behind us, and lie down behind her. Curling myself around her, I drape my arm around her shoulder and lace my fingers through hers. "We'll leave before daybreak," she says.

"Yes, sir," I say, and rub my nose in the back of her hair, savoring her earthy, herbal smell. Wishing I never had to move again, I breathe her in and close my eyes.

What feels like moments later, I open them again. Sunlight is streaming through the sides of the tent. *It's already morning.* "Juneau, wake up," I say, and pat around in the blankets for a second before I realize I'm by myself.

I unzip the tent door and look outside. "Juneau?" I yell. I scan the woods around the tent and see no sign of her. And then I spot a piece of paper skewered on a tree limb right in front of the tent. It's a note from Juneau. I know what it says before I even read it. I know what she's done. She's gone ahead and left me behind.

Miles,
I have decided to follow my heart
instead of my head. To barge in like
gangbusters. It doesn't make sense and

isn't strategically sound, but maybe I'm not the great leader I'm supposed to be. Maybe I'm just a girl who misses her family.

I can't take you with me. I've chosen the dangerous route—the one that will require me to use all of my gifts in order to hide, find my people, and survive. I've chosen to place myself in danger, but I won't choose the same for you—not when you aren't equipped with the same advantages I have. I almost lost you once. I won't take that risk again.

If you wait here, you won't be in danger: Whit wants me, not you. If I succeed, I promise to return. But if you need to leave the mountain, for whatever reason, I will come and find you.

There is, of course, the chance that I won't succeed. That I will be imprisoned with my clan. Or worse. You have your own battles to fight, Miles. Your own parents to save. You still have your mother, and, once she gets better, she will need you.

This is my fight. My clan's fight. You

are not yet a part of our world, and I won't pull you in before you're ready. I won't risk your life.

Don't forget that you're my desert island friend.
Juneau

27

JUNEAU

SWEAT STINGS MY EYES. I WIPE THEM AND GLANCE up to measure the angle of the sun. If it's this hot at 10:00 a.m., the afternoon is going to be sweltering.

I peer out from behind the boulder that hides me and watch the jeep full of camouflaged guards drive slowly along the inside of the perimeter fence. One sweeps the landscape with his binoculars, looking for anything that stands out against the brown-on-brown landscape.

They are the first sign of life I've seen today, besides a band of wild dogs I spotted early this morning, jogging just inside the fence as if they were doing their own surveillance of the land. They looked like the picture of hyenas in the EB, which, considering Avery's collection of zebras and antelope, fits right into the African theme.

I turn my attention back to the jeep, and watch the guards stop parallel to my hiding place and jump out. My heart seizes as the one with the binoculars yells and points in my direction. Even though I have masked myself to match the desert behind me, I duck down and shuffle sideways so my entire body is hidden. There is complete silence for a full ten seconds, and I am about to stick my head back up to see what they are doing, when I hear a rifle crack, and a few yards to my right something goes flying up in the air.

I hear triumphant shouts as I watch the rattlesnake fall to the ground, twisting in nerve-damaged death throes. Easing myself up, I see the shooter being clapped on the back by one of his fellow guards, and bumping knuckles with another.

"Ah, man, I want that rattle!" he yells, eyeing the dead but still-writhing snake through the fence.

"Yeah, well, we're not going to cut off the juice just so you can go get your trophy," says another.

"Why not?" the snake slayer asks. "We'll just tell the boss another deer got stuck in the wires and we had to reboot the section."

Two guards get bored with the conversation and head back to the jeep, leaving the shooter and his buddy to argue. "If anyone double-checks the video, they'll know we fooled with the fence. And I'm the one who'll catch shit for it."

The men stare at each other, one unsure and the other pleading. "Come on, Sergeant, I'll give you a bottle of my bootleg Oaxaca."

"Is that the tequila Sully drank when he mistook the cactus for a bear and unloaded a semiautomatic into it?"

"Same poison," the shooter says.

The sergeant rubs his chin, and then says, "Hell, Sanders, you've got yourself a deal." He pulls from his pocket an object that looks like Miles's cell phone, and aims it at the metal box affixed to the top of the fence. The red light underneath it stops its slow flashing and turns a steady green. Letting out a whoop, Sanders climbs three times his height to the top and scrambles halfway down the other side before dropping to the ground in a crouch. I squeeze myself tightly behind the boulder, my brown, cracked skin blending in like an extension of the rock as the man jogs over to the dead snake. Mere feet away from me, he draws a long hunting knife from a sheath at his waist and chops the rattle off the snake, leaving the stump spurting blood in the dust.

I can almost taste my anger: It is coppery like the taste of fear. My nose wrinkles in repugnance as I look at the rattlesnake's remains. Killing for sport is something I will never understand. Killing for protection . . . for food . . . that is the way of nature. Killing for fun is the vilest of crimes.

As Sanders pockets his prize he scans the landscape, looking right through me as he does, and then jogs back to the fence. In a minute he has scaled it and is climbing back down the other side. I see the guards joking among themselves, and the sergeant points the black box at the green light. "Let's see you jump, Sanders!" he calls, and the light switches to red. Sanders immediately lets go and drops the final ten feet to the ground.

Face scarlet, he turns to the sergeant and his two companions, who climb into the jeep roaring with laughter. "Goddamn it, you could have killed me, Sarge!" he yells, and though I can see he is shaking, I'm not sure if it's from fear or rage. Probably both.

"Get your fat ass in the jeep," the driver calls, and starts driving off slowly without him. Sanders runs, grabs the side of the vehicle, and swings himself over to land in the backseat.

I sit down, my back to the boulder. Unscrewing the top of my canteen, I take a swig, careful not to drink too much. I've been hiking since before dawn, and have eight more hours before nightfall. If my estimates are right, I'm halfway to where the two rivers end. And if my hunch is correct, that is where I'll find my people.

I think of Miles and wonder what he thought of my letter. I'm sure it hurt his feelings, but I didn't want him to follow me. And although I didn't come out and say it, I'm sure he read between the lines. I had no other choice. Miles would only have slowed me down. He could have gotten us captured. Or worse. Besides, knowing that he's alive and waiting for me is additional motivation for me to find my clan and get them out of there as soon as possible. *And after that?* I wonder.

I will go wherever my clan decides. Miles and I will say good-bye, and he will return home, make amends with his dad, and go to college. Get on with his life. That's what has to happen—I know it like I know my own name. So why does it make my heart twist painfully in my chest?

I can't think about that now. I need to stay focused. I scan the horizon and spot my next hiding place—a large patch of yucca in the distance. I adjust my backpack, and, unable to maintain my camouflage without concentration, I let it fade and get ready to run.

28

MILES

I CRUMPLE UP THE PAPER AND THROW IT ACROSS the clearing. "Fucking hell!" I yell. But there is no one to hear, and my words feel as empty as the hole in my chest.

Juneau didn't need to say it. I know what she was thinking. She doesn't want me along because she knows—we know—that if it comes down to fighting in the desert, instead of using the truck for surveillance and escape, I will be a liability.

Even if I always knew that I wasn't Juneau's equal, the fact that my incompetence is so insurmountable that she left me behind just confirms my utter lameness. I stop these thoughts in their tracks. *I'm not utterly lame,* I tell myself. I am exponentially less lame then a few weeks ago; Juneau said it herself. I can help her. I know I can. She needs me. I won't let her push me away just to protect me.

I pace the clearing, debating what to do. The sun is shining in through the trees at an angle, well up above the horizon. When did Juneau say the sun rose? Six a.m.? And if the sun is directly overhead at noon, then I guess it's around ten in the morning. Juneau's probably been gone since dawn, if not earlier. Even if I ignore her request and follow her, it will be impossible to catch up with her at this point.

I hold my head in my hands, squeezing hard, and let out a roar of frustration. What do I do? Can Juneau really free her clan by herself, or is she walking into a trap? What can I actually do to help? I can't just sit around and wait. But if I go after her, I could be a detriment: either slow her down or get her captured.

I head to the top of the mountain, ignoring the branches that whip painfully against my arms, the brambles that poke me through my jeans. And when I reach the crest, I find a rocky outcrop and sit down, surveying the land spread before me like a giant Western movie set. The woods thin out gradually as the land levels into foothills, until there are no more trees—only a dry brownish-green pastureland that quickly turns into desert scrub. Deer-type animals graze peacefully in the distance. It would look like they were living in some kind of untouched-by-civilization Disneyesque utopia, if it weren't for the twenty-foot fence sectioning off the ranch.

As I sit, my anger and shame melt away and my thoughts become clearer. What are my options? Stay or leave. And if I leave, I'll have to find a plan of my own since I can't catch up with Juneau.

Think about what advantages nature gives us, I hear her say. What advantages do I have? Although I can shoot a tree, I've never aimed at a moving target. And although I can build a fire, I'm not a wilderness survivalist like her. But I have one advantage she doesn't know about: I can Read. At least, I did it once. And I am determined to find out what that means. To add it to my short list of skills.

I stand and let the wind whip my hair around, close my eyes and breathe in the pure mountain air. *I can be one with nature,* I think. And then I open my eyes and laugh. Like hell I can. I'll let Juneau be one with nature. I'll just be myself.

Back at the campsite, I rifle through our supplies. Juneau left the tent and bedding, the cooking equipment, flashlights and dishes, and most of the food. It looks like she took the backpack, most of the water, and some food. The knife and her crossbow are gone.

My crossbow, however, lies where I left it last night by the fire. I decide to fit in one last practice with a tree before potentially having to aim it at live targets. At the edge of the clearing, I cock the bowstring and load a bolt into the tiller, like Juneau showed me yesterday. Pulling the crossbow up to my chin, I eye a tree a few yards away with a large, round knot about halfway up. Aiming for the knot, I squeeze the trigger and launch a bolt in its direction. Then one after another, I cock and load and fire, until all six of the arrows are embedded in the tree, although unfortunately nowhere near the knot.

At least I'm getting faster at loading, I think, as I gather the bolts and go back to my starting position. But I'm still not a sharpshooter like Juneau. Sometimes I'm good, sometimes I'm way off. I have no consistency, and don't understand what's tripping me up.

Too bad it's not a video game, I muse, and suddenly an idea comes to mind. I'm good at video games. Really good. Shooting in real life must be mainly a matter of hand-eye coordination, after you've gotten used to the weight and feel of the weapon. What if I just pretend I'm in a video game? Forget that I'm in the woods, out of my element, and pretend I'm in the comfort of my living room, all conditions under my control.

I let everything melt away, the sounds of the woods, the smell of dirt and pine. It's just me, the tree, and the crossbow. I breathe out slowly and squeeze the trigger. The bolt flies across the clearing and lodges firmly into the knot.

I whoop and dance around a bit before calming down and trying again. I put myself in the zone, aim, and fire. Another bull's-eye.

This is what I needed. If I make the environment my own, I can manipulate it with confidence. It makes perfect sense.

After practicing another half hour, I've gained a renewed sense of purpose. I'm no longer lost and out of my element. I'm in control. I look at the campsite with new eyes.

In gaming terms I would say this is a two-day mission with the goal of infiltrating an enemy camp. What supplies do I have at my disposal? I go through the bag and measure the food into small portions. Since I'll be on the go, I won't have time to stop and eat. Plus constant eating to keep my strength up is smarter than slowing my metabolism with three large meals. Bread, soup, canned beans . . . I'll be eating it all cold. No cooking supplies means a lighter pack.

Juneau left me a bottle of water, plus one empty bottle I can refill from the stream. I'll have to be careful with that—it won't be easy to find another water source in the desert.

The plastic shopping bag won't do the trick if I'm going to be hiking. I need something that will give my hands freedom. I look around at the scattered supplies. The nylon bag that the tent came in is just big enough to hold the bottles of water and the food, with a little space left over. I slip the lighter and the flashlight that Juneau left me into the tent bag and, remembering the lifesaving advice from *Hitchhiker's Guide to the Galaxy,* add one of the purple towels that Juneau's been dragging along since Seattle.

I take one last look around the clearing and, seeing the piece of wadded-up paper, I grab it and stuff it into the tent bag with the rest of my supplies. It seems masochistic to keep it, but it'll serve as my motivation to prove Juneau wrong.

29

JUNEAU

THE SUN IS DIRECTLY OVERHEAD WHEN I DECIDE to stop. I'm not tired, but I've spotted a group of trees far off on the horizon, and am heading directly for them. I know I should eat something and give my body time to rest. I might not find shelter again.

I jog for another twenty minutes before reaching the motley group of dried-out trees. Swinging my pack to the ground, I throw myself down in a patch of shade cast by the anemic tree branches. I close my eyes and after a few seconds I doze off.

I awake in alarm—there's something scratching at my chest. Sitting up abruptly, I send Poe flapping off me and onto the ground nearby. "Poe, you scared me to death," I scold.

He cocks his head to one side and lets out three loud caws. *Fair enough,* I think, *I scared him, too.* I check the sun. I couldn't have been asleep for more than an hour. Wiping caked-on dirt from the side of my mouth, I fumble with my bag and take a long swig of water from the canteen.

Then, unfolding the pouch on Poe's back, I draw out a small bundle of papers and shuffle through them. Three printed sheets. Tallie's done her work.

I pull out a rabbit leg and, handing Poe a small piece, eat as I read. The first sheet is an area map that is similar to the one I left with Miles. "It's all I could find" is written at the bottom of the page in red ink. "Hunting range isn't advertised on the internet. I only found it mentioned in a couple of articles on wild-game hunting. Both referred to it as a 'well-kept secret.'"

The second page reads "Forbes 1000" at the top, and shows a photo of a man wearing a suit with cowboy boots and a hat. The name under the picture is Randall Bradford "Hunt" Avery III, and the article beneath talks about how he transferred his father's Texas-based oil business into an offshore drilling outfit, more than tripling his father's fortune. It mentions a couple of ex-wives with children, and refers to him as a "playboy."

On the last sheet, Tallie has written "from Wikipedia" across the top. Several paragraphs follow, starting with this:

Amrita (Sanskrit: अमृत; IAST: amṛta) is a Sanskrit word that literally means "immortality," and is often referred to in texts as nectar. The word's earliest occurrence is in the Rigveda as the drink that confers immortality upon the gods.

Well, that confirms why Whit and my parents named the elixir what they did. I scan down the page for anything else of interest, and my attention is caught by this:

A Vajrayana text describes the origin of amrita . . . In this version, the monster Rahu steals the amrita and is blasted by Vajrapani's thunderbolt. As Rahu has already drunk the amrita he cannot die but his blood, dripping onto the surface of this earth, causes all kinds of medicinal plants to grow. At the behest of all the Buddhas, Vajrapani reassembles Rahu who eventually becomes a protector of Buddhism.

There is something about this passage that calls out to me, but I'm not sure what it is. I turn the page over and see more of Tallie's scribbling. Giving Poe my rabbit bone, I take another swig of water and begin to read.

I spent half the night throwing the bones for you. Thought of how my and my ancestors' readings are similar to yours, and more than ever I'm convinced that our answers come from the same source: the collective wisdom of all things, past and future. So I suppose you can consider me an oracle from your Yara. In any case, the answer

I've been getting for you has been the same, no matter how many times I throw.

You will be captured. There will be a battle. Whether a battle of wills or an actual physical struggle, I can't tell. But I see you at the center of it. And when the end comes, your regular weapons won't help you—I read that as meaning both physical and mental weapons . . . meaning your Reading and Conjuring. Instead you must Invoke.

Invoke! As in "call upon," but more powerful. And invoke who . . . or what? Damned if I know what it means, and I think it would be unwise for me to try to translate a message that is meant specifically for you. But you will need to figure it out—Beauregard's never been this specific. Otherwise, let's just hope that the message becomes clear when the time comes.

I lower the paper and stare out over the desert, thinking. So many new concepts. And somehow, they blend together. But with only a few notes of the melody, it's hard for me to decipher the song.

Poe squawks and reminds me that I'm not alone. I fold the papers and slip them into my back pocket—I'll have plenty of time to mull over things while I'm running. But there's no reason for me to keep Poe out here in this baking desert. I scrawl a message thanking Tallie and telling her I'll call Poe back when I need her help.

I send him off. Then, throwing everything into the pack, I swing it onto my back and leave my oasis of shade for the ruthlessness of the desert sun.

30

MILES

I HEAD OVER THE CREST OF THE MOUNTAIN LOOK-
ing for one of the streams I saw yesterday. I hear it before I see it,
and follow the sound of flowing water until I'm standing on the
bank of a crystal-clear mountain stream. Taking the empty water
bottle from my improvised backpack, I fill it, take a long drink,
and then fill it again.

I eye the perimeter fence a few yards away. Do I try to get inside
the ranch or do I follow along outside the fence, like Juneau suggested? I've decided that my role will be distracting the Avery guy
and his guards away from wherever it is that her people are being
held. But I won't be able to do a damn thing if I don't figure out
where he is.

I pull out the area map and trace the two rivers that Juneau
pointed out yesterday. She thinks that both the Avery mansion

and the adobe huts where her people are being kept will be in that vicinity, and she's heading there following the southern edge of the perimeter fence. At least I think she is. Doubt strikes me. How can I know what to do if I'm not even sure of her plan?

Juneau would try to Read, I think. She would try to get her direction from the earth. So maybe it's time to see how far my Reading ability works. I feel weird just thinking about it. This is so out of my comfort zone. *Everything from now on is going to be out of your comfort zone,* I remind myself. *Buck up.*

Closing my eyes, I press my hand to the ground. I try to slow my breathing. To concentrate. Almost immediately, a tingling sensation begins in my fingertips and spreads upward through my hands. I think of Juneau. I picture her in my mind.

And suddenly I'm experiencing her feelings: I am swept by a wave of fierce determination. I feel a sense of curiosity . . . alertness. She's watching . . . waiting for a sign. *Juneau's still on her way,* I think. If she had been captured, she would be feeling fear. If she had found her clan, there would be some relief. She's safe, for now, and is still looking.

I open my eyes and the tingling stops. I can't help the smile that spreads across my face. I did it. I Read.

Juneau is wrong. The Amrit *has* changed something in my brain. It's not a choice—a lifestyle change—like she's been taught. It's something that comes automatically with the drug. A side effect. Not only does Amrit make you immune to disease and slow your aging, but it somehow changes your brain chemistry so that you can perceive things you couldn't before. Or, saying it in Yara-speak . . . plug into the consciousness of the universe.

Why not? I think. My mom used to talk about how she got "dog nose" when she was pregnant with me. Being pregnant changed her perceptions enough that her sense of smell was sharpened. Why shouldn't a drug powerful enough to bring me back to life have a chemical effect on how my mind processes things?

It's just another weird quirk to accept about my condition. But at a time like this, if I can figure out how to use it to my benefit, it could be my greatest asset.

I decide to push a little further and walk into the woods until I find a place where trees grow thick enough to blot out the sunlight. In between a few old pines, I gather sticks and build a small fire. When it catches, I sit cross-legged in front of it and look just above the flames, like Juneau does.

I wait. I think about the map that Juneau said she saw in the fire, and try to imagine something like it, but nothing happens. No tingle, no picture, nothing.

My mom used to meditate as part of her stress therapy. She would focus on something like a candle or a mandala to empty her mind. I stare at the edges of the flames, watch the dancing orange light, and try not to think of anything. But the harder I try to clear my mind, the more my thoughts wander.

And then all of a sudden my fingertips are buzzing and an image begins to form in the shimmering heat above the flames. I'm looking at a guy in a cowboy hat standing on the porch of an elaborate white McMansion. He's got his thumbs stuck through the belt loops of his blue jeans and is talking to one of the muscle-bound camouflaged guys. An American flag is attached to a pole near the door, and it flutters back and forth in the wind. And in the distance, to the far right of the house, there's a tree-lined river.

Juneau was right. Avery did build his home near one of the rivers. In her Reading, she said that his house was a good distance from the adobe village where her clan was being kept. I think about adobe huts and keep watching the image, but nothing changes and after a few seconds the whole thing disappears and I'm looking at a plain old campfire once again.

Juneau said that the Yara shows you what it wants you to see. So if it showed me Avery's house, that's obviously where I'm supposed to go. Any doubts I had about leaving the mountain disappear. I have a mission. The Universe or Gaia or whatever has shown me what I'm supposed to do.

This strong sense of purpose is completely new to me. Adrenaline pumps through my veins as I trace a line on the map from where I am in the mountains to the two rivers flowing into the desert miles and miles away.

Scaling the fence and making a cross-country trek seems like a stupid idea now that I know where things are. My best bet is to do what I suggested to Juneau: take the truck past the other end of the ranch and come in from the east. It should only take a couple of hours to drive. I could get there before Juneau even reaches her clan.

That would give me time to scope the place out—to plan the best possible diversion before anyone knows Juneau's there. My mind made up, I throw the tent bag over my shoulders and begin the hike back over the mountain to where we left the truck.

31

JUNEAU

THE SUN IS SETTING WHEN I REACH THE TOP OF the ridge. I look out over the valley floor below, and see a dozen campfires burning in one small area. Not far from them, a river snakes its way through the valley, reflecting the sunset on its glistening rose-colored surface.

I throw my arms out and Read the wind. I think of my father, and campfire smoke fills my nose. He is down there. I have found my people. I scope the area for car headlights or any other sign of the guards, but I see no outsiders. What if they are stationed within the adobe village and living among my people? I wonder.

Although my body is exhausted from running all day, I can't stop and rest. I am almost there. I scramble down the ridge face, cutting my fingers on the sharp rocks in my haste, but I don't even feel the pain.

Trees hide the valley until I reach another outcrop and get an unobstructed view. I can now see people walking around, can make out the edges of the adobe houses silhouetted in the firelight. The southeastern corner of the perimeter fence is visible beyond the village, and atop a section nearer me the red light of an electrical box flashes slowly on and off. The sun slips behind the mountains in the west—*where Miles waits,* I think with a pang of guilt.

The moon that was bright enough to read by last night hides behind a bank of clouds. The night is dark enough for me to risk the last part of my journey exposed, and I jog the half mile across the valley floor to the perimeter fence. I follow the slow flash of the red light until I am standing beneath it. It is a whole twenty feet above me, and almost invisible in the dark of the night.

I have been thinking about how to scale the fence. At first, I had thought about trying to deactivate the box. But the way the guards talked, it sounded like there is a system that monitors when the fences are disabled. The last thing I want to do is set off an alarm and alert the guards to my presence. It wouldn't take long for them to reach the fence in a jeep, and even less time if some are already stationed among my clan.

I have to find some way to get over without setting off an alarm. My ignorance of how this type of device works puts me at a disadvantage. This is one case where Miles would have come in handy, I realize with remorse. *Don't think about it,* I tell myself. You made your decision, and it was based on keeping him safe. Keeping everyone safe. It's too late for regrets.

I wonder if I can wrap something around my hands and feet and climb—if the wires will only shock unprotected skin. I test the fence, throwing a piece of cooked rabbit against it. As soon as the flesh hits the metal, I hear a crackling sound and the meat falls to the ground with a line of black singed across it. I wrap it in cotton cloth and throw it again. The same thing happens, the cloth burning in the area that touched the metal. Climbing the fence while it is still electrified would be a very bad idea.

I think of the problem from every angle, and cannot come up with another way to get over the fence without disabling the box. This means possibly alerting the guards, significantly shortening the time I have to come up with an escape plan and see it through. So be it. I have no other choice.

I sit down near the fence and close my eyes, picturing the box in my mind as I summon my connection to the Yara. And as the connection is made, an image comes to me of lots of tiny multicolored wires coming together in a bundle and plugging into metal slots. I choose the bundle of wires attached to a large black cord and imagine a small flame underneath it.

I watch as the colored plastic sheathing begins to melt and drip, and the exposed wires grow red with heat. The inside of the shiny silver box glows until finally a few small sparks ignite and the whole thing explodes in a combustion of blue flame. I open my eyes and watch the flashing red light dim and disappear.

Around me, the night is silent. I can barely see the fence against the sky's velvet blackness. I rise to my feet and approach, carefully watching the now-dark electrical box high above me.

To be sure that the electricity is truly off, and it wasn't just the warning light that I affected with my fire, I do my rabbit-meat test again. The wrapped-up bundle hits the fence and falls to the ground unaffected. No noise. No sparks. But how can I be sure the surrounding boxes aren't programmed to take over for the disabled one?

I remember the shattered look of the guard when his colleague turned the fence back on before he was down. "You could have killed me," he said.

The charge is definitely lethal to humans. But I have no other choice. I'll have to risk it.

Fear sizzles through my chest as I move my hand an inch closer to the wires. Pulling my hand away, I back up a few steps. And then, running, I jump and fling myself as high up the fence as I can reach, grasping the wires with my fingers, and pulling myself up without pausing, my intention to reach the top and hurl myself over before the electricity can immobilize and kill me. I've scrambled halfway up before it registers that I am not being shocked. The fence is still disabled. I am safe.

I cling to the wires and allow myself one second pause to catch my breath before continuing my climb. Once at the top, I sling one leg over and scramble down the other side, hunching in a ball at the base of the fence, hopeful that no one noticed my acrobatic climbing feat. I readjust my backpack, and then, keeping low, sprint to a grouping of cacti and crouch behind it.

I am an arrow-shot away from the closest fire, where I see Galena cradling her baby, Aniak, in the firelight. I cast my gaze around the camp, but there's no sign of guards—I only see my people. My heart leaps to my throat as I allow myself to feel the excitement that has been building inside me.

I feel like whistling the notes that everyone will recognize ... my return-from-the-hunt whistle that brings the children running to meet me. But I'm still not sure my people aren't under some sort of surveillance, and don't want to be captured before I have to. Whit knows I'm near and that I'm coming for my clan. But has he yet alerted Avery's men to that fact?

Until he Reads that I'm here, I'm safe from him. Or until Avery's guards notice that I incapacitated a section of the fence. The amount of time I have to strategize with my clan about how best to free Badger and escape depends on how quickly either of those events occurs. Every moment counts.

A tall teenage boy walks out of one of the adobe huts carrying an armful of logs toward one of the campfires. I barely recognize him in jeans and T-shirt. I've only ever seen him in skins and furs. It's Kenai, and behind him is Nome, wearing shorts and a tank top. My heart feels like it's going to explode. I have missed them so much that I'm overwhelmed with emotion, and have to restrain myself from shouting their names.

As Nome bends over to pick up an armload of logs, I hurl my backpack to the ground, reach inside, and in seconds have assembled my crossbow. I hold it up to my eyes and aim to Nome's left, and a second later my bolt is lodged in the clay doorway, inches away from my friend. She turns to see what flew past her, and spotting it, pulls it out from where it is lodged and inspects it.

Her head jerks up as she looks around frantically, and it's not until I cautiously stand and wave that she sees me, drops the logs, and sprints in my direction.

"Oh my God, Juneau! Is that you?" she yells, and in an instant I am wrapped in a suffocating bear hug with a face full of blond hair. "We all knew you were coming. We just didn't know when," she says, searching my face as if she isn't sure it is me. "Oh, Juneau, your hair," she murmurs, and touches my pixie cut as tentatively as if it were made of snakes.

Others are running in our direction. Kenai reaches me and wraps me in his strong arms. "Junebug. You're here," he says.

"I missed you guys so much," I say, and then look over their shoulders toward the huts. "There aren't any guards?" I ask, and Nome pulls back from our hug and shakes her head.

"They're all back at the ranch house," she says. "They figured they didn't need to guard us once they seized all our amulets and took Badger after our last escape attempt."

"Why Badger?" I ask. "He's so young!"

"Exactly," Nome says darkly. "Too young to try to escape."

"Whit stopped by this morning," Kenai says, his nose wrinkling in disgust. "He told us to let you know that after you meet with Avery, Badger will be free to come back to his mother."

My father comes out of one of the adobe huts, and looks straight at me. I want to go to him, but I can't move. As he runs toward me, Nome and Kenai step back to leave him room. His face is haggard. He wraps me carefully in his arms, and pats me on the back in that reassuring way he did when I was a little girl.

"Oh, Juneau," he says, pulling back and looking intently into my eyes. "I told you not to come."

"But you knew I would," I say, and though I feel tears threatening to spill, I repress them and raise my chin in defiance. My father sees me do it, and he knows: I'm here for the fight.

"Yes," he says sadly. "I knew you would."

32

MILES

MY CALCULATIONS ARE WAY OFF. FOR ONE THING, the boundaries of the ranch aren't anywhere near where the gas station guy drew them on the map: I'm forced to backtrack twice and drive a lot farther east than I had expected. For another thing, no local roads seem to lead to the ranch.

At one point, the main road comes within view of the perimeter fence, and inside the compound I see what looks like an airstrip in the middle of a field. Avery's hot-shot customers probably arrive by private plane. But by road, the ranch seems unapproachable, which I know is impossible if all these army guys are coming and going. They must have to know exactly where the front gate is, because there's no signage, and no trace of an entry.

I park the truck at an abandoned rest stop, hike a mile back to the perimeter fence, and begin following it heading south.

Finally, an hour and a half later, I get to what looks like the main entrance. It's a security gate with a guy in a booth and a lifting bar to let cars in and out.

To one side is a big sign with AVERY RANCH painted in scrolling letters. The road is lined with trees, and I take advantage of them to hide as I make my way to the gate. Finally I am standing within ten feet of the security booth, and I can see the guy inside playing a game on his computer. He stops and takes a big swig of Coke, and then puts the empty glass bottle on the window ledge outside the booth. Propped underneath his chair is a big-ass machine gun.

I look behind me at the twenty-foot fence. I can't climb it—it's electrified. This security gate is the only opening I've seen. If the guy weren't there, it would be easy to duck down under the bar and slip my way in. It seems that, besides monitoring the cars driving in and out, Avery's not worried about people trying to break into the compound. *No one would be suicidal enough,* I think. A crazy Texan and his private army? Who would want a piece of that?

For the first time today, I realize that what I'm doing is actually dangerous. Sweat beads on my forehead, and my palms are clammy. Great. I'm not even inside the gate, and I'm already petrified. Which is probably a good sign: It suggests that I am, indeed, sane.

Here I am, an eighteen-year-old who never even did ROTC, trying to sneak into an armed compound. It was one of these private-army guys who shot me—almost killed me—while I was escaping my house with Juneau. I'm sure this front-gate guard won't hesitate to fire if he spots me. A crippling wave of panic almost makes me turn around and slink away, back to the safety of the truck.

With much effort, I ignore the flashing red lights of my innate fear, shoving my emotions aside, and try to focus on what will further my goal. Damned if I don't remind myself of someone.

I inch closer to the security booth, while still hiding from the range of the guard's viewpoint. I watch him intently, waiting for him to bend over or turn the other way. All I need is for him to be distracted for a few seconds, and I can be past the booth and out of his line of sight.

I pull the crossbow pieces out of my bag. Slotting them together, I cock the bowstring, then load it with a bolt. I aim at the guard's Coke bottle.

It's so small. How am I ever going to hit it?

Concentrate, I think. I squeeze the lever, and the bolt goes flying straight toward the bottle. It misses by just an inch and lands in the trees on the other side of the security booth. I exhale, brush aside my disappointment, and aim. I pull the trigger. To my amazement, the Coke bottle flies up into the air, lands with a loud clang on the pavement, and begins rolling away.

The guard swears and, stepping down out of the booth, chases the bottle down the drive. I dash out from behind my tree, crouch as I run under the toll-booth arm, and sprint into a thicket of tall bamboo plants on the other side. I watch from my vantage point as the guard scoops up the bottle and carries it back to the security booth. As he leans down to throw it into a trash can beneath the window, I turn and run at full speed away from the front gate. My arms pump by my sides as I dash through some pine trees and, at the point where the trees grow thin, throw myself (a little too forcefully) to the ground. Having knocked my breath out, I crawl panting to the point where the trees meet the road.

And there I see the ranch spread out before me. From where I lie, the road winds through pine trees, spans a river with a flat metal bridge, and leads to a big white McMansion with an American flag hanging on the porch.

Behind the mansion is a one-story L-shaped building with lots of windows and doors—kind of Motel-6 looking. Several Land Rovers and jeeps are parked outside. *That must be where the guards stay,* I think. Judging from the number of doors and vehicles, I estimate that up to forty men could be housed there.

The sun is just going down over the horizon. I decide to make my way through the trees up the hill and wait there until dark before crossing the river and making my way to the main house.

But what I'll do once I get there . . . I have no idea.

33

JUNEAU

THE CLAN CONVERGES, EACH WANTING TO HUG me: the children excitedly, the elders with sorrow in their eyes. A few even murmur, "I'm sorry," as they embrace me. The truth is out, then. I am torn by so many different emotions that I can't talk. I let the hugs speak for me—words will come later.

Finally, I follow my dad back to his hut. I gesture at the sparse furnishings. "Pretty basic," I comment, not knowing what else to say. I've never felt uncomfortable around my own father before.

Dad feels my tension, and plays along with my empty conversation. "One of the guards told me that Hunt Avery took these abandoned adobe huts, patched them up, and uses them to house the guests who want an 'authentic living-off-the-land experience.'"

I nod mutely and lay my weapons inside the door.

My father sits on the smooth clay floor, and gestures for me to join him. His expression is grave, and he looks like he hasn't slept in days. We sit in silence, until finally he says, "Go ahead."

"What do you mean, 'go ahead'?" I ask.

"I mean, go ahead. Scream. Shout. Tell me I'm a liar. Tell me you hate me. Say whatever you've been wanting to say for the last few weeks."

I close my eyes and breathe deeply. And when I open them, they are wet with tears. "Quite honestly, Dad, I'm pretty much equally divided between wanting to hit you and wanting to hug you. There's hate and love and relief and betrayal, all battling each other inside me. If I let myself feel it all, I'd probably explode."

"I don't blame you for hating me," he says, and the sorrow on his face is clearer than any apology he could make.

"You lied to me," I say. "Not just you. All of the elders lied to me. But you ... you're my father. How could you have raised me, cared for me, taught me right from wrong, and all the time have lied through your teeth?"

"Juneau," my dad says. "You don't have to accept my justification. But in this particular situation, I had to make the welfare of the world—of humankind and all living things, of the future of our planet—more important than my obligation to you. If lying to you meant ensuring your survival and that of your descendants, then I was willing to sacrifice my soul and lie to you and the other children."

"I hear you," I say, wiping away another tear. "But I don't agree.

You could have told us the truth. You could have trusted us with reality."

My father shakes his head. "Remember Kenai when he was thirteen? Rebelling against every rule; questioning every word his parents said? How do you think he would have handled the truth? Do you think he would have stayed in our territory, hiding from the outside world?"

I shake my head.

"And he's just one example, Juneau. We had to fabricate a story that would keep you all with us. Keep us separate from the world. And keep our secrets safe."

"It still wasn't right," I say.

"I know," Dad says. "But it's the best we knew to do. The other elders are having to deal with their own children and, worse for some, themselves. We all have to deal with the repercussions of our mutual and individual deceit. There has been forgiveness in some cases." He looks down. "Less in others."

My jaw clenches and my eyes sting. I squeeze my hands into fists.

"You're allowed to cry, Juneau," he says.

Wiping the corners of my eyes, I take a shaky breath. I can tell my father wants to hug me, but if he does, I'm afraid I'll start bawling and never stop. I wrap my arms around myself, keeping him at a distance.

"Why did you come here when I told you not to?" he asks softly.

"The clan is my responsibility," I say.

My dad rises and walks to the corner, where he picks up a bottle of water. Sitting back down, he hands it to me. "Juneau, ever since the clan was abducted, I've been thinking about you. Questioning how I raised you. You've grown up with the knowledge that you will be the next clan leader. I know the burden that Whit put on you. And I know how our clan members look up to you, but also treat you like you belong to them. Their own clan Sage."

My father reaches forward and runs his hand back and forth over my short hair. "Because of this, you've missed out on a childhood. You don't know what it means to be carefree. To not feel the weight of the clan's survival resting on your shoulders at all times. I was wrong to have raised you like this. But it was hard to refuse Whit and the other elders once your mom died. You were the only one who could take her place."

"Because I can Conjure?" I ask.

"That's a part of it," Dad says. "What's more important is something I have never talked to you about. I was waiting until you passed the Rite. But that might well never happen now. It's time I told you everything."

I hold up my hand to stop him. "And I should believe you because..."

"There are no more lies between us. No more secrets," my father says. "I swear it on the memory of your mother. It's up to you whether you believe me or not. But I assure you that everything I'm telling you is true."

I watch him, silent.

"How much do you know now about Amrit?" he asks.

"I figured some things out for myself, and Whit pretty much confirmed it all last night," I say.

He nods sadly. "I saw you talking to him in the fire. Did he mention our part in making Amrit? The part about your mother's legend?"

I nod. "Something about healing a she-wolf who went on to live a long time."

He takes a long drink from his glass and stares at the ceiling, as if trying to see back in time. "Both your mother's story, and several of the legends about eternal or extended life that we subsequently dug up, specified using 'the life force of a prophetess.' They called for a woman who was one with the earth—a daughter of Gaia.

"Your mother not only knew about her tribe's legend, but she was the right person to re-create it. That is the only reason we were able to succeed where scientists and scholars have failed over the centuries. It's the reason we, of all people, were able to crack the long-hidden code . . . to access the earth's secret."

"What do you mean Mom was the right person?" Goose bumps rise on my arms.

"What do you know of your mother's family?" my father asks, blatant guilt scrawled across his face.

"Well, before Whit told me she was from Mongolia, I thought they came from China."

"A part of China that used to be Mongolia," my father clarifies. "Your grandmother was from a tribe of itinerant farmers who worshipped the land they worked and lived on. Their women were famed shamans, medicine women.

"Your grandmother used to tell your mother their stories. She said your mother was special because she had priestess blood. The knowledge of her ancestors' nature-worship was one of the things that interested your mother in Gaian philosophy and the movement rising up around us. She was drawn to it through her heritage.

"In your grandmother's legend about the wolf, the life force the prophetess used was her own blood. So that's what your mother used when we made the first batch of Amrit. And for every batch afterward. No one else's blood worked."

In my mind, it's as if a stone dislodges from the base of a river-dam. As my thoughts come together, the dam cracks and realization comes flooding through. Her blood. My blood. The reason she and I were the only ones to give the Rite. But as I begin to understand, a host of new questions arises.

My father watches as I grasp the meaning of what he's saying. He waits until he thinks I'm ready, then continues. "We tried the Amrit on animals, and then on ourselves. And we ran as many tests as we could to try to pinpoint what was different about your mother's blood from every other sample. That was before we discovered the ocular mutation and the deceleration of aging on test animals, which is when we decided to flee—in order to protect our discovery from the outside world. Once in Alaska, we had none of our equipment to continue the blood-type experiments.

"However, when you were little, your mother took a sample of your blood to see if you too had the ability to 'bring the Amrit to life,' as she called it. You did."

"That's why Whit always had me prepare the elixir for the Rite?" I ask.

"Yes—you were the key to the Amrit. Without your mother . . . without you . . . it wouldn't have worked."

Dad's eyes are empty. I can tell he has been over and over this story in his mind, planning how he would explain it to me one day. "How could Whit think he could sell a drug that needs one person's blood?" I ask.

"I think he figured that if he brought it to a buyer with enough funding, they would be able to run tests on your blood and find a working alternative that could be manufactured."

I don't even know what to say. I just sit and let the pieces try to sort themselves into something recognizable. Something sane.

"What would the clan have done if I died, too—like Mom did? Would the formula for Amrit die with me?" I ask.

"Unless you had a daughter of your own, I suppose," my father says, smiling sadly.

That little bit of information finally tips the scales, and I am no longer able to think. I lie back on the ground and stare at the ceiling.

"What are you feeling, Junebug?" my father asks.

"Used. Lied to. Confused."

My father is silent. He doesn't try to explain any further, and I am thankful. Nothing he can say will make me feel better. Nothing he can do will erase the last seventeen years of my life. I wish I could talk to my mother. The same blood flowed through her veins. And she took that blood and made it into something she thought could save the world . . . until she realized that it had the potential to destroy it.

I hear the crunching of tires on the dirt road outside, and Whit's voice calling my name. I stand and walk to the door of my father's hut. Whit sits behind the wheel of a huge monster of a truck-like vehicle, while two of the armed guards step out.

I turn to my father, who has risen to stand behind me. "Keep these for me," I say, glancing at the corner where I stashed my pack and crossbow.

"You don't have to go with Whit," he says.

"I'm the life of the clan. Literally," I say, and though I want to reassure him that I still love him, I can't bring myself to speak the words.

I step outside the door and squint into the blinding beams of the headlights. I lift my empty hands in the air and, staring straight at Whit, say, "You wanted me? Here I am."

34

MILES

I ARRIVE AT THE EDGE OF THE TREES AND FIND myself on a hill overlooking the Avery ranch. From where I lie, I have a side view of the mansion and the guards' barracks behind. Between me and the estate is a fence that's about half the height of the one around the perimeter, and not nearly as scary looking. I can't tell if it's electrified or not.

The river runs along one side of the property, and disappears off into the distance. In spite of the moonlight, I can't see much. Though the buildings are lit up, the rest of the estate is draped in darkness.

This hill provides such a good vantage point that I decide to stay and watch for a while—to see if anyone's coming and going, and basically get a feel for the place.

I wonder how Juneau's doing. Where she is. I'm betting she

went straight to her clan, but have no clue what her next step will be. She didn't seem to know either—at least the last time we talked.

I unstrap the tent bag from my back and lie down on my stomach. Taking out one of the rabbit legs, I wash it down with the rest of the bottle of water. I only have one bottle left, but am not worried. Maybe I'll sneak down to the river later tonight and refill.

So I've got my plan for staying hydrated, I think. *How about one for deciding my next move?*

I try to channel my inner James Bond. I could sneak into the guards' quarters, steal one of their uniforms, and infiltrate the group. Yeah, right. Like they're not going to suspect anything when a puny eighteen-year-old suddenly appears among them.

How about something more direct? I could show up first thing in the morning and tell Avery that I'm a high school student doing my final paper on exotic-hunting reserves. Or not. Even if Avery was stupid enough to buy that, Whit's hanging out somewhere and would recognize me instantly.

Plan C. I could set a fire or trip an alarm. That would at least provide a temporary distraction. But since I don't even know where Juneau is or the status of her rescue mission, I might alert the guards at the wrong moment, and interfere with what she's doing.

My best bet is to wait and watch. And just as I make that decision, high-powered headlights appear far to the south. As they get closer, I can see it's some kind of enormous all-terrain vehicle—probably what Avery takes his clients hunting in. A toy for rich middle-aged men. At a fork, it turns and takes the road to the mansion. It pulls up into the circular driveway, and two guards climb out of the back.

Someone steps out of the driver's seat and moves toward the house. At first, he's too far away to see, but when he walks into the porch light I spot a head of black spiky hair. It's the devil himself: Whit.

A figure jumps down out of the passenger seat. It's a girl: She's about half the size of the guards. Her pixie haircut and the gliding motion of her stride tip me off to her identity. My heart drops. Juneau's been captured.

Well, it's too late now for me to infiltrate or talk my way into the house. And since Juneau's in their clutches, I can forget my plan to provide a distraction to her rescue attempt. She walks proudly up the porch steps and in through the front door. It doesn't look like she's handcuffed or bound, and the guards aren't brandishing weapons. I wonder why she's going along with them without a fight.

Once Juneau is inside and the door shut behind her, the two guards split off and walk around the mansion to the barracks. I watch as they join a picnic table of cardplayers outside their quarters; they unstrap guns, place them on the ground, and pull bottles out of a beer cooler. Their work is obviously done for the day.

I wonder if there are guards stationed inside the house, because none are visible outside it. Maybe Avery doesn't plan on any trouble now that he's gotten what he wants. Plus he practically has an army within yelling distance.

I need to get closer to see what's going on inside the mansion. To discover exactly what Avery's doing with Juneau—if he'll have her locked up or if she'll be able to escape.

I look down at my clothes: jeans, a black T-shirt, and dark blue tennis shoes. The white lettering and irate red bird on my Cardinals shirt glow in the dim moonlight, so I turn it inside out and put it back on.

Now only my skin stands out. Luckily, from all the action movies I've seen, I know how to fix that. I inch my way back to the trees, and once among them I use a stick to dig up some dirt. I pour a little bit of bottled water on it, then stir it around until it's thick. And then I spread it all over my arms and face. It dries fast—within minutes my arms are caked with dried mud.

I look through the tent bag to see if there's anything heavy I should leave behind. But, imagining that if I'm successful and somehow manage to spring Juneau, we might need the food and water. I leave everything in and, swinging the bag to my back, get ready to retreat into the forest. I'd rather backtrack and climb down the unexposed side of the hill, than go the direct route down and serve as target practice for bored guards with a few beers in them.

I'm only a few steps into the dark wood when I hear something that makes my blood run cold. A low growl comes from the blackness near me. My hair stands on end as my heart simultaneously leaps into my throat. What the hell was that?

I suddenly remember I am on a wild-animal hunting range. And it dawns on me that those ten-foot-high fences around the mansion and barracks aren't for intruders. They are meant to keep animals away from humans. Or, more specifically, to keep the animals in the zone between the perimeter fence and the living areas . . . which is exactly where I am right now.

Holy crap, what kind of animals did that gas station guy mention? Zebras and antelopes? I might not know much about animals, but I very much doubt it's one of them making these menacing deep-in-the-throat growls. This is a predator.

The only predators I've ever seen outside a zoo are the coyotes roaming around L.A. People are warned to keep their dogs and kids close by, but they don't usually attack adults. That is, unless you come near their cubs.

But this doesn't sound like a coyote. It's definitely more cat-like . . . in a not-so-cute-and-fluffy way.

What do I do? Stay here, frozen in place? Or walk calmly away? What if I'm walking directly toward its den? Then it'll definitely attack. For the hundredth time this month, I curse myself for not watching more National Geographic.

I summon every last drop of courage inside me and take a step backward. Then two steps. And, in a little patch of moonlight that's broken through the trees, I see a brown paw step cautiously forward not more than ten feet away. It is followed by a head the size of my torso. A brown-and-white head with black stripes. Oh my God, I'm being stalked by a tiger. That crazy-ass billionaire imported a fucking tiger to the middle of New Mexico. And I'm going to be its next meal.

There's no way I'll be able to dig the crossbow out of my bag, put it together, load, and shoot. I can't even move—my feet are rooted to the ground.

As if in slow motion, the tiger pulls its front paws together and crouches low to the ground. It flicks its tail jerkily back and forth, like my mom's cat did when ambushing a chipmunk.

My mouth is open. I try to scream, but nothing comes out. A lightning bolt of fear sizzles behind my eyes as I realize I'm about to die.

I clench my teeth. The tiger pounces.

35

JUNEAU

"WELL, NOW. WHO'VE WE GOT HERE?" CALLS A booming voice as I follow Whit into a cavernous front hallway. The light from an enormous deer-antler chandelier is reflected from a gleaming parquet floor.

A man walks toward me. He's a good head taller than anyone in my clan, and wears a fawn-colored cowboy hat and matching boots. He claps his hands and rubs them together like he's getting ready to eat me whole. He leans over to get a good look at my starburst and, satisfied, takes one of my hands in his big meaty fist and shakes the life out of it.

"You must be our little Juneau. My name's Randall Bradford Avery the Third, but for obvious reasons"—and he spreads his arms out to indicate the mansion, the shooting range, everything around—"everyone calls me Hunt. Let me tell you, I have been waiting to meet you for the longest time now. Haven't I, Whit?"

There are so many things wrong with this little introduction that I decide not to respond, and settle for a scowl. Avery laughs, like I've made a joke. Grasping me by the shoulder, he ushers me toward a door. "Why don't we all just grab a drink and get acquainted."

I don't even put up a fight. All I want to do is find Badger and get him out of here. If that means following this idiot around until I come up with a plan, well, so be it.

Whit follows us through a double set of doors, and then closes them behind us. I enter a room that could fit ten of my clan's yurts inside. The floor is thickly carpeted, and the walls are lined with mostly empty bookshelves and topped with mounted animal heads. Every species you could possibly imagine has a representative hanging glaze-eyed on the wall.

Instinctively, I look back at Whit in horror, and see him squirm. He doesn't like this violent display any more than I do.

"Welcome to my trophy room," Mr. Avery says, affectionately scratching the chin of an enormous tusked boar before walking over to a copper-topped bar installed in one corner. He squeezes behind it and makes conversation while lining up glasses and bottles. "Made my money in oil. This wildlife hunting range is just one of my little hobbies." Glancing up, he winks at me.

Although he is trying his best to display an easy manner, I can tell by the way he talks and moves that he is uncomfortable. He's trying to size me up, but doesn't know what to expect. And for a big-game hunter, not knowing your prey makes you vulnerable.

He drops some ice cubes into a glass, and pours in a caramel-colored liquid from a crystal decanter. "This is for you, Whit," he says, handing him the glass.

And as he extends his hand, I see the ice cubes tremble—the drink sloshes slightly back and forth inside the glass. Avery's hand is shaking. I glance to his face—his expression is neutral. He's not nervous or upset. Why is he shaking? His other hand clutches the side of the bar, anchoring him.

He is looking at me, shaking his head in faux-dismay. "Where are my manners? I should have served the lady first. Though I doubt you're a whiskey drinker, Juneau. You just don't have the look." He turns back to the bar and runs his hand over a stack of bottles. When he pauses over one, I see his fingers tremble again.

"I've got every alcohol known to man," he says. "Or if you're a teetotaler, I can offer you a nice cold tonic and lime."

"Sure, I'll have a nice cold tonic and lime," I say, and he gets this relieved look on his face, ". . . as soon as you have one delivered to everyone in my clan." I make my voice as blank as my face.

Avery takes his hat off, sets it on the bar, and rubs his hand over his thinning hair. "So we've got ourselves a vigilante," he says, the smile on his lips as cold and dead as the snakeskin on his boots. "If you're not feeling sociable, we can get straight to business. Wouldn't want to waste any of your time."

He pours himself a whiskey, and then leads us through his stuffed slaughterhouse toward a door at the far end of the room.

We walk in silence, with only the tinkling of the ice in the glasses accompanying our footsteps. Whit hasn't said a thing since he picked me up from the adobe camp, and that's been fine with me. If I get started with him, I know I won't stop, which is kind of too bad, because I've got an overwhelming urge to hit him hard enough to break something.

We pass out of the trophy room and into a hallway, where Avery stops in front of another door. A rectangular box with numbered keys is fixed to the wall next to it. Switching his drink to his other hand, Avery presses a few keys, puts his hand flat on a screen, and turns to me, once again wearing his false joviality. "Those eggheads at NASA don't have anything on my technology."

I have no clue what he's talking about, but keep my face unreadable, and when the door swings open, I follow him in.

We step into a blinding white room. Everything is white: the floors, the walls, and all of the equipment inside. There are machines from wall to wall, and a low humming noise comes from a large electrical box in one corner.

"Welcome to the North Pole!" Avery bellows and waves his free hand around. "Now I reckon you haven't seen anything like this before, taking into account the way you've been living." He stops and winks at Whit, who is ignoring him and walking around inspecting the machines like he's never seen them before, which I greatly doubt.

"This is my cryonics lab. I, like your parents and Mr. Graves here, have a great interest in preserving endangered species. However, the species I'm most concerned about is me!" He gives another laugh, and I realize that it's not feigned: He actually thinks he's funny.

He sees my blank stare, and harrumphs unhappily. "Please, do have a look around," he says.

I stay where I am, and fold my arms across my chest.

Avery takes a mouthful of whiskey, and sets his sweating glass on a sterile white counter. He turns to me, and though there's still a smile on his lips, his eyes have grown cold. "Miss Newhaven, there is a little boy somewhere under this roof, who has been crying because he misses his momma. It would be in his best interest, as well as your own and that of your clan, if you can find it in yourself to be amenable to any propositions that I make you."

"If you so much as touch a hair on Badger's head—" I growl, but Avery cuts me off.

"The boy has everything a child his age could want: warm clothes, food, toys, and a whole mountain of DVDs. And he'll have his mommy, too, as soon as I get what I need from you. So . . . are you ready to cooperate?"

I ignore him and turn to Whit. "How could you do this to Badger?" I ask, controlling my fury.

My old mentor lifts his chin and says, "I did nothing to Badger."

"Nah, that was my idea, little lady," offers Avery, "as was the plan for bringing your clan here to our lovely ranch. Whit didn't seem quite ready to do business with me, so I figured I needed to sweeten the deal. The only thing we were missing was you, and I didn't yet know how important you were. But now that we're all here, let's get down to business.

"As I was saying, please have a look around." Placing a hand on my shoulder, he steers me deeper into the room. A giant transparent tube containing a single white-leather bed lies propped on a plinth in the middle of the room. "This here compartment is for full-body cryonic preservation. I like to call it my 'life insurance.' Top of the line, just waiting for me to kick the bucket so they can put me into deep freeze."

His grip tightening on my shoulder, he guides me to another bed: this one metal framed and cloth covered like the one I saw Whit lying in when he was in the hospital. A handful of complicated-looking devices are arranged around it. "And over here are all the fancy do-dads doctors will need to keep my organs functioning once I die in order to freeze me." He turns to me with a broad smile. "But it doesn't look like I'll need that now, thanks to you and Mr. Graves."

Wait, what? I turn to Whit, my eyes wide, but he pretends like he doesn't see me. So *that's* what this is all about. Avery wasn't joking before: His interest in the elixir is personal. I should have guessed.

Before I have time to let this sink in, Avery steers me to a far corner of the room, where a silver metal box the size of my pup tent sits atop a table. "Being close to nature and all, you're going to love this part," he says.

Whit speaks up for the first time. "I'm sorry for interrupting, but I don't think this display will help you plead your case with Juneau." He looks worriedly at the box.

Avery narrows his eyes at me, his frostiness returning, but a mocking smile is planted on his lips. "Miss Newhaven doesn't need me to plead with her. I think we're playing for the same team at this point. We're on little Badger's team, aren't we now, Juneau?"

I remain silent, and taking that as agreement, Avery pries open a door on the front of the metal box. There's a hissing noise, and smoke rises in a cloud from inside. "Of course, before full-body cryonics were perfected, the best method was neuro-preservation," he says.

Within the box, positioned side by side, are three bucket-sized clear canisters filled with ice. As the warm air hits them, they immediately cloud over. Avery takes a cloth from the top of the box and wipes the frost off the side of one of the canisters, and I can see something large and dark suspended inside the ice. "Meet Daisy, best friend a man could ever have," he says fondly.

And then I notice the fur and the long snout, and the clean line where the neck was severed from the rest of the body.

Avery shakes his head sadly. "Never was a hunting dog like this ol' girl. Hope to bring her back someday. Her and her kin," he nods at the two other canisters. "Now ain't that a noble cause to undertake?"

Daisy's frozen eye stares out at me, and something inside me snaps. I twist out of Avery's grip and make it halfway to the door before I'm on my knees, heaving up the scarce contents of my stomach onto the sterile white floor.

36

MILES

I BRACE MYSELF TO BE KNOCKED DOWN AND TORN to shreds. Instead, a loud squawking noise rips through the darkness and I am blinded by a face full of flapping wings. Finally able to move, I dive through the underbrush and run full speed through the woods until I reach the steep hillside, then slide down it on my butt.

I run for safety to the middle of the road, like it's a no-man's-land where nothing can hurt me. As if a huge man-eating tiger would stop for pavement. But nothing moves up on the hill, and I stand there for what seems like forever before I see a dark shape hurtle downward toward me. This time I recognize it and, crumpling over in relief, drag myself to the ditch at the side of the road.

"Poe!" I say, as the raven lands next to my hand.

He spreads his feathers and caws a hello.

"Man, you just saved my life up there!" I want to pet him, but he waddles backward out of my reach. "And now I'm talking to you," I say, "but that's okay, because no one's around to hear." I grin like a crazy person.

"How the hell did you find me here?" I ask. I know he has some kind of draw toward Juneau, but why would he come to me?

Poe eyes me as if weighing me up, and then takes a step toward me. I reach out, and he lets me pick him up. I set him on my lap and open the little leather pouch that's on his harness. There's a paper inside. I unfold it, to read in big, curly writing,

> *Your bird-child is driving me insane. Doesn't want to stay with me. Send him back with instructions when you have something for me to do.*
>
> *P.S. I've been trying to Read the fire, but can't get a thing out of it. Either I'm not close enough to nature (as if), or your Yara is a bit more selective about who can use it than you thought.*

I fold up the note and stick it in my pocket, rehashing what Tallie wrote. She's figuring out what I've already discovered. Amrit is the key to connecting to the Yara.

That still doesn't answer the question of why Poe came to me instead of Juneau. Maybe I can Read his memory like Juneau did.

Carefully, I cradle the bird in both hands, and feel its heart-beat patter against my fingers as I raise it to my chest. I close my eyes, and—here comes the Yara buzz—suddenly find myself flying up into the air, and over a city in a desert. I catch a glimpse of a woman with fiery red hair in a curly cloud around her head as the bird looks down at her. I recognize Tallie, and the town must be Roswell. Poe and I fly high over the desert until we slow and begin circling over a valley with a river running through it. In the distance we spot another river. It must be the one right down the hill from where I'm sitting.

There are several campfires burning in the valley, and as we swoop down we smell the smoke through our beak, and feel the air separating our feathers for landing. We alight in the middle of an encampment of adobe huts, just as a huge vehicle with a blinding row of headlights pulls up to one of the huts. Juneau is in the doorway, and our heartbeat speeds up as we see her. She's the goal. She's what we flew here for.

But then she gets into the truck and drives away, and we are once more in the air, following her trail. When we arrive at the big white mansion, we spot Juneau following Whit into the house. We cannot follow. We get ready to peck on one of the windows, but then something else catches our attention. It's like a glow—like a warmth inside our breast, and it's coming from atop a nearby hill. We fly toward it, and once in the trees, we see Miles . . . me . . . standing mere yards away from a tiger. The tiger pounces, and we dive, flapping our wings in its face, distracting it while Miles runs away.

The tiger swipes at us, but we are too fast, and fly up to perch in a tree above. The tiger sniffs the air and growls in frustration before turning around and pacing back to the tree where its two cubs wait. We fly after Miles until we find him here, sitting in the road, and here I come, back up to the surface of the vision. The buzzing in my arms gets lighter, and here I am holding a bird and feeling this amazing feeling because . . . *I was flying*! I, Miles Blackwell, was up in the air, soaring over the earth.

I jump up and whoop. Poe flaps away, and then turns and peers at me like I'm the most fascinating thing he's seen in a long time. "I know. I've changed. I'm like Juneau and her people now. All Yarafied and immortal and shit," I explain.

I pull my bag up over my shoulders, and make the clicking noise that I heard Juneau use with Poe so that he'll follow me. He flaps up and lands on my shoulder, digging his talons into my shirt to keep his balance.

I talk to him as we start toward the mansion. "So, you only came to me because I'm your sloppy seconds, huh? No offense taken. Let's go find your first choice."

37

JUNEAU

AVERY PICKS UP A PHONE. "GLORIA, WE'VE GOT A mess to clean up in the cryo room," he says, listens for a second, and then yells, "For God's sake, you can leave the damn kid for fifteen minutes. He's not going to self-destruct if someone's not watching him twenty-four/seven. And on your way down, tell O'Donnell and Nursall to get in here."

He hangs up and, yanking a white towel from a drawer, hands it to me, scowling. "Clean yourself up, Miss Newhaven. We've got work to do."

There is a knock on the door, and a man in a blue jeans and a checked cotton shirt walks in.

"There you are, Dr. Canfield," Avery says, marching up to him and shaking his hand. "Thanks for coming so quickly."

Avery turns to me. "My trusted medical advisor dropped what

he was doing in Roswell and rushed on over as soon as we knew you were over the fence. See how important you are to us?"

The man gives us a little bow, grabs a white jacket off a peg on the wall and pulls it on over his clothes.

"Now let me make introductions. This here is Dr. Whittier Graves," says Avery, slinging an arm around Whit's shoulders like he owns him. *Which he does.* "Graves was involved in the creation of the drug I have told you about. However, he is not a medical doctor, are you, Graves?"

"Philosophy," Whit says.

"He is the person who administered the drug to the members of his community, along with the indispensable assistance of this young lady, Miss Juncau Newhaven."

The door opens and in walks a middle-aged woman wearing a white uniform and carrying a roll of paper and a spray bottle. As she mops up my vomit, she glances up and holds my gaze for a couple of weighted seconds. And then, as quickly as she arrived, she's gone. All the while, Avery continues talking as if she's not there.

"So, friends, as of this moment"—he looks up at a clock on the wall—"ten thirty p.m., on Thursday, May ninth, everyone in this room is entering a contract situation. I would say it was legally binding, but that's not how I tend to do things. I prefer to handle compliance to terms myself. So let me explain things as clearly as I can so that everyone understands what they're agreeing to.

"This is the drug that Mr. Graves approached me with, hoping to make a deal with me for an amount that I will not disclose."

He opens a drawer and pulls out a tray containing several plastic bags and vials. I recognize them immediately: They are the ingredients for the Amrit.

Avery continues. "After an alternate deal was precipitated by the appearance of a competitor, Mr. Graves revealed that one vital component was missing—the blood of this young lady, who we needed in person since a workable alternative has not yet been found." He pauses and frowns at me before continuing.

"I am willing to meet his price, as long as I know for sure that this elixir works. Sure, I've got the proof that this man is what he claims to be. He looks the same as when I met him in the sixties, and a thorough medical examination gives pretty clear evidence that he has not aged in the last thirty years. And Dr. Canfield, you yourself have analyzed blood samples from members of Mr. Graves's community, and have found them to be immune to every disease you tested."

The doctor nods his agreement.

"However, being that I'm fond of that old dictum, 'I'll believe it when I see it,' I prefer to test the drug myself. Therefore we will proceed as follows: Mr. Graves and Miss Newhaven will carry out the procedure under the surveillance of Dr. Canfield."

My face becomes numb as I understand what is about to happen. I glance over to Whit, and his blasé expression informs me he already knows about these arrangements.

"As I agreed with you, Dr. Canfield, if it succeeds, or even if it fails, and you are able to revive me, you will receive one million dollars. If not, all you stand to lose is one day out of your busy schedule. Are those terms amenable to you, good doctor?"

"Yes, they are," says the man, adjusting his glasses.

"Good, good," says Avery. He turns to Whit. "Let me confirm in the presence of Dr. Canfield that the immediate effects of the drug are violent and resemble a poisoning. I will then be without breath or heartbeat for eight hours . . ."

"On average. The maximum we have seen is nine hours," corrects Whit.

"All right then, if at the end of nine hours my breathing resumes, it is understood that I will be aware, but paralyzed for a maximum of four days. At that point, I will regain my mobility and test negative for all known diseases. In this case Mr. Graves will receive the sum he has requested. The boy will be returned to his mother, and the entire community will be free to leave. They will have my assistance getting wherever it is they want to go."

Avery stares at the dregs of his whiskey as he twirls his glass, then tosses it back in one gulp. "However, if I do not regain consciousness after nine hours and Dr. Canfield is unsuccessful at reviving me, my guards have instructions for how to take care of you"—he focuses on me, and the cold in his eyes freezes my soul—"you," he says looking at Whit, "and the boy. I don't think we need to go into specifics. Let's just say that your community will be free to leave my ranch . . . if they are able."

"Wait a minute," Whit says, looking as shocked as I feel. "You never mentioned any of that last part before!"

"I didn't need to," says Avery, "because you're going to make damned sure that this thing works. Then all those nasty consequences just disappear."

"And what about our other agreements?" Whit asks.

"Such as?"

"The promise that for each dose of serum sold by you on the market, you will provide one free dose to the underprivileged in developing countries."

"We can speak about that issue later. I might not want to sell any of the drug at all. As I have always maintained, the main concern here is my own longevity. If the drug works on me, then I will consider its possible distribution later."

"But . . . ," Whit starts.

Avery strides past him and opens the door. "Please join us," he says, and two guards step into the room. "Since I'm counting on Dr. Canfield to monitor my vital signs while I am 'dead'"—and he uses his fingers for quotation marks—"I have asked a couple of my men to personally accompany you wherever you wish to go. Within my house, that is. You can grab a meal in the kitchen. And you each have a room assigned to you if you need to rest. *Mi casa su casa*: You are my honored guests. How's that sound to you?"

Not waiting for a response, he claps his hands and rubs them together expectantly. "Good, good. Men, please take a seat. Everyone, please excuse me while I change." He goes to the back of the room and steps behind a screen, while the two guards pull out chairs and, laying their guns across their laps, sit down. Whit walks past me and, pulling a mortar and pestle out of a cabinet, begins grinding the herbs and minerals together. I want to jump on him, beat him with my fists, shake him until he turns into the old Whit I knew . . . not this cold, emotionless monster.

I glance at the guards and see that one is staring holes through me. Something looks familiar about him. His gaze locked on mine, he pulls aside his jacket to show me a bandaged upper arm. My heart drops. It's the man I shot in Salt Lake City.

Avery steps out from behind the curtain wearing paper clothes: blue pants and a short-sleeved shirt. He notices my stare-down with the guard. "Ah yes. You recognize Mr. O'Donnell, Juneau. I thought since you were already acquainted, I would ask him to be your personal escort."

O'Donnell's lips curl into a cruel smile. But Whit interrupts this tender moment by calling my name. I walk over to see what he wants. "It's time, Juneau. Remember, you're doing this for your clan." He pauses and, for the first time today, he looks me in the eyes.

"Give me your hand," he says, and picks up a scalpel.

38

MILES

THE NIGHT IS SO DARK THAT I TAKE MY CHANCES on someone driving up behind me and walk in the middle of the road. At least I'll have some hope of spotting a dangerous predator before it has a chance to attack. Poe grips my left shoulder as we walk, and his raven talons pinch enough to give me a double dose of alertness.

It takes us around twenty minutes to get to the fence, and probably another fifteen minutes of walking back and forth along it before I decide it's electrified. The part that crosses the road looks like a swinging gate, and a yard or so in front of it is a pole with an intercom.

I'm a good way off the road, trying to see if there are any trees close enough to the gate that I might be able to climb over (there aren't), when I see headlights coming. Poe flaps down from my shoulder as I duck behind some undergrowth to hide. A car pulls up to the intercom. The window comes down, and the driver pushes a button. "Yes?" a tinny voice says.

"Dr. Canfield," the driver answers, and the gate swings slowly open. *This is my chance,* I think, as I sprint toward the gate, hunching over as I get near. The car is waiting for the gate to open wide enough, and I scramble up behind its back bumper as it begins to drive through. Staying low, I follow it through the gate, and immediately head for some trees off to my right. I hide there and watch the car pull into a parking garage. The driver gets out and jogs over to the front door, letting himself in without knocking or ringing a bell. The good doctor has obviously been here before.

I judge the distance between myself and the house, and secure my crossbow for another run. Since my face-to-face with the tiger, I've kept it slung across my back. This time I'll be ready if something or someone attacks. But I wonder if I will actually be able to shoot a person, if things really come down to it. I remember how Juneau aimed for the guards' arms back in Salt Lake City, and reassure myself that I would be capable of shooting if I weren't aiming to kill. But honestly, unless someone was attacking me, I'm not sure I could even go that far.

I've been in one fight in my entire life, and that was when I saw one of my middle-school friends get punched by a bully. I remember the rage I felt—the blinding red fury that came over me at the big-kid-hurting-little-kid injustice of it. If I can channel that, then I might be able to shoot someone. These people are keeping Juneau's clan captive, and the guns they're toting make my crossbow look like a slingshot. They're the big kids, and I'm definitely the little kid in this case. Even so, I think I'll opt for hiding as my first line of defense.

There is a light on over the mansion's front porch. A decorative fountain the size of one of those aboveground swimming pools sits lit up in the middle of the drive, a massive sculpture of two stags fighting perched in the middle. The road winds in a circle around it. I make my way toward the fountain, scrambling from tree to tree, until all that's left between me and it are a few yards of grass.

I take the last stretch standing up, running as if my life depends on it, which, in fact, it does. Because just before I reach it, two guards walk around the side of the house from the barracks. I hit the ground and crawl the last yard, then crouch behind the outer rim of the fountain, which is just tall enough to hide me. I wait, wondering if they saw me, until I hear the front door slam. After a few seconds I inch my head up to see the coast is clear. I scramble to my feet and crouch-run the rest of the way to my destination: the thick hedges that border the front porch. There's just enough room for me between the hedge and the porch, and I wedge myself in and lie down.

My heart feels like it's going to pound its way right out of my chest. For the first time I seriously doubt the wisdom of this rescue mission. If those guys had seen me hiding behind the fountain, they could have walked right over and filled me full of bullets. And—*bam*—I would be dead. After days of angsting about my immortality, I'm suddenly wishing that the Rite had given me bulletproof skin as well.

The night isn't cold, but I'm shaking from my second near-death experience of the day. Who do I think I am, anyway, to think I can take on someone's private army?

Stop! I command myself. I can't keep thinking like this, or I'm going to psych myself out. And what good's that going to do me?

What have I got to work with? A crossbow, a map, a flashlight, and a lighter. Oh, and a towel. Fat lot of good that's going to do me.

What else do I have? I hear a flapping noise and Poe lands on the porch three feet above me. He perches on the edge, peering down at me as if to say, "What the hell are you doing down there?"

Okay . . . I've got a raven. And—oh, right, I almost forgot—I'm magic. Not that I know what I can do with that besides figure out how a certain girl is feeling, see visions in fire, and read a bird's mind.

I close my eyes and try to let go . . . to dislodge the panic inside me. What good is being able to communicate with all of nature if I can't even beam a message to Juneau? I have a huge beef with Gaia, or whoever it is who came up with the Yara rules.

After a while, I calm down enough to feel twigs sticking into my back, smell the piney scent of whatever kind of bush I'm lying under, and hear mean-sounding rough-guy laughter coming from the guards' barracks. My eyes have adjusted to the dark, and I raise my head cautiously to have a look around.

The front of the house is lined with windows, most of which

are lit up from the inside. Besides the porch light, there are no outdoor lights, so feasibly I could see in without the people inside seeing me, unless I got too close. But that damned porch light pretty much ruins that plan.

Then all of a sudden, I remember Juneau's electronics-frying trick. She said she imagined heat or fire or something in order to fry my phone. And then she imagined moisture to flood the spark plugs on my car. A lightbulb must fit into the "fry-able" category. Might as well give it a shot.

I peer up at the bulb, visible inside its glass fixture. In my mind I focus on the filament, fragile and thin like a thread. And as I slow my breath and feel the buzz of the Yara kick in, I imagine a flame underneath it, heating it, messing with the electrical current. I keep this up until—*pop*—the filament explodes and the light is suddenly extinguished.

No. Way.

I can't believe I just detonated a lightbulb with mere thoughts. It might sound ridiculous, but I suddenly feel all-powerful. I could join the X-Men. Like SuperNatureGuy. Or the Yara Avenger.

And then I stop. I realize what I've just done. Yes, I plugged into the Yara to Read Juneau's emotions, to Read what the ranch looked like in the campfire, and to Read Poe's memory. But what I just did doesn't fit under the category of Reading. I just Conjured. I "manipulated nature," as Juneau described it. And from what she said, only she, her mom, and Whit were able to do that.

Oh my God, I can Conjure, I think with amazement. That means I must have a whole arsenal of weapons at my disposal.

If I just knew what they were. What did Juneau Conjure? The cell phone fry, the levitating rocks, turning invisible, she got Poe to do stuff for her, too . . . what else? I can't remember. But I'm buzzing with excitement and fear and awe and don't know if the tingling all over my body is the Yara or a huge adrenaline rush owing to the fact that the rules of nature no longer apply to me.

No time to think about it now. Juneau's been in the house for about an hour, and I need to find out if a diversion's going to help her or hurt her. It's time to find out just what Avery's doing in there.

I jump up to the now-dark porch and begin the surveillance phase of my not-quite-yet-a-plan.

39

JUNEAU

"THAT IS ONE NASTY-LOOKING CONCOCTION," says Avery, glancing with disgust at the spoonful of the Rite elixir . . . Amrit. "But, hell, I figure I've eaten every kind of wild animal hunted by man; a little girl's blood mixed with rocks and plants won't kill me. At least not permanently." He chuckles at his joke.

Whit hands him a glass of water, and Avery raises it like he's making a toast. "Well, here goes everything," he says. "Bottom's up!" He sticks the spoon of elixir in his mouth, swallows every last drop, and then follows it quickly with the glass of water. I watch his Adam's apple move up and down as he drinks the whole glass, and then holds it back up to Whit for a refill.

"That stuff's downright vile," he says, wiping his mouth with his arm and making a face like he's bitten a sour apple. "And you got every single person in your clan to take it?"

"Every person over twenty," Whit confirms.

"Well, here's to you," Avery says, and drinks down the second glass of water. He hands Whit the glass, and then lies back down on the bed, while the doctor fiddles with the devices attached to the billionaire rancher. There are silver disks attached to wires stuck all over his chest, head, arms, and legs, and a black cuff around his arm. These are all connected to machines that are beeping and making up-and-down lines that measure, I suppose, Avery's blood pressure, heart rate, and other vital signs.

"Do you want me to give you something for pain or nausea?" the doctor asks.

Avery turns the question on Whit. "Do your people take anything?"

Whit shakes his head.

"Then no," the rancher says. "I want conditions to be the same as they are for you. Can't take the risk that one small change might mess up the whole process."

Whit can't help but look at me at this point.

"But all of the conditions *aren't* the same," I find myself saying.

"What's different?" Avery says, crooking his neck so that he can see me.

I pause and glance at Whit, whose face is a blank page. "We surround the head with candles and prepare the body with minerals, herbs, and precious stones. We sing, and the children dance," I say. "Vows are taken, and sacred words are spoken."

"Yeah, well, I know a sacred word, too. 'Bullshit.' That's what you and your clan have been swallowing along with your price-less elixir for the last three decades. Whit here told me the whole story. You all served as a field trial for the drug, and like with any religion, your leader kept you pacified by lies and spiritual juju."

I turn to Whit, who is rubbing his forehead with his fingers. Once again, I want to slap him halfway to Antarctica, but that would give Avery the pleasure of knowing he had upset me. I fight to pull a blank expression over my shock and turn to leave.

"Where you think you're going?" my assigned guard, O'Donnell, grunts.

"My job's over. And your boss said something about food."

"No one's leaving until I say they are!" Avery bellows, and the electronic beeping kicks up a notch as the doctor tells him to calm down.

I have to leave this room. I can't stand being this close to Whit anymore without wanting to hurt him. I eye the scalpel that Whit used to cut my palm—it's lying on the counter where he left it. Since I abandoned my crossbow and knife in my dad's hut, everything has looked like a weapon to me—the silver tongs Avery used to pick up ice, the metal poker standing next to the fake fireplace in the trophy room—everything sharp or heavy or potentially lethal has been calling out to me.

Being unarmed in this situation reminds me of the defenseless-ness I felt in my old nightmares about surprise brigand attacks. But in those dreams I found the closest weapon I could and fought them. I don't have that option now. Because Avery has a hostage, and I don't dare do a thing until I know Badger is safely back with his family.

But that doesn't mean the scalpel can't come in handy later on. I lean back against the counter, positioning myself directly in front of the instrument, and slide my arm back toward it. My eyes flicker to the guards. O'Donnell watches me with a smirk on his face.

Just then Avery lets out an anguished cry, and the guards are on their feet, looking his way. I grab the scalpel, retract its blade, and slip it into my back pocket. By the time O'Donnell looks back at me, the deed is done, and I'm making my way to Avery's side. He's holding his stomach and cursing loudly, using word combinations I never knew existed.

"Stomach pain is a typical reaction to the drug," Whit reassures him as the beeping noise and wavy lines go berserk. My old mentor looks back at me with a question on his face, and I shake my head. He knows I can ease the pain. But he'd have to shoot me to get me to do it. The song I sing while I'm in my trance, the way I touch the person's face, arms, and feet, the aromatic plants I hold under their nose—they all help to ease the suffering. But if Avery says he doesn't want any juju, well, by Gaia I'm not going to give it to him.

Retreating to a corner of the room, I sit on the floor and glance up at the clock. Avery's got a good half hour of intense pain before him, and I feel like enjoying every minute of it. I lay my head against the wall and close my eyes and think about Miles back at our camp at the top of the mountain. I hope he's forgiven me for leaving him behind. He's probably fast asleep, snuggled under the blanket on the tent floor. What I wouldn't give to be back there with him, just for a moment.

40

MILES

CROUCHING IN THE DARKNESS OF THE PORCH, I peer through a window that looks into an office. Everything is made of wood and leather: The room is like a set for *Masterpiece Theatre*. For a minute, I'm tempted to break in and use the phone or even the computer sitting on the leather-topped desk. If I could reach the police I could tell them what was happening, but what would I even say? That a crazy rancher has kidnapped forty odd people and is keeping them hostage on his exotic-animal gaming reserve?

The police probably already know Avery, and would laugh it off. Hell, he probably owns the local precinct anyway.

Scenarios pass through my mind like action-movie trailers. I need a better plan. Something that's not going to end up looking like a scene from *Kill Bill*.

Moving through the hedges to the left, I look in on a bedroom. Although the light's on, no one's in there and nothing is out of place—it looks unused. I don't dare turn the corner to follow along the back of the house, since I'm pretty sure I could be seen from the barracks if I did. So, shuffling behind the hedges I head back to the porch the way I came, passing the office and a huge front hallway complete with winding marble staircase.

To the right of the hallway is this vast library-looking room, with taxidermied heads of every sort of animal you can think of. I move from window to window, getting a full view.

There's a big fireplace, complete with fake fire glowing inside the hearth. Though bookcases line the walls, there are very few actual books. Instead, the shelves are filled with guns, knives, and other hunting objects placed on little stands like they're works of art. At the far side, there's a door, and through the next window I see that it opens into a long hallway with doorways on either side. The door across from the library leads to a multi-car garage. A Hummer, a Rolls-Royce, and the doctor's sedan are parked inside. Outside is the ATV I saw Juneau arrive in with Whit and the guards.

I make my way around the side of the garage, and see that the house continues behind it. The only window on that side looks into a kind of den-looking space. The lights are off, but by the glow of a cable box I make out an enormous flat-screen TV.

And I don't dare go farther, since the barracks are just down the hill from the back of the house. I step back and look up at the second floor. It is dark, except in the corner room above the den, directly above me, where a soft light glows from the window.

Poe has been following me around the house, hopping from position to position as I peer into the windows. I wonder if I can send him up to look through the window and then Read his mind when he comes back. "Go up there," I whisper, pointing toward the window. He cocks his head to one side and stares at me.

I make the clicking noise and bend down to pick him up. I hold him against my chest and look up at the window, and then close my eyes and picture him flying up to it. I let him go. Squawking and flapping a bit, he lands on the ground and walks a safe distance away from me, then resumes his staring. *Bird wrangling is obviously not one of the skills the Yara provides,* I think.

I glance back up at the window. It looks like I'll have to do this the old-fashioned way. I shake the drainpipe running down from the roof gutters to see how sturdy it is. Sturdy enough.

Placing my crossbow on the ground, I grab the pipe. And using the white bricks as footholds, I shuffle my way up the side of the building until I'm at window-level. Leaning sideways, and grasping the sill for stability, I find myself looking into a bedroom lit only by a small lamp. Next to it sits a woman in a white uniform—the kind a housekeeper or nurse would wear. She reads a book and casts occasional glances toward the bed.

I lean farther and see a young child in pajamas lying on top of the covers. The lighting is too dim to make much out besides the fact that it has dark hair, and is toddler-age. *So Avery has a kid,* I think. Either his wife's not around, or they have a full-time nanny, which wouldn't surprise me. And then I remember the note that Poe brought from Juneau's dad. Avery took a three-year-old from the clan when they tried to escape. This must be that child. I've seen all there is to see in the room, so I slide back down the drainpipe and take a minute to mull over things.

Juneau and the others must be in one of the interior rooms. I didn't see a kitchen, so it must be on the far side of the house facing the barracks. They could be there. They're not on the top floor, unless they're sitting around in the dark. Judging from the depth of the rooms, and the enormity of the house, I'm guessing there are one or two rooms in the middle.

I walk back around the garage and peer in the window looking into the hallway. Halfway down, there is a door on the left-hand side with a security panel next to it—the kind with numbers to type a code into. A windowless room could be a bathroom, but I doubt even Avery's bathroom holds something valuable enough to need a password. Could be a prison—his own personal dungeon—or a safe, or something else he doesn't want his goons to wander into.

As I watch, the door flies open and people start walking out. I duck down for a second, and then pop my head back up when I realize they're walking away from me, down the hall. Leading the group is Whit, and just behind him walks a camouflaged guard holding a gun. Then comes Juneau—my heart squeezes painfully when I see her—and following her is another guard with a gun. Juneau isn't carrying anything—neither her backpack nor her crossbow. Which isn't surprising. It's not like they'd let her bring weapons with her.

But again, I wonder why she hasn't thought of some way to disarm them. Or disappear and slip away. Is it just because of the boy?

When I saw them outside, I had thought that maybe Whit would defend against any tricks Juneau could come up with. But the guard behind him doesn't seem to be obeying his orders. It looks like Whit himself is being kept against his will. Which is a total about-face from when he was driving the jeep and ordering the guards around.

I see them disappear down the hallway and take a left before the TV room. If my hunch was right, they could be going to a kitchen. But they could just as easily be going to a cellar or even upstairs.

I've got two people unaccounted for: Avery and the doctor. I realize they could appear at any moment. But I know I have to make my move while I'm sure Juneau and the guards are away.

I creep around the corner into the garage, toward the door that leads inside the house. I turn to look for Poe. He has trailed me and is standing a few feet away.

"Can you avoid squawking or making any loud bird noises?" I whisper to him. He angles his head with the same you're-crazy look, and then with a flap, launches himself into the air onto my shoulder.

I turn the doorknob slowly. As I suspected, it is unlocked and doesn't set off an alarm. Who needs security with an entire army within shouting distance? I ease the door open and glance down the hall. No one's around. I shut the door quietly behind me, tiptoe across the carpeted floor and enter the bookless library.

It smells like a mixture of Old Spice cologne and cigar smoke, and I have the overwhelming urge to sneeze. Pressing hard on my nose bone, I creep the entire length of the room, past all the animal heads, which I imagine are turning to stare at me as I pass. Taxidermy is so freaking creepy.

I pass the fake fireplace on my right, and then a big copper bar that looks like it was stolen straight out of a saloon on my left. Poe is digging his claws into my shoulder, squeezing for all he's worth. Maybe being surrounded by dead things is as traumatic for him as it is for me. I ease open the door to the front hallway and peer out before closing it behind me and tiptoeing across the hall toward Masterpiece Theatre. I'm not even halfway across when I hear voices coming my way.

"You're following me to the *bathroom*?" I hear Juneau say. "Do you realize how weird that is?"

I book it through the hall, steadying Poe with one hand and my crossbow with the other, and throw the office door open, thanking the WD-40 gods that the hinges don't squeak.

"I've been told not to let you out of my sight," comes a man's voice. I inch the door inward until it's open just a crack.

"You're holding Badger hostage. Your boss made it clear I have to wait here until he awakes. That's more than eight hours guaranteed that I'm not going to run," Juneau says. I hear a door in the hallway open. "But suit yourself, pervert," she says, and the door slams shut.

Badger. That's the name of the kid—now I'm sure he's the one

I saw in the bedroom upstairs. As for the rest, it doesn't make sense. Why would Avery bring Juneau here and then go straight to bed? Unless . . .

I shudder as a new thought grabs me. Maybe Avery doesn't own a pharmaceutical company. Maybe he wanted the Amrit for himself. And maybe he's just taken it.

Juneau said she usually performed the Rite, and Whit's excuse about wanting her to be safe was obviously a sham. What if he can't do the Rite without her? And what if she's just been forced to do it for Avery? It took me around eight hours to regain consciousness after the Rite. That's got to be what Juneau's talking about. Avery's lying dead somewhere in this house, and Juneau's being kept here until he awakes.

I hear a toilet flush and a door open. "Still here?" Juneau asks in an eat-dirt voice.

"Just shut up and get your ass back to the kitchen," the guard says as their voices disappear down the hall. Easing the door closed, I breathe a sigh of relief. I set Poe carefully on the floor, and crane my neck to inspect my shoulder. "Dude, for a raven you're acting suspiciously chicken," I say, touching the spot tenderly. "I think you drew blood."

There is a grandfather clock ticking in the far corner. It reads ten thirty. That means Avery will be waking up around seven.

I've got all night to do something. But I don't even know where to start. *How about with something you're good at?* I think. And sitting down in front of the computer, I click the mouse and pull up Avery's desktop.

41

JUNEAU

I'M NOT HUNGRY. FOOD IS THE LAST THING ON my mind. I'm only eating to keep my strength up for whatever comes next. Because at the moment, I have no idea how things will play out.

I chew the pasta and vegetables that I found in the refrigerator in a bowl labeled "pasta salad." It looks appetizing, but once in my mouth tastes like sawdust. I can't get past what I just witnessed. I can't believe that Whit told Avery—a man we don't even know—things he never told me. The betrayal leaves me wounded, like a fiery brand has been pressed against my skin.

I shove these thoughts aside to think about later. It won't help to dwell on them. I need to be thinking about things I can control. There are so many different scenarios I need to plan for. I categorize them in my mind.

Scenario 1: Avery wakes up in eight hours. There's no way he'll let us go while he's still paralyzed, so that's another four days of sitting around. And once he's up and about, *if* he actually does keep his word, my clan will be released and he'll help us get to our next destination—wherever that is. I'll think about it once we're outside the electric gates. Or maybe the clan has already decided. But that's the rosy version of things. We could be stuck with:

Scenario 2: Avery awakes, we wait four days for the end of his death-sleep, and he decides to default on the deal. I find a way to escape, get Badger, and rescue my people without getting shot by Avery's troops.

Scenario 3: Avery doesn't awake. I find a way to escape, get Badger, and rescue my people without getting shot by Avery's troops.

Whatever happens, I should prepare for the worst. While imprisoned in the house, I can at least locate Badger and scope the building for escape routes. I pat my back pocket to check that the scalpel's still there, and make sure the back of my shirt is covering it. It's not much of a weapon, but it's all I've got.

I sense someone approach from behind me and wait until I feel a tap on my shoulder. I turn and see the eyes of my former mentor, inches from my own.

"So what's wrong with him?" I ask.

Whit doesn't even have to ask what I'm talking about. "How did you know?"

"His hand shakes, and he tries to hide it."

"He has Parkinson's, stage one," Whit responds.

I don't remember reading about that in the EB. I wonder if it existed in 1983. "It's a degenerative disease," Whit fills in. "I didn't know he had it when I offered him the Amrit. I didn't know that's why he was interested in buying it from us—he'd been working on options for life extension even before he was diagnosed. It's just made the matter more . . . urgent for him."

I nod, wondering if that would really have made a difference to Whit if the price was right. "You've gotten what you want from me," I say, "now go away."

Whit gives a slight shrug, and I can see in his eyes that it's not true: He hasn't gotten what he wants from me. He still needs me, or he'd be too chicken to come over and talk to me.

"Oh, of course," I say, realization dawning. "You need more blood. Am I going to be your own personal supply from now on? Or, make that Avery's?"

"No, of course not," Whit says, looking pained. "We only need enough blood from you to serve as a sample for testing so that we can find a functional substitute."

"So now you and Avery are a 'we'? It's comforting to hear that your new 'partner' knows more about the clan and our beliefs than I do." I can't tear my gaze from his neck—I'm longing to grab it and squeeze as hard as I can.

"Juneau, there are so many things I couldn't tell you," he says, clasping his hands together like he's pleading.

"Whit, there's a difference between not telling me something and creating a whole system of lies."

"Like, for example?" he asks.

"Don't even get me started," I say. "We already had this discussion up on the mountain."

We sit in silence for a moment, and then I can't hold it in any longer. "How can you say that the Yara is a lie when there is solid evidence that it works?"

"If you're referring to Reading," he says, "I didn't tell Avery about that—or Blackwell either. I thought it would complicate the sale of Amrit if I mentioned a side effect that probably wouldn't be discovered by most of its users."

He gives me a significant look, and my stomach falls. "What do you mean, 'side effect'?" My voice is hollow, like it's coming from far away.

"Before we left for Alaska, we—I and your parents—noticed during our experiments that Amrit widens the brain's sensory receptors. I had already been developing my theory of the existence of the Yara and its relationship with Gaia. After taking the Amrit, we found that we were able to actually tap into the Yara and Read, and in the case of your mother and I, Conjure. We discovered that only because it's something we already believed in and practiced—in a way—in our everyday life. It just seemed to make sense. There might be other uses of the widened sensory receptors, or even other side effects, that we don't even know about."

I just stare at Whit, jaw dropped. "Our gifts are a side effect of the elixir," I say. He nods.

More lies. I can't believe it. But then again, what hasn't been a lie up to this point?

Whit tries to pacify me. "I'm not saying the Yara doesn't exist, Juneau. You know how everyone in the clan believes their own version of the Gaia story. Some have practically turned it into a religion, others, like myself and your father—"

"Don't you ever compare yourself to him."

Whit holds up a hand and nods. "Okay. But just hear me out. The Gaia and the Yara are constructs: devices that help explain something difficult to understand. The ideas of Gaia and the Yara embody concepts that most people don't know about—or perhaps call by another name.

"It's like describing the Yara to the children using circles. That's putting a complicated idea into symbols they can understand. And even for adults, attaching the name Gaia to the complicated concept of the superorganism makes the whole thing more digestible. As does using the concept of being one with the Yara to explain the clan's extrasensory perceptions.

"If what you're asking is 'Does one's closeness to the Yara and to Gaia really affect how well we Read?' my answer is no. However, the power of persuasion is great, and the more one believes in their skills, the more control they have over them. Thus, the value in teaching the clan that a closeness to the Yara and to Gaia strengthens their ability to Read."

"Why couldn't you just tell everyone the truth, and leave it up to them to draw their own conclusions?"

"It's not like I wasn't telling them the truth. It's more like I was telling the truth through metaphors. Through story," Whit says.

"My dad knew this the whole time?" Heat flares across the surface of my skin as the weight of the betrayal sinks in. I push the bowl of pasta away. I can't eat any more.

Whit eyes me sadly. "Yes, as did some of the elders. But after a while, it worked so well that they decided to embrace it. As Marx said, religion is the opiate of the people. Life is easier if they believe in an almost physical goddess and spiritual system."

"Well, if our powers can just be put down to a chemical reaction, then why is it that you and Mom and I can Conjure? We all took the same elixir, didn't we?"

"Your mother and I were the first to take the elixir, at your mother's insistence. Your father gave it to us from the same batch. He watched over our bodies while we death-slept. And once we survived and tested immune to disease, your mother let your father take the elixir. In between time she adjusted the formula's measurements to see if the painful side effects could be avoided. Less blood was used. And your father had an easier time with his death-sleep than we did. So that's the formula we stuck with. You, of course, received the side effects of your mother's consumption of Amrit, which I guess we could call the 'powerful batch.'"

I shake my head. "I had always thought it was something innate in us—a sign that we were made to be leaders."

Whit bites his lip. "I'm sorry to tell you, Juneau, that it all comes down to science. There is nothing else."

I squeeze my temples with one hand and try to calm the raging storm inside me. "That's enough," I say.

"What's enough?" Whit asks.

And something moves inside me . . . wells up from the deepest part of me and comes crashing to the surface. "That's enough!" I yell. "That's enough! Get away from me, you lying bastard. I don't believe anything you say anymore. You've fed me lies since I was a baby. My whole life has been a farce. Just get away from me and stay away from me!" I'm screaming now, and Whit's guard approaches, his weapon raised. O'Donnell rushes in from the front hallway.

"What's going on?" he yells, and points his gun at me.

Whit backs up with his hands in the air. "Everything is okay," he says to the guards.

"No, it's not," I say, looking from Whit to the guards and back. "It'll never be okay—*we* will never be okay—again."

42

MILES

I'M CLICKING RANDOM FILES ON AVERY'S DESK-top, when I hear footsteps outside the door. I leap out of the chair and dive behind a nearby leather couch. I gesture desperately at Poe to come down from his perch on a bookshelf. He sees me, but stays where he is. The door handle turns, and in walks one of the guards. I get just enough of a glimpse to recognize him as the guy who grabbed me in Salt Lake City—one of the guards accompanying Whit.

He walks to the desk, sits down in the chair, and dials a num-ber on his cell phone. He waits. I wait. Poe stands still enough to pass as stuffed, if the guard can even see him in the darkened room.

"Yeah, it's me," he says. "I was with Avery, so I couldn't call before. The girl's here." He pauses. "Got it. I'll turn the airstrip lights on." He hangs up.

What the hell was that about? I think. This guy—one of Avery's own guards—must be working as a double agent.

He types something into the computer, and takes his time, clicking around for a couple of minutes. He's on his feet in a second, though, when a shriek comes from the kitchen. At first, I'm afraid that Juneau's hurt, but she keeps yelling and I know that tone. It's her pissed-off voice, and I am very glad that, for once, I'm not the one she's mad at.

The guy runs out, slamming the door behind him. I stay hidden behind the couch for what seems like five minutes, then ease my way back to standing. I walk to the desk and click the computer's mouse to get out of the screen saver: a photo of Avery kneeling next to a dead lion. *The guy's obsessed with death,* I think as the desktop comes up. The window that's open reads at the top "AHR Security Client Center *** Operator: Administrator." Running across the upper nav are dozens of icons, and down the left are lists of locations with links like "Lights," "Fences," and "Ranch House." A window with a CCTV image takes up the rest of the screen.

The camera shows the airstrip I spotted earlier today from the road. It's all lit up in the image, and the link that was last clicked is under "Lights/Airstrip." So the guard had finished what he was trying to do when Juneau distracted him. Which, I hope, means he's not coming back.

I click on the link at the top of the "Fences" list, and then down each one under it, watching the images of sections of fence flash by. All feature identical red lights blinking slowly atop the fence until I get to one section that has an orange exclamation mark next to its link. "Southeast corner" it reads, and the box perched atop this section of fence is dark. This must be the one that Juneau took out to reach her clan.

I wonder how many more of these security systems exist. There's presumably one at the front gate, if not one in the barracks as well. More importantly, is anyone paying attention to them? And if they are, can any of them override this computer, since it's got administrator access?

The double agent guy obviously didn't think that anyone would notice the airstrip lights were turned on. *I might as well take the same chance,* I think, and one by one start clicking "disable" next to each of the fences.

I continue with the list under "Ranch House," disabling all of the alarms and security locks. And then, with another click, I turn the airstrip lights back off.

I click the icon for "Perimeter Map" and get a scale model of the entire ranch, complete with roads, fences, and outbuildings. I zoom in to the eastern half of the ranch, and then even closer, studying the area around the ranch house, barracks, and something labeled "Guest Village," which is in the area where Juneau's clan must be located.

Finally, I pull back the window with the CCTV image of the airstrip in case the guard comes back. He'll only see the screen he was on and, unless he clicks through, won't be aware that anyone's fooled with the fences.

I take a pen and piece of paper and write a note to Tallie. Folding it, I turn to see Poe still doing his stuffed-bird impression on the bookshelf. "Ready to play messenger raven again?" I whisper, and tuck the paper carefully into the pocket of his harness. I ease the window up, glad I disabled the alarms, and step out onto the porch, letting Poe hop out before me.

I close the window as quietly as I can, and then sit on the porch, holding the bird in my hands and closing my eyes. I connect to the Yara, think about the mountain woman with the wild red hair, and then throw Poe upward, as I've seen Juneau do.

He flaps his wings and flies off into the night.

43

JUNEAU

I'VE BEEN SITTING IN THIS ROOM, WATCHING MY guard stare at a television for the last two hours, thinking that this is the worst torture imaginable. The grunts and guttural noises he makes as he alternates between watching a football game and checking his cell phone are making me crazy. I'm beginning to think I'd rather be shot than spend another six hours with a TV-watching Neanderthal.

I brought it on myself. The guards decided to separate Whit and me after I attacked him. O'Donnell said there was a bedroom assigned to me, but when he made it clear that he'd be staying with me inside the room, I refused.

I asked if I could see Badger. Another no. And he didn't even answer me when I asked if we could go outside. So we came down here to the "media room" as he calls it. I tried to watch television, but it gave me a throbbing pain between my eyes.

I scoped the room for anything I could use to Read, but there's no fire, no water, not even a potted plant. In our yurts, the floors were dirt, we had fires in our stoves: Nature was all around us. This room doesn't even smell natural. There's a sweet artificial smell—like dying flowers—that's making my headache even worse.

Unable to do anything useful, I'm distracting myself with a book on jaguars—the books in the room are all about hunting and animals—sitting on the couch the farthest away from the windows, as per my guard's instructions. I don't know what he thinks I'm going to do—break the glass and use a shard to persuade him to let me go? An idea I wouldn't completely dismiss if it weren't for Badger being kept hostage somewhere in the house.

As the minutes go by, O'Donnell gets more and more nervous, until he's just sitting there staring at his phone. I'm almost relieved when it finally rings: The tension in the room's as thick as goat curd.

"Yes? Where are you?" he asks anxiously, and then yells, "What the hell?"

He's on his feet in an instant, and grabbing me by the arm, says, "You. Come with me, and keep quiet." Pocketing the phone, he shoves me down the hallway, through the room of heads, past the front hall, and into a dimly lit office. He closes the door quietly behind us, and then throws himself in front of a computer sitting on a dark wooden desk the size of a rowboat.

He clicks a button, and the screen lights up. "What?!" he

exclaims in surprise when he sees a dark square on the screen. He clicks something else and the picture goes from black to hazy white, and a road appears with spotlights lining it on either side.

He picks up the phone and punches a couple of buttons. "You see it now?" he asks, and then breathes a sigh of relief. "I have no idea how that happened. They were on before. Must be some sort of glitch in the system." He waits. "Gotcha. We'll be right there."

He hangs up and, taking me roughly by the arm, leads me into the hallway and out the front door.

It's pitch-black outside. O'Donnell leans back in the door and flips a switch up and down while staring at a nonfunctioning light on the porch ceiling. "What the hell's going on around here?" he mutters, and giving up, yanks me down the front steps.

"Where are we going?" I ask.

"I have an errand to run, and you're coming with me," he says.

His grip is so tight it hurts, but I don't let him know. He seems like the kind of man who would find it amusing to inflict pain on someone smaller than him. O'Donnell leads me to the same huge vehicle I was brought here in, steers me into the front seat, and closes the door behind me. He jumps behind the wheel and clicks a button, locking us inside.

We make our way up the drive, through the electric gate, and go west at the crossroad instead of south, where my clan is. "Where are we going?" I repeat, but O'Donnell doesn't answer. He turns on the radio and drives.

I can't see a thing beyond our headlights, the night is so dark.

But my driver seems to know the way by heart. After a while, he looks at his phone and murmurs, "Ten minutes. We're almost there."

We come over the top of a ridge, and spread below us is an airstrip, lit up on either side by white lights. I recognize it as the road I'd seen on the computer: O'Donnell just turned these lights on for someone. I check the sky and see flashing lights coming toward us—a plane flying low—and feel a surge of the shaky anxiety that almost crippled me in the Mojave.

This is a small plane, like the one I took to Los Angeles, but with no markings besides numbers on the tail. As we near, the plane eases down and lands on the runway, its tires screeching as it bounces a couple of times and then comes to a stop.

We follow the road in and park near the airplane, just as its stairway lowers, unfolds, and touches the ground. O'Donnell gets out of the car and comes to my side. He opens my door, and holding me tightly by the arm, marches me toward the plane. I look up at the door, and my heart plummets when I see a familiar figure appear in the doorway.

"Ah, Juneau," Mr. Blackwell says. "So good to see you again."

44

MILES

I HAVE BEEN FOLLOWING THE ROAD TOWARD THE "Guest Village" for what feels like a good half hour. The night is so dark I can't see much of what's around me, but the little moonlight there is shines off the pavement and leads me along.

I have a harder time when the pavement ends and a gravel road picks up where it left off. But after a minute, I see firelight in the distance, and heading toward it, I pick up my pace.

I can almost make out the adobe houses in the firelight when, from right behind me, a man's voice says, "Stop right there and drop your weapon."

I freeze, and then slowly place my crossbow on the ground and lift my hands in the air.

"Who are you?" the voice asks.

"A friend of Juneau's," I say, not daring to turn around.

"Why are you carrying a loaded crossbow to our camp, then?"

"I was afraid of wild animals," I reply.

I hear a low laugh. "Fair enough," the voice says. "I was able to get within two feet of you—you'd be easy prey for whatever's out there. You can drop your hands and turn around. I've seen you before. I know who you are."

I turn to see a tall thin boy with a close-cropped Afro. The moonlight reflects off the star in his right eye. He stands there, arms crossed, with a bemused expression on his face. "You don't even have a weapon," I say.

"Looks like I didn't need one," he responds, holding up his empty hands and wiggling his fingers. He points to my face. "Nice war paint. Trying to camouflage yourself?"

I ignore him, glad he can't see me turn red under the dried mud. "What did you mean you've seen me before?" I ask.

"I fire-Read you. Saw you with Juneau a couple of weeks ago—before they took our amulets away. Don't know your name though."

"I'm Miles."

He sticks out his hand. "Kenai," he says. I shake his hand, and he bursts out laughing. "No way . . . this really works? Dennis told us people used to greet each other shaking hands . . . I mean still do. You know what I mean."

I can't help but smile. "Yeah, I know what you mean," I admit.

"Juneau's not here—Whit took her to the ranch house," Kenai says, suddenly serious.

"I know," I reply.

"So what are you doing here?"

"I need to talk to the clan."

"Well then, come on."

I bend over to scoop up my crossbow, and Kenai leads me toward the fire where a dozen or so people are gathered. They watch as we approach, and one man stands to greet me. No starburst in his eye, so I figure he must be one of the elders, although he looks the same age as everyone else—between twenty and thirty. He is looking at me closely, more closely than the others are . . . checking me out. Looking at me intently, like he's trying to read me from the outside in.

And then I see something familiar in his face. "You're Juneau's dad," I say. He nods and shakes my hand like he's actually done it before.

"You're her travel companion," he says. "We've seen you."

"I just came from Avery's ranch house," I say. "I was able to get in without being noticed. Juneau and Whit are both being guarded. I heard them talking. Sounds like Avery made them give him the Rite. He's death-sleeping and they're being forced to stay and wait until he wakes up."

No one says a word, although a lot of looks are thrown between the people around the fire. "There's a small boy being kept in the ranch house—Badger, a boy from our clan," Juneau's father says.

"I saw him asleep in one of the upstairs rooms," I say.

"Is he guarded?"

"A woman is in the room with him. But she's not armed."

Juneau's father exchanges looks with a woman in the group.

From her anxious expression I guess she must be Badger's mother.

Just then I hear a cawing noise coming from above, and look up to see Poe descending in the firelight. He lands on the ground in front of me, and ducks his head as I reach for the pocket on his harness. There are two notes inside, and after glancing at the first, I stick it into my pocket for later. I read the second one quickly and then look up at the group in front of me.

"I came to tell you that I turned the electric gates off." I hold the note up. "And less than a mile away a friend is waiting with her truck. She's willing to make a few trips back and forth to take people to a nearby city, where the guards can't find you. I thought the children and those accompanying them could go with her."

I look Juneau's father in the eye. "And I was hoping the rest of you would go back with me to get Juneau and Badger."

45

JUNEAU

I AM LIMP WITH SHOCK FOR A GOOD FEW SEC-onds. Then I try to jerk my arm away from O'Donnell, but he's got me in a death grip. He grabs my other hand and pins them both behind my back as Mr. Blackwell walks over to me, looks me up and down, and sighs.

"Oh, Juneau. You could have saved me so much trouble by staying under my roof. If you had cooperated, I would have been happy to help your people escape from Avery. But as things are, I'm going to need all of my resources getting you away from here and won't be able to help them."

"What are you doing here?" I ask, still incredulous that these two separate worlds are colliding.

"O'Donnell here's been very generous with information about

you—since the very beginning, isn't that right, O'Donnell? Otherwise, I would never have known how important you were and would have gone after Whit instead. Not that he's not important, too, of course. Where is he now?"

"Back at Avery's ranch house," says O'Donnell from behind me.

Blackwell nods thoughtfully. "Well, Juneau, let's not beat around the bush this time. Would you like to tell me why you're so necessary? Just what part do you play in the making of Amrit?"

I glare at him, wishing he were a few inches closer so I could head-butt him.

"Claiming the First, are you? You, then, O'Donnell—have you figured out why Juneau here is so important?" he asks, though he's still looking directly at me.

"Yes, sir. When Mr. Graves was fixing the Amrit to give to Avery," my guard begins.

Blackwell cuts him off. "What?" he bellows.

"Mr. Avery insisted that Mr. Graves try the Amrit out on him as soon as Juneau arrived."

Blackwell stands there looking horrified, and then regains his composure. "That crazy bastard," he says, rubbing his chin with his hand. "Trust Avery to test a new drug on himself … I've never known anyone so obsessed with death. How long ago was the drug administered?"

"Approximately three hours ago."

Blackwell calculates. "Delightful," he says. "That buys us a little more time, then, doesn't it? Go on, O'Donnell. You were saying . . ."

The guard starts his story over. "When Mr. Graves prepared the ingredients for the drug, he cut the girl's hand and added her blood to it."

A light goes on in Mr. Blackwell's eyes. "Aha! The magic ingredient. Graves mentioned that something in the formula was so rare that a synthetic replacement would need to be found. So it's blood. But not just any blood. What's so special about you, Juneau, that no one else in the clan could provide the missing ingredient?"

I narrow my eyes and remain silent.

He ignores my reticence. "That's why Graves insisted that Avery get him Juneau. Because the formula doesn't work without her *vital* input!" Blackwell laughs.

"I don't suppose you know how to make Amrit by yourself?" Blackwell asks me.

"No," I lie. "Whit always prepares it."

Blackwell nods. "Just as I thought. Well, you'll need to go back to get him," he says, giving O'Donnell an impatient look.

"What?" O'Donnell asks uncertainly. "You only said you wanted the girl. And you told me you'd take me with you. I can't go back there without her."

"Who's going to care?" Blackwell asks. "Avery's unconscious."

"My boss is watching Mr. Graves. The two of us were ordered to keep them in the house until Avery wakes up. He's not going to let me come in without the girl and demand the other hostage as well."

"Then I suppose you'll need to use force," Blackwell responds with a blithe shrug.

Sensing O'Donnell's confusion, I take the chance to try to jerk out of his grasp again. To no effect. He gives a grunt of frustration and asks, "Can I cuff her?"

"Yes," Blackwell says.

O'Donnell lets go with one hand, and cold metal clamps around my wrists with a disturbing clicking noise, fastening my hands behind my back. He steps to my side, grasping me by the upper arm. "We've got twenty-five fully armed men in the barracks behind the ranch house," he explains. "If my boss called for them, two dozen men would be on top of me and Graves within minutes."

"Well, we wouldn't want to cause a fuss," says Blackwell, looking annoyed. "Why don't I come back with you and see if I can speak some sense to your colleague. I suppose he might be open to the same sort of deal you were?"

"Who wouldn't be?" says O'Donnell, looking relieved. I wonder just how much Mr. Blackwell has given this man to play double agent for him. "But if anyone sees us coming . . ."

"You'll just say that I'm a guest of Mr. Avery's who arrived early for a hunt. Why would anyone question that?"

O'Donnell thinks it over and finally nods his agreement. "You going to leave her in the plane?" he asks.

"I will not be leaving this young lady's side for even an instant,"

Blackwell says, eyeing me once again. "Not until I have what I want from her. She's entirely too slippery to be entrusted to anyone else."

Blackwell turns toward the plane and gestures toward two other men who have come down the steps and are standing side by side, awaiting his orders. They walk past us and get into the vehicle. "But . . . ," O'Donnell says, dumbfounded. "What are they doing?"

"Coming with us," Blackwell says. "Don't tell me Avery's clients never bring their own security details."

"Yes, they're usually invited to hunt with us," O'Donnell replies.

"Well then," Blackwell says succinctly. And with O'Donnell leading me by the arm, he follows us to the car.

46

MILES

WITHIN MINUTES, THE CLAN HAS MOBILIZED. Juneau's father seems to be in charge, but he barely needs to do anything. You can tell these people have been preparing for emergencies their whole lives.

The children are awakened, dressed, and out of the huts within minutes. There are about a dozen of them, and it seems that one parent has been chosen from each family to accompany their kids, bringing the number of people meeting Tallie up to seventeen.

For some reason, in my head, it was women and children who would be going with Tallie. But there are more men going with the children than women, and I wonder if Juneau's group was able to move past the typical male/female family roles along with the rest of society's "ills."

A tall girl with blond hair pulled back into a braid walks up to me, looking like a female Viking: suntanned and bold and outdoorsy. She has the same fearless aura that Juneau has, and I know who she is before she even opens her mouth.

"Nome?" I ask.

She smiles broadly and hands me a wet cloth. "Kenai said you might want to wash your face."

I take it and scrub my skin until she nods. She crosses her arms and brazenly inspects me. "So you're the guy Juneau's been hanging out with," she says. "You're cuter than you looked in the fire."

"Um, thanks?" I say. Juneau told me her people say exactly what they think. *She wasn't lying,* I think, as I feel my ears get hot.

"You'll have to excuse my friend here," says Kenai, walking up with a big pair of wire cutters. "No manners. It's what you get from growing up in the wild. Try to stop drooling, Nome. He's with Juneau, remember?"

Unembarrassed, she just winks, takes the wire cutters from Kenai, and strides toward the fence. "Can't ask the little ones to climb that high," Kenai explains. "Cutting an opening's a better option."

"Where did you get wire cutters?" I ask in astonishment.

"Stole them off the back of a jeep. They were to be used in our last escape attempt, but once Badger was taken we buried them. Saved them for a rainy day." Kenai laughs, and his teeth glow white in the firelight. "Walter needs you back there, by the way. Wants you to draw them a map to where your friend with the truck is waiting."

"Walter?"

"Juneau's dad. Mr. Newhaven, for outsiders."

"Oh, right," I say. Would he still consider me an outsider if he knew I'd gone through the Rite? I wonder if I would ever be able to fit into this group. I doubt anyone could, unless you were born into it.

"Miles," Juneau's dad ... Walter ... calls. I meet him by the fire, take the piece of paper and pen he offers me, and sketch where I remember the road was in relation to the adobe village.

By the time I'm done, the children and accompanying parents have gone through the hole Nome cut in the fence and immediately set out to find Tallie.

Those who stay spread out and begin preparations. The woman I guessed was Badger's mother walks up to me. "Holly," she says, introducing herself. "How did my son look?"

"He was asleep in bed. He looked fine to me." She nods, relieved, and swings a crossbow over her shoulder. I look into the nearest hut, and see one of the men digging in the earth floor and pulling out a homemade crossbow of his own.

Holly sees me watching. "We haven't just been sitting around."

"Were you preparing to attack?" I ask.

"We were waiting for Juneau. Seeing how things played out. So not planning for attack per se, but readying ourselves for any contingencies. Our strategy has always been to be prepared for anything."

"Everyone ready?" Walter says to the group, and counts us: twenty-four. About half are armed. They huddle around us, waiting for instruction.

"What is the situation with the guards?" Walter asks me.

"Besides the two in the house watching Juneau and Whit, the only others I saw were sitting outside the barracks, playing cards and drinking," I say, loudly enough for all to hear.

"They have been doing random checks on us throughout the night," Walter says, "so we'll have to be careful, but if Juneau's just given Avery the Rite, I doubt his people will be focusing much on us." He looks up into the clear night sky. "Storm's coming," he remarks, and the others nod their agreement. "Okay, people, let's go. Miles—take us the way you came in."

I sling my crossbow over my shoulder and begin walking, hyperconscious of the fact that I am leading two dozen people toward danger. Leading anyone at all is a foreign-enough concept. But these are Juneau's people, and they know more about the land than I do.

Fear pricks my skin and dread sharpens my senses. But I feel an overwhelming sense of being where I am supposed to be. Finally doing what I'm supposed to be doing.

47

JUNEAU

NO ONE TALKS ON THE WAY TO THE MANSION. The smell of rain is in the air, although the sky is clear and the stars burn brightly overhead. I sit in the backseat with Blackwell's guards, and think about how much Miles looks like his dad. Will he grow up to be like him, I wonder? A businessman so driven by success that he would resort to abducting a teenage girl in order to get what he wants? No. I can't imagine it.

Blackwell's not as bad as Avery, I think. The hunter's use of force goes beyond a show of strength into the realm of threatened violence. I can't imagine Blackwell actually killing someone to get what he wanted, although driving into the heart of a fortified ranch with his two burly security guards doesn't seem the most peaceful of statements. But that's what makes me doubt his intentions are violent. There's no way he'll try to strong-arm

Avery's men into giving me and Whit up. He's counting on talking his way into what he wants. Making Avery's men an offer while their boss is out of the picture.

My wrists chafe from leaning back against the metal cuffs. I lean forward and flex my fingers to get my circulation going. The guard sitting next to me notices. He gets the keys from O'Donnell and unlocks me, and I massage my wrists with my thumbs.

We drive over a hill, and the house and barracks lie spread before us. In the mansion, the ground floor is lit up as before but two additional lights are on in the top floor. O'Donnell takes us down the drive and around the fountain, parking the car outside the front door. The men pile out, the guard sitting next to me positioning himself behind me as I walk in front of them.

Before we can even get to the door, Whit's guard steps out, and stands, gun in hands before us, face twisted in anger as he berates O'Donnell. "What's she doing out here? Where have you been?" He waves his gun toward Blackwell. "And who are they?"

O'Donnell gestures toward Miles's dad. "This is Mr. Blackwell. Mr. Blackwell, Ben Nursall, Head of Security."

"What the hell is going on?" Nursall says, taking a step forward. Blackwell's men do the same, puffing themselves up to look more menacing.

Whit walks out the door behind Nursall. "Blackwell," he says, his voice steeped in shock.

"You know him?" Nursall asks.

"Let me introduce myself properly and tell you why I'm here," Blackwell says, raising his hands to show he knows he's on Nursall's turf. "It is in my interest to take these two guests of yours with me. Since I hear that your employer is currently indisposed, I will take a rather unfair advantage of the situation to offer you double what Avery is currently paying you to come work for me in L.A., as well as a substantial finder's fee for handing over Mr. Graves and Miss Newhaven—which is the same deal I have offered your colleague here."

Nursall looks at O'Donnell, raising an eyebrow as if to ask, "Is this guy for real?" O'Donnell nods.

"I have air transport available for all of us, and am ready to leave immediately," finishes Blackwell, clasping his hands together and awaiting the burly guard's response.

Whit speaks up before his guard can respond. "I'm not sure we will be able to work with you, Mr. Blackwell, since we have a very specific deal arranged with Mr. Avery."

Blackwell fixes Whit with a cynical stare. "Have you seen any of that money yet, Mr. Graves?"

Whit is still for a moment and then shakes his head.

"To be quite frank," Mr. Blackwell says, "I think Mr. Avery has already gotten what he wants: virtual immortality. I very much doubt his interest was to reproduce and distribute the drug, no matter what he told you."

I speak up, surprising everyone. "I don't care about money. I'm not going anywhere while my people are being held prisoner." As if I have a choice.

Blackwell raises an eyebrow. "Really?" he asks, emphasizing the plain-as-day state of my powerlessness.

"I'll fight you every step of the way," I promise, clenching my fists by my side. I know how ridiculous I look. Five foot five and unarmed, up against these giant men with guns. But I give it all I've got and exude every ounce of resistance inside me.

Blackwell rolls his eyes, and holds up his hand to Avery's guards, asking them to excuse us for a moment. They shift uncomfortably. "As I said before, if you had cooperated back in L.A., I would have been happy to help your people escape. But as things are . . ."

He looks quickly from scowling me to cautious Whit and back, and I can tell from the change in his posture when he switches tactics.

"All right. Although I've been described as a snake, I am not a monster. Since my move leaves you without negotiating power to get your people out, once you are safely within the care and employ of Blackwell Pharmaceutical, I am willing to make a deal with Avery—let's call it an act of goodwill—which should soften the blow of losing the two of you, and ensure that your people are free to leave his hospitality. Now how does that sound to you all—Messieurs Nursall and Graves, Miss Newhaven?"

The situation has been defused. Whit's guard's posture has relaxed, and he seems to be considering Blackwell's offer. Whit too has lost some of his defensiveness and the guards standing behind Blackwell have deflated slightly, when, in the open door, Avery's doctor appears, his face as white as his lab coat. "He's awake! Avery's awake!" he says, and everyone is once again on alert.

"That's not possible!" exclaims Whit. "It's barely been four hours."

"But he *is* awake, and he's ripped all of his monitors off. He insists on getting up. And the way he's talking . . . it seems to me like he's having a psychotic break."

Avery's huge form appears behind the doctor, hair wild and eyes wide. Something is tucked beneath his arm, and for a moment I can't tell what it is. And then I taste bile as I realize it's the dog head, defrosted and dripping a thick, glutinous fluid.

Avery slams his fist against a button inside the front door, setting off a high-pitched alarm. Lights shoot on around the property, illuminating the yard in an artificial yellow glow. Shouts can be heard coming from the barracks, and an armed guard comes barreling down from upstairs.

"They're coming," Avery gasps, and pushes past the doctor to stand outside. Clasping the dog head by its soggy fur, he yells, "They're after me!" His cheeks are hollow, his look haunted. He lets go of the dog head, throwing his arms up to shield himself, as if to fend off a flock of attacking birds. The head rolls around at his feet, trailing dark liquid across the porch floor.

Everyone looks at one another in astonishment, no one knowing what to say. I take a step toward him. "Who's after you?" I ask. Avery's crazy eyes fix on me, and he stretches an arm forward tentatively, as if afraid to touch me.

"The animals," he says. "They want their revenge, and they're coming for it. I heard them. They spoke to me."

Whit reaches up to put a hand on Avery's shoulder. "Mr. Avery, you are hallucinating. You're not supposed to be up yet. You need to get back to the lab, lie down, and let the drug run its course."

The alarm sounds again—a loud wailing noise piercing the velvety silence of the dark night.

"Didn't you hear me?" Avery roars. "They're coming! Nature herself is rising up against me. They say I've exploited her—stolen lives that aren't mine to take." He shakes off Whit's hand and pushes past Blackwell without even seeing him.

Blundering down the front steps, he plants himself firmly in the middle of the drive and bends over, grasping his head in his hands. "It's over," he moans, as his paper shirt flaps in the strengthening wind.

Responding to the alarm, guards pour in from around both sides of the house, outfitted in combat gear with guns at the ready. Others sprint across the yard and disappear through the trees. The siren wails again, and Nursall ducks into the house and shuts it off, and then jogs down the steps to confront his colleagues. A dozen guards group around Avery, watching him with worried expressions. Nursall pushes through them and speaks.

"Mr. Avery isn't well. His doctor is here. The alarm was set off by accident. You can return to barracks."

"It's no accident," yells Avery, and shuddering violently, he slumps to his knees.

Nursall takes him by the arm. "O'Donnell," he calls, "help me take Mr. Avery back inside." O'Donnell leaves my side and runs to help.

"Get off me, you bumbling dipshits," Avery growls, trying to shake them off.

Just then a shout comes from the trees to the south. A pair of guards with guns drawn walk toward us, herding before them three people with their hands raised in the air.

One is a woman—and as they near I recognize her. It's Holly, one of the clan elders. Badger's mother. And with her are two people I recognize even before they come into full view. My heart beats wildly as they grow nearer and I see defeat written on their faces. It's my father, and beside him walks Miles. I feel like pinching myself. The two of them together? I must be dreaming.

"The inner fence was turned off!" one of the guards yells when they get closer. "These three got across and were headed this way."

The wind whips against us, sending a cloud of dust into the air. A second later, the heavens open and rain dumps down, drenching everyone instantly. "Everybody inside!" yells Nursall. He and O'Donnell make their way up the steps supporting a weeping Avery between the two of them. Whit disappears inside the house with the doctor, and Blackwell and his men take shelter on the porch, in spite of the fact that the wind blows the rain almost horizontally.

I wait until Miles and my father are closer and, ignoring their guards' protests, throw myself on both of them. "Miles! You're here!" I yell, the noise of the storm snatching my words away. My father gives me a grim smile and kisses my forehead before continuing on with Holly toward the house, their guard steering them ahead with the barrel of his gun. Miles drops his defeated look and stands there looking supremely proud of himself. With a conspiratorial grin, he winks at me and then, prodded by the second guard's gun, makes his way toward the house.

48

MILES

I TAKE THREE STEPS ONTO THE PORCH AND freeze. My dad is standing there under the porch roof, sheltering from the rain. We're both surprised, but I'm staring at him like he's a ghost, and his expression is more one of startled inconvenience. *What is he doing here?*

And then, it all falls into place. The phone call I heard O'Donnell make—he was talking to my dad. Of course, I should have realized it sooner! Who else had a vested interest in Amrit? Whit told us last night that he had only offered it to two people. This O'Donnell guy must have been playing both sides from the beginning. He's probably the one who my dad called his "source," feeding him information from Alaska, and alerting him that Juneau must be found.

Dad has known where we were heading this whole time.

I think of how I must look to him now: I haven't showered, besides rinsing off in the river, for a week, and my arms and neck are still caked in mud. I've got to look pretty rough.

He marches over and, grabbing me by the arm, pulls me toward the front door. The guy guarding me yells and swings his gun toward us. My father's men step forward, like they're ready to tackle the guy, but Dad doesn't budge—only stares him in the eye. "Follow us if you like. I'm not taking him anywhere." My guard looks confused but lowers his gun and pushes us through the door into the entranceway.

The storm inside the house is wilder than the one raging outdoors. Avery's fighting the doctor and Whit, who are both trying to subdue him. The guy who was guarding Whit is now in the office berating O'Donnell, as O'Donnell fumbles with the computer, trying to reset the electrical fences. Without orders, the two guards who brought us in seem confused about where they're supposed to take us. And before they can do anything about it, Holly heads up the stairs on her own.

"Stop right there," one of our guards says.

"Fat chance," Holly replies, and continues climbing the stairs.

"I mean it, come back here—now," he insists.

"Go ahead and shoot me," she responds as she arrives at the top. She glances at me, questioning. I point to the right, and she disappears down the hallway. Stage One of our plan is complete: reunite Holly with Badger. Now to get both of them out of here and find a way out ourselves.

I glance over at Juneau. She saw the exchange between Holly

and me and is staring like she doesn't recognize me. I grin and she narrows her eyes. She can't figure out what's going on, and I know how much she hates not having complete control over her situation.

One of the guards leaves to follow Holly upstairs. The other gestures with his gun for the rest of us to move into the book-less library. My father keeps his grip on my arm and stands his ground. "My son and I need some privacy," he tells the guard. The guy looks like he's about to blow a fuse, but O'Donnell's boss sticks his head out of the office and says, "Do what the man asks." Dad's already got the guards in his pocket. How unsurprising.

The guy gestures to the door next to the office and says, "You can use the bedroom. But don't go anywhere else in the house."

My father jerks me toward the bedroom. I turn to see Juneau's guard wave her and her father into the library with his gun.

My father's men are standing guard next to the bedroom. "Wait outside," Dad orders, and they take position on either side of the door as he closes it behind us. And before I even see it coming, his hand shoots out and he slaps me. Hard.

I want to touch the stinging skin—I can't believe that Dad actually laid a hand on me. But I keep my hands by my side and let the anger inside me bubble and boil and rise up from my stomach, through my chest, to sizzle and spit inside my head. I am a volcano of pain. Thousands of atoms of repressed hurt have been scattered throughout my body for years. I've kept them buried and spread out so they wouldn't join up and trigger a cataclysmic explosion. But in one second, Dad's slap pulls all those particles together and molds them into a fiery core of lava. I stand there, steam rising from every pore of my body.

"What the hell have you been doing?" my father hisses.

"The right thing," I respond, not daring to move a muscle. *Keep it inside,* I think, and stare at a vein pulsing in Dad's neck.

"'The right thing,'" my father repeats. Crossing his arms he stalks past me to sit on the edge of a dresser. "And the right thing in this case is going against your own father, undermining one of the biggest deals of his career. No, make that *the* biggest deal of his career.

"I asked you to help me. And what did you do? You stole my contact right from under my nose and delivered her to my competitor."

"Do you even hear yourself?" I ask, incredulous. "That is the most ludicrous spin on what actually happened. You kidnapped a teenage girl and kept her hostage in your home!"

My father shakes his head. "It's all a matter of perception. Yes, I was applying pressure, but she was always free to leave . . . *if* she chose to. And without your intervention, I am sure she and I could have come to an arrangement. In fact, I'm still hoping to do so."

"You are deluded, Dad. Juneau will never willingly help you. You'll have to force her. Which makes you as bad as this Avery freak," I say, gesturing at the door. From somewhere in the house, Avery's still yelling.

"Force is always vital in negotiating, whether subtle or more"— my father weighs his words—"overt."

I just stare at him, wondering when dishonesty became so ingrained in him that he began to believe his own lies. Dad is waiting for a response, but I don't give him the pleasure. Finally he shakes his head.

"Miles, you don't understand how dangerous this situation is that you've gotten yourself mixed up in."

"Really?" I ask, and pull up my T-shirt.

My father gasps as he sees my bullet wound. "My God. What happened to you?" For the first time today he looks genuinely shocked.

"I got shot," I say.

"By whom?" My dad's voice is faint.

"One of Avery's guards. They were chasing us in L.A. when we left your house."

"What?" My dad leaps up and throws open the door. "O'Donnell!" he yells. A second passes and O'Donnell appears in the doorway. "Were you aware that my son was shot?"

"I didn't do it," the guard says, eyes wide.

"It wasn't him," I confirm.

"Your partner shot him?" Dad asks, sounding dangerous.

"He shot *at* him. But I didn't know the boy was hit," O'Donnell says. "And just after, our Jeep flipped, so I was too busy saving my own life to think about his."

"That will be enough," my father says, and shuts the door in the guard's face.

"I almost died," I say. "Juneau saved my life."

I see a flash of pain cross my father's face. A split second of concern. It's the closest thing to love that I've felt from him for years, and my volcano cools a few degrees. Just enough for me to let my mask down. Like the shark he is, my dad spots my weakness and darts at it.

"You have feelings for the girl, don't you?" he asks. "You think you love her."

I hesitate, then nod.

"You're young," he says in a quiet voice. "You don't know what love is."

"Well, I know what it isn't," I say. "It isn't deserting someone when they're sick. When they're desperate."

"So that's what this is all about," Dad says with a cold glint in his eye. "You're angry at me because your mother left. *She* left *us,* Miles. I didn't force her to go."

"How hard did you try to stop her?" I ask.

My father sighs. "It's very hard to live with a person who is depressed. You can't understand how difficult things can be."

"Try me," I say. "Explain. For once."

Dad shakes his head, mournfully. "I bought your mother the best care possible while she was with us. But I have a multibillion dollar company to run. It's not like I could sit around and take care of her myself."

"It all comes down to you" I say. "Your business. Your success. Your money."

"That money pays for everything you have." Dad puts his

hands up to slow things down, and sighs.

"Listen, Miles. Help me convince Juneau, and we can all go back home."

"Why would I do that?"

"I think the question you should be asking is why wouldn't you do that. Like I said, everything you have comes from me. Your future is in my hands. Who else is going to pay for college, support you until you get a degree, find you a decent first job?"

I cross my arms and stare at him, struggling to keep my voice steady. Fighting the volcano. "No, Dad. My future's in my own hands now. I don't want your money. I don't want your help. And I'm not going to help you. Now, are you going to keep me prisoner, or am I free to go?"

"You realize what you're saying? If you walk now, that's the end of you and me."

"'You and me' have been over for a long time." I open the door and am immediately blocked by my father's men.

"Let him go," Dad says. They step aside to let me pass.

I touch my fingers to the burning slap mark on my cheek and, without looking back, I leave my father to go to Juneau.

49

JUNEAU

DAD AND I ARE USHERED INTO THE TROPHY room. The guard instructs us to sit down at a table in one corner. He moves a chair so that he has a direct view of us and sits down, setting his gun across his knees.

I speak in a low voice, but it doesn't matter. The guard isn't paying attention. "What's going on?" I ask.

"Miles came to us and told us he had turned off the electric fences. He got your friend Tallie to drive somewhere nearby so that she could ferry people from the ranch to Roswell. All of the kids and some of the parents went with her, and the rest of the clan is waiting in the woods for a sign from us."

"A sign for what?" I ask.

"For attack. We came here to rescue Badger. We were ready to try negotiation or flat-out escape. But if it takes an armed attack to save him, our people are ready and waiting. Once Badger's safe, our only goal is to flee this place with the least casualties possible."

I nod, one strategy after another forming in my mind. Dad catches my eye. "He's a good one, Juneau."

"Who?" I ask, confused by the abrupt change of subject.

"Miles. That boy shows signs of being a true leader," he says. "Might not know anything about nature. Or fighting"—Dad smiles at a memory, probably something ridiculous Miles did on the way here—"but he's got a good heart. And he cares about you—enough to come here and stand by your side. That says a lot."

"Thanks, Dad," I say, grateful for his opinion. For his approval.

Dad watches me with a look of sadness and resignation. Like he knows things aren't ever going to be the same. "Dad?" I ask.

"Yes, Junebug."

"Whit told me that our ability to Read the Yara comes from the Amrit—that it widens our brains' sensory receptors."

Dad nods. "Your mother and I discovered that during the drug's testing phase."

"So it has nothing to do with our closeness to the Yara and Gaia?" I ask, trying to hide the note of pain in my voice.

"Is that what Whit said?" my father asks.

"He said that the Yara and Gaia are only metaphors, but by encouraging our faith in them, he made the clan stronger. He also told me that my Conjuring is just a result of having a stronger batch of Amrit than everyone else."

"Do you think that's true?" my father asks.

My face melts, and a tear runs down my cheek. I wipe it angrily away. "I don't know what to think anymore. You and the elders lied to us. We were brainwashed." Dad raises a finger, but I cut him off. "And don't tell me that you did it for the good of the clan. I understand that, but it still doesn't make it right. Nothing will make up for the fact that I grew up in a world of lies."

My father nods sadly. "I know. But as for what you're going to believe from now on, that's up to you. You can believe like Whit does . . . that the Yara, Gaia, Reading, your Conjuring . . . that it all comes down to science. Or you can choose to believe that there is more to it than meets the eye."

"What do you believe?" I challenge.

"I believe that Amrit returns us to a state we were meant to be in. A state that humankind was in at the beginning of time. Communing with nature, living long, disease-free lives. It is only over the ages, and with our misuse of the earth that our brains' sensory receptors have narrowed and we lost communion with the Yara. And humankind has suffered the consequences through disease and premature aging. There were men in the Old Testament who were recorded as living for several hundreds of years."

Dad rubs his hand over his head as he considers what to say. "I think that the notion of Gaia had disappeared, but we recovered it. Science doesn't get in the way of that. Science and belief go hand in hand as far as I'm concerned. But it doesn't matter what I think," he concludes. "You have to decide for yourself."

I shake my head and, unable to hide my anger, I cast around

for another subject to discuss. "Saying we get out of here alive, where has the clan decided to go?"

Dad looks down at the floor.

"What?" I ask.

He looks back up at me. "There have been several discussions. Some of the young considered splitting away from the clan. But the general consensus is that if you lead, the clan will follow you."

I shake my head. "That's not going to happen."

Dad nods. He understands. "What do you want to do?"

"I haven't decided."

"I have," he says. "If you decide that you're done with the clan, I will leave them. With you. We can go off on our own somewhere and start a new life."

"But, Dad—" I start. He holds a hand up to stop me.

"But if you don't want to have anything to do with any of us, I will understand. It might be time for you to go off on your own. To discover who you are without us. What your purpose is on earth. If you decide to do that, then I will stay with the clan and go where they decide to go." He reaches toward me and grasps my hand in his.

"It's up to you, Juneau. You don't owe the clan anything. You don't owe me anything." He sighs. "You alone are in control of your future."

I put my arms around my dad, and we sit like that for a very long time, holding on to each other without speaking—because words aren't necessary for what we are telling each other.

50

MILES

I PUSH OPEN THE DOOR TO THE TROPHY ROOM and see Juneau and her father in a corner with the guard sitting across from them, looking annoyed. I pick up a chair and gesture toward them. "May I?" I ask him. Not knowing what to expect any longer, he just rolls his eyes and nods.

I set the chair down next to Juneau. She raises her head from her father's shoulder. "You left the mountain. You came," she says. From her neutral expression, I can't tell if she considers that a good or bad thing.

"Well, I would have felt pretty useless sitting around by myself in the woods," I reply, unable to repress a grin. And although the tension is thick enough to cut with a knife, Juneau gets her quirky half smile and leans forward to give me a hug. And let me tell you, that hug fills every inch of void inside of me left by the conversation with my dad. I don't want to detach. But Walter is sitting there, so I squeeze her hard and then lean back.

"So you met my clan?" Juneau asks.

I nod, smiling. "I like Kenai. I can see why you guys are so close."

"And Nome?"

I feel my face flush, and glance, embarrassed, at her dad. "Let me guess," Juneau says, with a huge smile. "She hit on you."

Now I'm blushing again. I nod, and look around the room to deflect attention from myself. Walter bursts out laughing. "She didn't actually hit on me," I scramble to explain. "She was just . . . complimenting me, I suppose . . ."

But before I can continue my feeble explanation, the sound of a gunshot comes from somewhere inside the house. The door at the end of the library flies open, and Avery steps in, gun in hands. He marches the length of the room, and out into the entryway, shouting to our guard, "Come back me up!"

"But, sir, what about the hostages?"

"I don't give a flip about them, come back me up!" He yells the same thing to the guards in the office, and storms out onto the porch, gun raised.

Walter is on his feet in a second. "I'm going up to Holly. As soon as the coast is clear, I'll get her and Badger out of here." He disappears into the hallway, and Juneau and I are left alone.

"We should go," she says, taking my hand.

"Just wait," I say, "this is important." And digging in my back pocket, I pull out two objects. The first is her opal necklace. "I've been keeping this for you since Salt Lake City. Didn't think you needed it, but I wasn't sure you wanted me to throw it away."

Juneau turns the stone over in her hands, its colors glowing in the low light of the room. Without a word, she pockets it, and looks at me expectantly.

"And this is from Tallie," I say and hand her the note.

"Dad said you had her come pick up the children and others." She pauses and watches me, appraising. "Good move."

"Thanks," I say. "Although I would have preferred you'd said, 'Good move, you extraordinary man. I couldn't have planned it better myself.'"

"You took the words right out of my mouth," Juneau says with a hint of a smile. "I'm not very effusive, am I?"

"'Effusive' isn't the first word that comes to mind when I think of you," I admit. "Which is fine. Effusiveness is totally overrated. I tend to dig the more restrained chicks myself."

Juneau's smile widens. *I'm glad to give her a light moment before she reads Tallie's note,* I think. Reading my mind, she tears her gaze from me, unfolds the note, and takes in the words that I saw back at the clan's encampment.

Juneau. I read the bones one last time before setting out to pick up your people. The battle that I saw coming? It's a physical one. And it will be bloody: Some will die. I'm sorry to tell you that, but once again, I saw that the outcome rests on you. Remember the concept Beauregard gave you: invoke. When it's all over you will have some decisions to make. Know that my house is open to you. My goddesses and I will welcome you, sister in the Sight.

Juneau's jaw clenches as she reads. She does her grow-up-a-decade-in-seconds trick, as all of the problems of the world settle onto her shoulders. I can almost see her sink in her chair as it weighs her down.

She sticks the note in her back pocket with the opal.

I raise an eyebrow. "So?"

"A bloody battle. With deaths."

"And what about the last part?" I ask.

"It's nice to know I have an option," she says carefully.

"You have all the options in the world," I say, and can't wait any longer. I take her in my arms and kiss her. Now that I've met her family and her clan, all the separate brushstrokes of Juneau's life are meeting up and taking form. I see the whole picture. And it's a picture that I love. That I want to be a part of.

Juneau takes my face in her hands and kisses me fiercely, like she knows it might be the last time. Land mines explode through my body as the same powerful energy ricochets between the two of us. I don't want to stop kissing her. I want to stay here, connected to Juneau, generating enough power to light up a city as my lips press her face, her mouth, her neck. But finally she pulls back from me. Taking my hand, she says, "I'm sorry I left you."

"Don't even start," I say. "No explanation needed. I totally get it."

"But I abandoned you," she says with regret.

"You were trying to protect me." She nods, acknowledging. "Just don't do it again," I say. "I don't need protecting."

Juneau presses her lips together.

"What?" I ask.

"You don't have to be a part of this, Miles. Tallie says it will be bloody."

"Are you kidding me?" I say, and catch her up in a my arms. "I'm with you in this," I whisper into her ear, the fuzz of her hair tickling my face. "In everything. Besides, as you might have noticed, you can't stop me. You can only slow me down."

Juneau gives me a wistful smile and grabs my hand. "Let's go then," she says.

We step outside onto the porch and a second later Whit and the doctor crowd out behind us. Everyone is frozen in place, watching the guards who had gone out to patrol the woods and are now heading back toward the house at full speed.

Behind them, Juneau's people are coming, chasing Avery's army out of the forest. The battle has begun.

51

JUNEAU

My people begin the battle by fighting clean—shooting to debilitate. Aiming for limbs. And they are fast enough to avoid the shots of the guards, using trees, bushes, anything they can to shield themselves while they wait for the best possible shot. They have been preparing for a fight against armed brigands for decades. They know what they're doing.

I can tell by their formation—their spread across the yard—what they're trying to do: clear an escape route for my dad and Holly to get Badger out. After that, they too will leave.

If they can, I think, and my heart lurches as, in the glare of the yard's spotlights, I see bullets fly and one of my people fall. It is Sterling. She presses her hand to her leg and crawls behind one of the boulders used in the ranch's landscaping. I breathe a sigh of relief. She's not dead. Yet.

But that one shot changes everything. The time has come—it is a true fight, as Tallie warned. Her words to me weren't just an empty warning. They were a call to action. She was given a message for me, from her own version of the Yara. Or maybe, since all things are indeed connected, from the Yara itself. "Don't Read, don't Conjure," she said. "Invoke."

As the battle rages before me, I feel like time has stopped. I force my mind to clear and immerse myself in the question Tallie's prophecy posed for me. *Invoke what?*

What do you believe in? asks a voice inside. I think of my experience in the last eight weeks. The crumbling of my entire belief system, and my rebuilding of it, stone by solid stone. "Doubt everything," Tallie had told me. "What you decide to keep, you'll be able to be sure of. And what you decide to ditch, you'll replace with what your instincts tell you is true."

My instincts told me that I had a direct link to the Yara—one that is stronger than I ever imagined. That doesn't necessitate the use of totems . . . props. The Yara—the force that flows through all things—flows directly in and out of me.

My father urged me to consider what I believed. To make my own choice about the nature of Gaia and the Yara. And I realize that I already have.

I know—from the depths of my being—that Gaia is made up of more than atoms. Gaia is more than mere science. Gaia—the superorganism—is a living, sentient being that uses its children—those who are one with the Yara—to protect her. Gaia empowers us for a reason and rewards us by preserving us—keeping us safe from disease. From typical human aging.

Whit thought that Amrit would work on anyone—even those who are not Gaia's children. But I watch Avery drop to one knee and begin shooting at the marble stags atop his fountain, and know that Whit was wrong. Gaia knows who will serve her and who won't.

I look up to where the moon glows through the storm clouds and discover that a truth has been born in my mind. Is on the tip of my tongue. Our relationship with Gaia is symbiotic. She uses us to protect her, and in turn she protects us. It is the power of Gaia that I am meant to invoke.

And with that realization, I throw my head back and stretch my arms wide, like I do when I Read the wind. And with everything I am, I call the mother. The source. The vessel for everything that exists. I call her to come to the aid of her people. To protect herself and her own. And, when I open my eyes, she has responded.

The rain intensifies, and torrential winds make it difficult for the fighters to stand their ground. It looks like a monsoon has descended on this patch of the New Mexico desert.

My people know how to deal with the elements. We've lived our lives outdoors. I watch as they use rocks and trees as hunting blinds and the weather as camouflage as they move from position to position. Meanwhile, Avery's army falls apart, scrambling for shelter while shooting haphazardly in all directions.

And then—barely visible through the streaking rain—dark shapes begin to emerge from the forest, slowly separating from the trees. Animals! Gaia has sent the animals. And they are heading directly toward us.

The rain is whipping down, animals are chasing guards out of the woods, and all hell is breaking loose. I make out the forms of large cats, wolves, and even a bear. But the only action that can be clearly seen is within the circular areas lit up by the floodlights stationed around the lawn.

Avery and four guards crouch behind the fountain, guns raised, trying to get a bead on the animals without shooting their own men.

A shot rings out from Avery and his group, and I see a tiger drop to the ground, snarling and injured. "They're killing the animals!" I yell.

Miles has been standing beside me this whole time, but I was so concentrated on my task that I forgot he was there until he takes a step in front of me. He seems to be calculating something as he peers out at the scene, and then I see him narrow his eyes. Suddenly, one of the floodlights explodes, plunging the area around it into pitch dark. My mouth drops open. "Miles!" I exclaim. "Did you do that? Did you Conjure?"

Miles turns his head and gives me this look . . . one I've never seen. It must be what my dad was referring to when he said Miles had the makings of a leader. This is strong Miles. Proud Miles. Miles who is in his element. And I am overwhelmed by a fierce pride. He is with me, this self-assured man who cares for me. *Maybe even loves me,* I think. Because I'm beginning to realize that's what I feel for him.

He sees my emotion and, taking my hand, pulls me next to him. "It's a conversation for another time," he says and points to one side of the yard. "You take those, and I'll get the rest." In under a minute, we have disabled all of the floodlights and submerged the scene into darkness.

"I hope your people can see in the dark," Miles says.

"Oh, trust me . . . they can," I respond, as a familiar whistle comes from behind us. Through the open door I see my dad running down the stairs with Holly, who is carrying a wide-eyed Badger. The white-uniformed housekeeper is with them, leading them down the stairs and then right into the trophy room.

"You go with them," Miles says, and rockets out into the dark, keeping against the front of the house, well out of the line of fire.

"Be safe!" I call.

"Always!" I hear him yell.

I leave the porch and run in after my father, following them through the animal-head room, into the hallway, and through a door into the parking garage. "We'll take the Hummer," the housekeeper yells. "They leave the keys in the ignition." She weaves her way past the other cars toward a monstrous vehicle. She opens the back door for Holly, who climbs in and begins attaching a seat belt around Badger. The housekeeper jumps into the passenger seat, and my father climbs in behind the wheel.

From outside, yells and screams, both human and animal, split the night air. My father turns to me. "Juneau. Come with us."

I shake my head. "I'm staying here. The fight is just beginning.

But you have to follow the plan: Evacuate Badger and his mother."

My father steps down to put his arms around me. He hugs me firmly and says in my ear, "I just want you to be safe."

I lean back and look him in the eyes. "I'll be safe. I promise."

He gets back into the car, strapping himself in and starting the motor. Rolling the window down, he asks, "You'll come meet us in Roswell?"

I nod automatically and then, looking down, shake my head. "No, Dad. I won't be coming."

He nods sadly. "Don't forget that I love you, Junebug," he says.

"I won't forget. Love you, too, Dad."

Putting the car into reverse, he backs up slowly into the gravel drive. In the backseat, Holly pushes Badger's little head down, and leans over out of sight. The housemaid points the way out to my dad, he flicks the lights on, and with a roar tears around the circle, scattering Avery and his guards as he shoots by them and up the driveway. Their escape is so sudden that no one reacts for a few seconds, and by the time shots are fired in their direction, they are too far away to be hit. Wheels screech as the Hummer knocks down the security gate, and continues on, taking a turn onto the main road and disappearing behind the trees.

Out of the corner of my eye, I see three shapes slip into the far end of the garage, and I dive for cover behind one of the remaining cars. I pull the scalpel from my back pocket and push up the blade. I've never stabbed anyone before, but after what I've seen tonight, I'm ready to take out a whole army with just this one tiny blade. My heart beats like mad as I wait for a sound.

A voice pipes up, echoing hollowly through the vast room. "It's us, silly!"

I rise and peer out over the top of the car, to see Nome walking toward me with Kenai beside her and Miles on her other side.

"We come in peace, oh wielder of deadly medical tool," jokes Kenai, and lances something large toward me. I drop the scalpel and catch the crossbow in the same hand. "And here's your knife," Nome says, holding up my bowie in its sheath.

I can't help the smile that spreads across my face. Shaking my head in disbelief at seeing my three favorite people together, I gesture with my head toward the chaos outside. "Ready to fight some brigands?"

52

MILES

WE MOVE OUT OF THE GARAGE TOWARD THE BAT-
tle, and I can't distinguish between the clan members and the
army guys, with the animals just blurs of movement in their
midst. In the dark and the driving rain, the mixture of fur, camouflage, and mud make it hard to see anything at all.

"Do we shoot to kill?" yells Kenai.

"No," calls Juneau, strapping the belt Nome hands her around
her waist, and holstering her bowie knife. "Shoot to maim."

"But, Juneau, these are the guys who killed our dogs. Kidnapped us. Kept us imprisoned," shouts Kenai above the noise.

"Shoot to maim!" Juneau repeats.

"They're probably wearing Kevlar," I shout at her.

All three turn to look at me with blank expressions. I guess

Kevlar's not in the EB. "Bulletproof vests," I say. "It'll be covering their chests and backs."

"Okay," yells Juneau. "Then aim for the arms and legs, Kenai. Nome, slingshot to the faces." And they're off, Juneau with her crossbow, Kenai with a powerful-looking mini-bow and arrows, and Nome with a slingshot and some sharp-looking rocks.

Seeing Juneau and her friends fight is like watching some crazy ninja film where everything is choreographed. It's like they're one person—every move is synchronized with the others.

I lag behind, not daring to fire. I'm scared I'm going to hurt someone on our side. I don't know how Juneau and her friends are doing it, but out of the darkness I hear yells and screams of pain as they pick off one guard after another.

Not far away from me, a one-on-one battle rages between one of Avery's guards and a big guy who was introduced to me back at the camp as Cordova. The guard must have run out of ammunition because he's using the gun like a club, warding off the knife-wielding hunter. Meanwhile, a cougar-looking cat paces back and forth behind the guard, as if waiting for its turn to fight.

And then it dawns on me. The animals are actually fighting *with* the clan.

But that doesn't make any sense. Juneau told me about one of her clanspeople being killed by a bear—they kept one gun in case of animal attack. The clan can Read animals. But the only influence over them I've heard her speak about is her and Whit's recently discovered ability to direct Poe to one place or another.

Something has changed. It seems like nature is on our side

today. And a strange thought comes to mind. Maybe nature *has* come to the rescue. Not nature, but Nature with a capitol *N*. As in Gaia. The torrential rain and wind, just as the clan's attack began. The animals joining in the fight. Maybe Gaia not only exists, but this superorganism thing that Juneau keeps talking about might just have a will. And a means to execute it.

Both guys fall back for a second. I take that chance to lift my crossbow and aim low at the guard, shooting to maim, like Juneau said. It's hard to see clearly, but I focus and exhale and shoot.

For a split second nothing happens, and then the guard drops his gun and falls to the ground, holding his leg in his hands. The cougar pounces, landing in a sprawl on the guard's back, and goes directly for his neck. It whips its head back and forth with a force that reminds me of my mom's cat with its prey, trying to break its neck. The poor chipmunk never had a chance. And neither does the guard.

Cordova leans forward, hands on his knees, trying to stay upright. Looking at me, he nods his thanks, and then collapses to the ground. I throw my crossbow over my back and run for him. "Are you hurt?" I ask, as I sling his arm across my shoulders and help him back to his feet.

"Bullet," he groans, and lifts a hand he's pressing to his side to show oozing blood washing away in the rain.

"Let's get inside," I say, and half carry him to the garage, where the doctor's dark sedan is just starting to back up. I sit Cordova down where the Hummer used to be and walk over to the car. The windows are completely steamed up and the doctor's sticking his head out the driver's side in order to see.

I bend down and knock on the half-open passenger window. "I've got a patient for you," I say.

"Go to hell," the doctor yells.

I raise my crossbow and stick it through the window. "I said, I've got a patient for you," I state. The doctor turns and sees me and sticks his hands in the air. "Turn the car off," I order, "and hand me the keys." The doctor quickly obeys my command. "Now get out of the car and come take care of this gunshot wound. I'll give you your keys back as soon as our man is stable."

Juneau runs in out of the rain. "I saw you come in with Cordova. Is he okay?" she asks breathlessly.

"I'm fine," Cordova says, lying flat on the ground. "It'll take more than a bullet in the side to send me back to Gaia."

The doctor pops his trunk, gets a first aid kit out of the back, and begins to work on the wounded man.

From where it's parked at the side of the garage, the ATV starts up with a roar. Without turning its lights on, it backs up and parks right next to us. One of my father's security men is behind the wheel, the other in the passenger seat, and in the back are my dad and Whit. Juneau's old mentor opens the door and steps down into the shelter of the garage.

He waves his arm toward the backseat and says, "Get in, Juneau."

"You're more delusional than I imagined if you think I'd ever come with you," she replies, and reaches backward for her crossbow. But before she can grasp it, Dad's guard swings a gun out the window. "The man told you to get in," he grunts, and aims the barrel at Juneau's head.

"Hey!" I yell, and make a lunge toward Juneau, but she holds a hand out to stop me.

"Drop your weapon," the man insists.

Juneau unstraps her crossbow and lays it on the ground at her feet. Her eyes never leaving the guard's, she carefully stands and folds her arms over her chest.

"Go ahead," she says. "Shoot me."

53

JUNEAU

"NO NEED FOR HISTRIONICS," WHIT SAYS, QUICKLY stepping between the gun and me. "Just let me talk to her for a second."

"Fine," Mr. Blackwell says sarcastically. "It's a bloodbath out there, but really, Mr. Graves, take your time."

Whit ignores him and, taking my hand, says, "Juneau, we have to talk."

I try to pull it back, but he's got a viselike grip on me. He shoots Miles an annoyed look, and then peers outside where the torrential rain has abruptly stopped, and the noises of warfare are suddenly audible. "Juneau. Come outside and talk to me just for a second. At least say good-bye." And he gives me a sad smile that reminds me of all of the gifts he's ever given me, of the care he took in teaching me, of the last twelve years he's spent preparing me for my role.

"Okay, I'll talk. But, Miles, keep your crossbow trained on Whit, and shoot at my signal."

"Thank you for that vote of confidence, my dear," Whit says, looking ruffled. He lets go of my arm, and I follow him outside to stand a few yards to the side of the garage, away from the fighting. Miles trails behind us, leans against the garage's outer wall, and aims his crossbow at Whit's back.

Whit stands close to me and speaks earnestly. "Juneau, we need you," he pleads.

"You need my blood," I respond.

"Yes, we do. But it's not only I who will profit from it—the whole clan will be rewarded lavishly, as I've tried so hard to explain to you."

"Whit, once the clan is safely out of here, my duty toward them has ended."

"How can you say that?" Whit says, truly surprised. "The clan is your family. Your world."

"My world is deceitful. My world decided for me how I was supposed to think. And I've pretty much had it with being manipulated. Once we're safely out of here, I'm gone."

Whit covers his eyes and exhales deeply. Then he drops his hands and shakes his head. "When it was decided that your mother would be my successor, I knew she would be as powerful a Sage as I had become. We were equals in so many ways.

"But right from the very start, you outshone her. Your gifts were as powerful at five years old as hers were at forty-five. And although her death was tragic, she left you behind to follow what she started. To one day lead the clan.

"Your mother was so proud of you, Juneau. And she would be even prouder if she knew what you were capable of today. You don't understand how important you are. You have the ability to change humanity."

Whit's words are like honey to me. He knows just what buttons to push to make me jump through his hoop. Or at least, he used to. But there is something that is nagging at me, an itch that's just out of reach. I go over the last few minutes in my mind. There's something wrong with what Whit said. And then it occurs to me, and it's like I've been punched hard in the stomach. All of my breath is gone. I just stare at Whit, my eyes bugging out of my head.

"What?" he asks, looking concerned.

I close my eyes, and press my hand against my heart as I try to breathe. "You just told me that it was decided that my mom would succeed you. But every time you've told me this story before, you told me that you chose her to be your successor."

"Well, it's the same thing really," Whit explains quickly.

"No!" I say, cutting him off. "It's not the same. Who decided my mom would succeed you?"

"Well, the elders decided that it was better for power to be alternated instead of being in one person's hands. Your mother, as the only other Conjurer, was the obvious choice to follow me as Sage until you came of age."

"Whit, that's not at all the same thing. My mother was going to replace you." My thoughts are a puzzle, all of its pieces falling together. "And you didn't like that, did you? She tested my blood before she died. You knew then that I could take her place and Amrit could still be made. What would have happened if she had become Sage? Would you have lost your opportunity to go out into the world? To sell the Amrit that she believed was better hidden from the rest of humanity?

"However, if I became Sage, after all of your tutelage, you knew I would be loyal to you. That I wouldn't go against what you wanted . . . to sell Amrit. You didn't do it for the money. Or for the clan. You did it for yourself. For the fame. I know you, Whit. Ensuring that your name would go down in history—that all of those old academic colleagues you always talked about who thought you were crazy would put you on a pedestal—that would be worth more to you, Whit, than any fortune Amrit could bring you."

Whit's eye has started twitching, and the look on his face says that he wants to shut me up.

"You killed my mom, Whit. Didn't you?"

When he speaks, his voice is low and menacing. "I had nothing to do with your mother's death, Juneau."

I study his face. Take a good long look to interpret his features, like he taught me to. "No, you didn't kill her. But you Read that she would die. No one would have thought to Read into the future for her death . . . there was no reason for anyone to think about it. Except you. You sought for anything that might harm her in the coming years. You Read it, and you did nothing to prevent it." I watch his expression and know I am right.

Whit's face contorts into a mask of fury. "That doesn't matter now!" he screams. He grabs my shoulders and starts shaking me. "I trained you, Juneau. Everything you know . . . everything you can do is because of me. You are mine. And you are coming with me right now." He grabs me by the arm and starts dragging me toward the car.

With a keening screech, Poe flies down out of nowhere and dive-bombs Whit's head. Whit drops my hand, and starts swatting the attacking bird away. And then he lets out a shriek and falls to the ground.

A crossbow bolt sticks out of the arm he was dragging me with, and Whit is clawing at it, trying to pull it out. I leap on top of him, knocking him flat on his back, and pinning his shoulders to the ground. Unsheathing my knife, I hold it beneath his chin.

"You let my mom die. You manipulated me. You betrayed our clan."

"Juneau, I did everything for your good, and the good of our people, I swear," Whit says, clenching his teeth in pain. Angry red scratches from Poe's talons crisscross his face, and the stitches in his forehead have torn. The wound from the crash is once again bleeding.

"Liar," I yell. There is a rumbling noise coming from the direction of the forest. A noise that I recognize. I look up and see a shape lumbering toward us in the dark, and I tighten my hold on the knife, grazing the skin under Whit's chin and watching the trickle of blood run down his neck.

Whit's eyes narrow. "What are you going to do, Juneau? Kill

me? Are you going to go against everything you've ever learned and murder a defenseless human being?" He is spitting out the words, daring me to do what he thinks I'm not capable of. *He's right,* I think. With that realization, I make a decision. I'm leaving his fate up to Gaia. I loosen my hold on him, and stand up, straddling his body with my legs.

He stares up at me, victory written on his face. I begin to walk away.

"I knew you couldn't do it," he yells.

"I'm doing what I think is fair," I say. "You didn't kill my mom, but you let her die. I'm just returning the favor."

Whit stares at me, confused, and then follows my gaze as I look behind him. He has time to scream once before the bear is upon him.

I turn and head toward Miles, who is coming across the lawn toward me, crossbow in hand. Tears are streaming down my face, and Miles takes me in his arms and holds me tight.

The car starts up with a roar of the engine, and reverses over the grass toward us, kicking up clods of mud as it comes. Mr. Blackwell's face is illuminated by the interior light, and is twisted in rage.

"Your dad," I yell. "He's coming back for us!"

Miles whips around to look, just as a volley of gunfire blows out the car's windows, and hits one guard who slumps, motionless, out of the passenger window. "Get us the hell out of here!" I hear Mr. Blackwell bellow. The car slams into gear, and Miles and I watch in shock as it speeds away from us. As it passes the house on its way out of the compound, its headlights illuminate the fountain, next to which Hunt Avery lies, writhing on the ground.

He holds one leg with both hands—his paper pants are soaked with rain and blood and have half disintegrated. He meets my gaze and yells, "Help me!"

I pull back from Miles and watch as Avery holds up both hands. "I swear, I'm unarmed," he yells, and groans pitifully. None of his men are anywhere nearby.

I look at Miles, gauging his reaction. "Let him bleed out," he says, stone-faced. I say nothing. He looks back at the pitiful spectacle and then back at me. "Ugh. We have to help him, don't we?" he asks. I nod and we begin walking toward him.

"Okay," Miles says as we approach, "we're going to help move you to the garage, where your doctor is tending the wounded." He positions himself near Avery's head and sets our two crossbows on the ground, while I lean down to grab the injured man's feet.

"That's not going to happen, because I'm the one giving orders here," Avery says, and digging a gun from beneath himself, points it at Miles's head. I reach automatically for my knife, but Avery sees me and, cocking the trigger, says, "Drop it."

I let the knife fall, and copying Miles, hold my hands in the air and back away. Avery presses himself against the side of the fountain, and inches up to a standing position, keeping the gun directed at Miles's face. "You two are going to help me over to those cars over there and get me the hell out of here," he says, gesturing to the garage.

From my left, I hear a familiar sparrow call and, without moving, shift my eyes to see Nome crouching behind a nearby boulder, just out of Avery's sight. Amid all the chaos, she's the only one who's spotted what's happening. I cock my head in Avery's direction, prompting her to shoot him. But Nome holds up her slingshot and pouch, and shakes it to show me it's empty.

She points to her eyes, and then away, indicating that she's going to make a run for it to get backup. I shake my head. If she leaves her hiding place, Avery will see her and could shoot Miles.

As I rack my mind for a solution, I instinctively reach toward my neck to finger my opal like I used to in times of distress. *It's gone*, I remember. And then I freeze.

I watch Avery put one arm around Miles's shoulder and shift his support from the fountain, training the gun on Miles's head. Avery shouts to me, "Miss Newhaven!" and I move toward him as if to give my assistance. For a fraction of a second, he lowers the gun to stretch his arm around me, but it's all the time I need.

I reach into my back pocket, pull out my opal, and throw it toward the rock where Nome is hiding. She stands, catches it, and in one smooth movement, cradles it in her slingshot, pulls the band back, and fires. Avery screams and, dropping the gun, falls backward, tripping over the edge of the fountain into the water. He rises, flailing in the water, as blood spurts from where the gemstone is lodged deep in his eye socket. Then, just as suddenly, he collapses and falls face-first into dark water. His body pops up like a cork and he floats facedown as a cloud of red forms around his head.

54

MILES

THE AFTERMATH IS MESSY. THE CLOUDS HAVE moved away, and the moon is once again visible, casting a silvery light on the lawn. It looks like the scene of a Civil War battlefield, with dead animals and people strewn around, and wounded lying groaning in the mud. The animals that weren't hurt have disappeared into the forest. It's over.

Juneau's people have captured a group of eight guards. The men stand in a circle, hands in the air, as Nome and Kenai point guns at them and wait to be told what to do.

Juneau's expression is haunted as she turns to go to her people. No matter how she felt about Whit in the end, his death traumatized her. Her eyes are red from weeping, and she presses the heels of her palms into them and takes a deep breath. "I have to take care of things," she says.

"I'm right here beside you," I say and scoop up two industrial-sized flashlights that I just scrounged from the garage. Juneau runs her hands through her dripping hair, straightens her clothes, and marches over to the group of prisoners. They squint and frown in the beam of my flashlight.

"Who's here?" she asks, and looking around the darkened battlefield, lets out a loud musical whistle.

Her clanspeople run over to join her. They've swapped their rustic weapons for their enemies' guns.

"I'm going to organize getting us out of here. Is everyone okay with that?" There is a general murmur of consent.

"Elders, do you grant me authority?" Juneau calls. There is an uneasy silence, and one woman steps forward.

"Juneau, dear, during your absence we gave up all authority we once held and abdicated our right to make decisions for the clan. You're in charge here." She steps back, taking her place among the rest of the clan.

Juneau looks uncomfortable, but nods. "All right. Let's start. Is anyone wounded?"

"Sterling's shot in the leg, but she's going to be okay. Palmer's with her," someone says.

"There's a doctor in the garage taking care of Cordova," says Juneau. "Go tell him he'll be tending to Sterling next." The woman nods and jogs away from the group.

Juneau points to two teenage boys that are standing by. "Homer, Tok, you do a sweep of the lawn. Pick up the weapons, even from the dead, and pile them on the front porch. We don't want anyone regaining consciousness within reach of a machine gun." The teenagers whisper a few words to each other and then take off in different directions.

"Elders, take one of these men down to the barracks. Have him show you where the vehicles are. Drive three of them back here." The three elders nod and, taking one of the guards by the arm, lead him away.

Juneau faces the group of prisoners. "This is how it's going to work. We're giving you three vehicles. You take care of your dead and wounded. Load them into the vehicles, and then leave immediately."

She turns to a tall, thin woman with sandy hair pulled back into a ponytail. "Esther, look after the animals. The rest of you, assist her. Animals that are dying, send them back to Gaia. If any need more care than you can give them here, load them into a truck and take them into Roswell."

Juneau turns to one last clan member. "Lakes, come with me." She takes the gun Lakes is holding and hands it to me. "Guard the captives with Kenai and Nome," she orders, and then whispers, "Please," and gives me a secretive wink.

Juneau and Lakes walk a ways away, and Juneau begins explaining something to him. After a minute, it looks like they're arguing. Lakes is upset about whatever she's telling him. But in the end, he seems to give in, and the two walk back to us, Juneau with her chin-up expression and Lakes looking grim.

From the barracks comes the sound of motors starting, and in a minute three utility trucks pull around the drive and in front of the house. The elders step out from behind the wheels, and with Lakes, Nome, and Kenai, they spread out with the guards to pick up their wounded and dead and load them into the vehicles. And although they follow the guards with guns in hand, it looks like they don't even need the weapons. The guards just want to get out of there. As they work, they throw apprehensive glances at the corpse of their ex-boss floating in the fountain.

Finally they all take off in a slow-moving convoy and disappear from sight. The clan members organize in front of Juneau, and she holds up a hand to signal that she's going to speak.

"Go back down to the barracks and take all of the vehicles you can. We've got four elders here, but anyone else who wants to try their hand at driving is welcome. Once you get to Roswell, you're going to need as many vehicles as possible.

"That's the last instruction I have for you. From now on you're on your own. Whether or not the clan decides to stick together is up to you. But I won't be coming along."

There is a gasp from those assembled. "Not right away," Juneau clarifies. "You've all had weeks to work this out among yourselves. To think about the past and talk about the future. To forgive one another," she says, looking directly at the elders.

"I've already discussed this with my dad," she continues. "He told me you were all ready to follow me. Thank you for being willing to entrust your future to me. But I can't lead you in wisdom if I don't even know the truth myself.

"I need time to think things out. To figure out what I believe apart from what we've been raised with. I'm sure a lot of you will be doing the same thing, and I want to know what conclusions we all come to. So I'm not abandoning you. Just . . . taking a break. I'll keep in touch with you through Dad. So this is just a good-bye for now."

Her people take her one by one into their arms, hugging her and then letting her go. Juneau fights to stay composed as she exchanges words with her clan members.

Kenai and Nome hang back. Juneau's obviously already spoken to them, because they show no surprise.

Once the last person has embraced Juneau, she holds up her hand once again. "I've asked Lakes to organize the practical matters for those of the clan who decide to stick together. As leader of the hunters, he'll serve best as your tactical planner and will work with the elders, who know about this country and how things work."

Juneau looks around the group. "I send my love with you on the path we all will take." And then she turns her back to them, takes my hand, and with Nome and Kenai silently following, leads us back toward the house.

55

JUNEAU

SAYING GOOD-BYE TO MY PEOPLE SO SOON AFTER finding them is one of the hardest things I've ever done. Part of me wants to go with them—to join them in Roswell. To catch up on the time we've lost. To talk through it all until I understand more: why the elders did what they did, and how their children are dealing with it.

Instead, I take Miles's hand and walk away. Leave them to clean up the mess—both on the battlefield and in their own lives. Nome and Kenai fall in behind us. They are dirty, wet, scratched-up . . . and their eyes are shining like sunlight on gemstones. After a month of captivity, they had been yearning for a fight, and the post-battle adrenaline makes them both look ready to jump out of their skins.

One car remains in the garage, and the way Miles is staring at it—like he wants to eat it whole—makes me smile. "Is it something special?" I ask.

He nods. "A classic Rolls-Royce Silver Shadow."

I shrug. "A car's a car, isn't it?"

Miles shakes his head, and though his face is smudged with dirt, sweat, and blood, he is glowing with awe. "No," he says. "Not this one."

It's amazing—even after all the trauma we've lived through today—Miles is able to make me smile. I wrap my arms around him and give him a quick, sweaty kiss.

Turning to include the others, I ask Miles, "How far away did you park the pickup truck?"

"About a half-hour drive," he replies.

I nod, thinking. "Okay, Nome. You get behind the wheel. Miles has fifteen minutes to teach you to drive, and then we'll switch and have Kenai learn. I'll need you to drive yourselves to Roswell once we get the truck."

I've never seen Nome move so fast. She's behind the wheel in seconds flat, and Miles has to physically restrain her from pushing all of the buttons. Kenai and I climb in the back and within minutes we are backing out of the garage and making our way across the battlefield.

Our buoyant mood dissolves as we pass the destruction. Oddly, looking out at it from behind the car windows makes it feel more real. More horrific. Some of my clan members look up from what they're doing and solemnly wave as we drive by. Others don't even look up. The cycle of truth telling and forgiveness has just begun. Who knows where it will lead? Will the clan band together like survivors of yet another catastrophe, or will the past be too painful for some to reconcile? Not all will stay. And those who do will have to start from scratch. Begin something new that is based on truth.

As we reach the top of the hill and turn toward the exit, Kenai breaks the silence. "So, great leader, you said we needed to talk." He cracks his knuckles to let off excess energy.

"I'm not the leader anymore. Won't ever be," I say.

"Yeah, right," Nome says, turning around to look at me, and the car swerves to the right.

"Eyes on the road!" Miles yells, and grabs the steering wheel.

Nome adjusts the car and peers at me through the rearview mirror. "If you're not leader, who's going to be? Me?"

"Gaia help us," murmurs Kenai, and Nome gives him an indignant "hey!"

Kenai nudges me gently. "Can I assume these emergency driving lessons mean you definitely can't be talked into coming to Roswell with us?"

I shake my head. "No, but I'd like you to go—to help with the regrouping of the clan. Stay while decisions are being made. Decide where you want to go. And once everyone makes their choices, I want you to come find me and tell me."

"I know the reasons you gave the group for not coming," Kenai says, "but there's more, isn't there?"

I lean my head back against the seat and sigh. "They're going to make me be leader whether I want to or not. If I go to Roswell, everyone will look to me for direction. I don't even want to be a factor in their decision-making. I can't be there." I look Kenai in the eyes, and see that he understands. Agrees, even. "I'll decide what I'm going to do, though, once I hear the decision of the clan."

We ride in silence, until a few minutes later Miles has Nome pull over to the side of the road, and shows her how to put the car in park. Kenai takes the driver's seat, and Nome climbs into the back with me, leaning over first for a meaning-laden hug. Kenai pulls onto the road with a jerk, and I quickly show her how to put the seat belt on.

She watches me with wide eyes. "Where will you go?"

At this, Miles turns around, and a whole wordless conversation takes place between us. Finally he says, "I'm going wherever you're going."

"Are you sure?" I make my expression blank and wait. It doesn't matter what I want, this decision is up to him.

He nods, showing me that his choice is made. "Besides, you need me. I'm your oracle—how are you going to figure out what to do without me?" He raises one eyebrow, and I can't help but crack a smile.

The tension broken, Nome says, "Okay, then, Oracle. Enlighten us as to what Juneau is planning."

Miles flashes a smile at me. "I don't have to say it as a riddle, do I?"

I laugh. "No. I prefer straight-out prediction, please."

He makes sure Kenai is doing okay with the driving, and then turns back to us. He squints, as if he's looking at something far in the distance, and strokes his chin seriously. "I see a very cold place in Miles and Juneau's immediate future. A road trip to Alaska. A plane would be more convenient, of course, but since Juneau has no ID"—Miles glances at Nome and clarifies—"identification papers, without even taking into account her acute hatred of air travel, they will travel by car and boat."

He looks at me for reassurance, and I grin. "Sounds good so far. Go on."

"Once in the land of tundra, they will proceed immediately to a certain dog shelter, where a very joyful reunion will take place."

Tears spring to my eyes, and I cover my mouth to hold in my emotion. Miles pretends he doesn't see and continues.

"With their enthusiastic dog companions, Juneau and Miles will venture to the emergency shelter and on to the yurt encampment to retrieve everything of value, thus ensuring the economic future of the clan."

I compose myself and say to Nome and Kenai, "He's right. With what I've seen our gold can buy, we'll all have enough for a good start in this new world."

"And finally," Miles says, wrapping up, "the companions make their way back to the mainland, traveling to Utah to stay with a crazy mountain woman in her ecologically correct cabin in the woods, allowing Juneau time to . . ." He hesitates and glances at Nome and Kenai.

"Go ahead and say it," I urge.

"De-brainwash—" Miles chances.

"We could all use some of that!" Kenai says, roaring with laughter, and the car swerves slightly before he straightens it out.

Miles smiles and continues, "While she awaits word from her faithful friends about the fate of her clan members. The end."

"Bravo!" Nome shouts, and we both give him a round of applause.

Miles looks pleased with himself. "Did I get close?" he asks me.

I'm awestruck by his accuracy. Fake oracle prophecies aside, this boy really knows me. "It's exactly what I was thinking," I reply.

"What did I tell you?" Miles says. "You need me." He shrugs, as though it's obvious, and turns to point at something ahead of us.

Our headlights illuminate the forest-green pickup truck ahead, and Kenai pulls smoothly over to park next to it. As we get out of the car, a cawing noise comes from above, and Poe swoops down to land on the roof of the pickup. "Look who's been following us," I say to Miles. "You didn't figure him into the prophecy."

"Well, of course he's coming with us," Miles says, shrugging as if it were obvious. "What would a trip to Alaska be without our favorite messenger raven?"

"How about you?" I ask Nome and Kenai. "Have you thought

about what you'll do when this is over?"

Kenai looks at Nome, and back at me. "We've been talking about it since we were kidnapped: what we would do in every possible scenario. We decided that if we all got out of there alive, we would set out on our own for a while, hopefully with you and"—he makes a welcome gesture toward Miles—"with whatever random men you happened to pick up along the way, of course." Miles rolls his eyes but nods, accepting the sidekick role.

Nome speaks up. "At first, we were both pretty bitter and twisted. We've forgiven our parents now . . . at least we've started to. But we both think we need time away from them. They and the other elders are still learning how to live with themselves." She wrinkles her nose. "It could be messy."

"Where will you go?" I ask.

"Why don't we consult the oracle?" Nome suggests, and nudges Miles.

"Let's see," he says, and closes his eyes. "After you two bring the clan's news to Juneau, we form our own mini-clan and take off for a year or so on an epic road trip of adventure." He opens one eye to see my reaction, but quickly closes it again as Nome throws herself on him, hugging him around the neck.

"I am totally up for that plan," Kenai says, nodding in approval.

"Me too," says Nome, and leans back to look Miles in the face. "You are perfect for Juneau. And, seeing that I've known her since we were both toddlers, I don't give that compliment lightly." She leans in to kiss him on the cheek, and then skips away with the keys to the car, which Miles had been holding in his hand. "I'm driving first!" she crows, dangling the keys in front of Kenai before leaping into the driver's seat and slamming the door behind her.

Kenai sticks his hand out to Miles, who shakes it, much to Kenai's amusement. I look at him quizzically. "Inside joke," he tells me, and then gives me one of his signature Kenai bear hugs. "We'll get directions from Tallie," he says. "See you in Utah. Stay safe."

He disappears into the car, and the tires screech as Nome turns around and heads back in the direction we came from.

"We couldn't have taken the Rolls?" Miles asks.

"Would it stand out parked at the foot of a mountain in Utah?" I respond.

"Point taken," he says, sighing, and watches until the car disappears around a corner.

Poe caws loudly, and flies from the top of the pickup to land on my shoulder. Miles takes the truck keys out of his pocket and holds them out, offering. I shake my head. "You drive," I say. "I have a lot to think about."

We get into the pickup. Poe perches on the seatback between us, and immediately begins cleaning his feathers. "Is he like our bird-child now?" Miles asks, nudging Poe closer to me get the tail out of his face.

"As long as he wants to hang around," I say with a smile. Miles shrugs his acceptance and starts the engine. He pulls out into the road and turns the truck around to steer us back toward Albuquerque.

We drive in silence for a few minutes before I speak. "There were some things you left out of that prophecy," I say.

"I know," Miles admits. "I only said the things I was sure of. I left out the rest."

"Like . . . ," I prod.

"Amrit," he replies. "I know what a negative thing it is to you now that Whit sold your people out to make a buck off it."

"Or make his name from it," I add. Miles just nods. Waits.

I sigh. "Part of me wants to never make it again. To make the Rite a thing of the past. But I know I want to use it first."

Miles breathes a sigh of relief. I take his hand. "Because of you. Because of my people. Because it's what I've shaped my life around. I'll offer it to Nome and Kenai, too . . . for the same reasons."

"How about . . . other people?" Miles asks, and something in his voice tells me exactly who he is thinking of. His mother. I've thought about her, too.

Could Amrit cure mental illness? What if it didn't and she took it? Would it consign her to hundreds of years, or more, of unabated depression? I choose my words carefully. "That's something we'll both have to think about."

"Would you like to meet her?" Miles asks, glancing over at me.

"I was thinking that could be the first stop on our epic road trip of adventure," I say. He puts his arm around me and pulls me close.

"So what about Yale?" I ask.

"Looks like I'm going to have plenty of time to get a degree," he replies. "Or ten. I don't need to start right away."

I lean my head on his shoulder and watch the landscape speed by. We drive in silence for a while before Miles speaks again. "This is a weird place to be in. For both of us, but more for you than for me."

"What do you mean?" I ask.

"When we were talking about an epic road trip, I thought of how your life up to now is already like an epic story. Your old life in Alaska is like an entire book that you've already worked your way through from start to finish. It's over. Done. I know you'll want to read it and reread it until you understand what happened—to make sense out of everything. But pretty soon you'll be able to close it and move on to a new one. One you haven't even cracked open. It's your new life. Just about to start."

My heart is in my throat—I can't even talk. This boy knows me better than I know myself.

"So we're in a weird place right now," he concludes. "It's a no-man's-land between two epic stories. After the end of one . . . waiting until the beginning of the next."

"What kind of book will the new one be?" I ask, leaning back to look at him—this muddy, brave, *wise* boy who doesn't even resemble the person he was a few weeks ago. He earned my respect. He earned my friendship. And now he has earned my love.

"A mystery," he replies with a grin, "with a kick-ass heroine, a hero who is so hopelessly into her that he'll follow any crazy plan she suggests, and a bit of magic and action thrown in to keep things interesting."

I can't help but beam. "Mysteries are my favorite."

Miles gives me his quirky smile. "Finally it looks like we've got something in common." He pulls me close to him, and we begin our drive across America. Away from the darkness of our old lives and toward the bright sparkling future of the new.

ACKNOWLEDGMENTS

THIS BOOK WAS NOT CONCEIVED IN A VOID. MY own childhood provided me with a fierce will to survive and a need to search for my own path to truth. Although I didn't have Miles, Poe, and the Yara to accompany me on that path, there were others who helped me along my way: Madeleine L'Engle, Robert Heinlein, Isaac Asimov, C.S. Lewis, Ursula Le Guin, J.R.R. Tolkien, Mark Helprin, Charles Williams, Ray Bradbury, Walker Percy, George MacDonald, Anne McCaffrey, and a host of others. These individuals helped me escape my internal world and learn to see the one outside me through different eyes. They saved me. Books saved me. Story saved me.

As for bringing the story of another survivor and truth-seeker to the page, I want to thank Tara Weikum and Christopher Hernandez for helping me organize my thoughts on Juneau, and prodding me about the ideas that weren't quite true until I took them further. Thank you for your guidance and wise advice.

Once again, thank you to my agent, Stacey Glick, for finding the perfect home for Juneau and Miles.

My friend and beta reader Claudia Depkin had the patience and grace to read the story chunk by chunk as I churned it out, and then read it all over again . . . several times. Thank you for your encouragement and feedback, Claudia. Gratitude as well to fellow writer and wereboar sister Anna Carey for reading, reassuring, and advising.

Thank you to my assistant, Alana, for all of her help in organizing me, proofreading, coming up with discussion group questions, and all of the other tasks I set for her. I forgive you for leaving me for university, and have no doubt you have a very bright future, whether in books, physics, or whatever else you put your mind to.

Thank you to everyone who contributed to *Until the Beginning*'s final package. Copyeditors Melinda Weigel, Alexandra Alexo, and Anne Heausler helped clean things up inside, while the outside was treated with grandeur and beauty by Jenna Stempel, Alison Donalty, and Craig Shields.

There were several batcaves used in the making of *Until the Beginning*: besides my regular haunt in Paris was a brownstone in Brooklyn with Lisa Steiner; a cozy flat on the Isle of Bute, Scotland, with Lisa O'Donnell; a home in the desert in Lake Havasu, Arizona, with my cousin Diana Canfield; and a convent-school-turned-artist-retreat near Reims, France, the Performing Arts

Forum, run by the indefatigable Jan Ritsema. It seems that one must travel in order to create a road-trip book.

Finally, and most important, I want to thank my readers for loving my stories and for telling me so. Your enthusiasm and support means everything to me.

PROLOGUE

THE FIRST TIME I HAD SEEN THE STATUE IN THE fountain, I had no idea what Vincent was. Now, when I looked at the ethereal beauty of the two connected figures—the handsome angel, with his hard, darkened features focused on the woman cradled in his outstretched arms, who was all softness and light—I couldn't miss the symbolism. The angel's expression seemed desperate. Obsessed, even. But also tender. As if he was looking to her to save him, and not vice versa. And all of a sudden, Vincent's name for me popped into my mind: *mon ange*. My angel. I shivered, but not from the cold.

Jeanne had said that meeting me had transformed Vincent. I had given him "new life." But was he expecting me to save his soul?

ONE

MOST SIXTEEN-YEAR-OLDS I KNOW WOULD DREAM of living in a foreign city. But moving from Brooklyn to Paris after my parents' death was anything but a dream come true. It was more like a nightmare.

I could have been anywhere, really, and it wouldn't have mattered—I was blind to my surroundings. I lived in the past, desperately clinging to every scrap of memory from my former life. It was a life I had taken for granted, thinking it would last forever.

My parents had died in a car accident just ten days after I got my driver's license. A week later, on Christmas Day, my sister, Georgia, decided that the two of us would leave America to live with our father's parents in France. I was still too shell-shocked to put up a fight.

We moved in January. No one expected us to go back to school right away. So we just passed the days trying to cope in our own desperate ways. My sister frantically blocked her sorrow by going out every night with the friends she had made during our summer visits. I turned into an agoraphobic mess.

Some days I would get as far as walking out of the apartment and down the street. Then I found myself sprinting back to the protection of our home and out of the oppressive outdoors, where it felt like the sky was closing in on me. Other days I would wake up with barely enough energy to walk to the breakfast table and then back to my bed, where I would spend the rest of the day in a stupor of grief.

Finally our grandparents decided we should spend a few months in their country house. "For a change of air," Mamie said, which made me point out that no difference in air quality could be as dramatic as that between New York and Paris.

But as usual, Mamie was right. Spending the springtime outdoors did us a world of good, and by the end of June we were, if only mere reflections of our previous selves, functional enough to return to Paris and "real life." That is, if life could ever be called "real" again. At least I was starting over in a place that I love.

There's nowhere I'd rather be than Paris in June. Even though I've spent every summer there since I was a baby, I never fail to get that "Paris buzz" as I walk down its summer streets. The light is different from anywhere else. As if pulled straight out of a fairy tale, the wand-waving brilliance makes you feel like absolutely anything could happen to you at any moment and you wouldn't even be surprised.

But this time was different. Paris was the same as it had always been, but I had changed. Even the city's sparkling, glowing air couldn't penetrate the shroud of darkness that felt superglued to my skin. Paris is called the City of Light. Well, for me it had become the City of Night.

I spent the summer pretty much alone, falling quickly into a solitary routine: eat breakfast in Papy and Mamie's dark, antique-filled apartment and spend the morning entrenched in one of the small dark Parisian cinemas that project classic films round-the-clock, or haunt one of my favorite museums. Then return home and read the rest of the day, eat dinner, and lie in bed staring at the ceiling, my occasional sleep jam-packed with nightmares. Get up. Repeat.

The only intrusions on my solitude were emails from my friends back home. "How's life in France?" they all started.

What could I say? *Depressing? Empty? I want my parents back?* Instead I lied. I told them I was really happy living in Paris. That it was a good thing Georgia's and my French was fluent because we were meeting so many people. That I couldn't wait to start my new school.

My lies weren't meant to impress them. I knew they felt sorry for me, and I only wanted to reassure them that I was okay. But each time I pressed send and then read back over my email, I realized how vast the gulf was between my real life and the fictional one I created for them. And that made me even more depressed.

Finally I realized that I didn't actually want to talk to anyone. One night I sat for fifteen minutes with my hands poised above the keyboard, searching desperately for something even slightly positive to say to my friend Claudia. I clicked out of the message and, after taking a deep breath, completely deleted my email address from the internet. Gmail asked me if I was sure. "Oh yeah," I said as I clicked the red button. A huge burden lifted from my shoulders. After that I shoved my laptop into a drawer and didn't open it again until school started.

Mamie and Georgia encouraged me to get out and meet people. My sister invited me along with her and her group of friends to sunbathe on the artificial beach set up next to the river, or to bars to hear live music, or to the clubs where they danced the weekend nights away. After a while they gave up asking.

"How can you dance, after what happened?" I finally asked Georgia one night as she sat on her bedroom floor, putting on makeup before a gilt rococo mirror she had pulled off her wall and propped up against a bookcase.

My sister was painfully beautiful. Her strawberry blond hair was in a short pixie cut that only a face with her strikingly high cheekbones could carry off. Her peaches-and-cream skin was sprinkled with tiny freckles. And like me, she was tall. Unlike me, she had a knockout figure. I would kill for her curves. She looked twenty-one instead of a few weeks shy of eighteen.

"It helps me forget," she said, applying a fresh coat of mascara. "It helps me feel alive. I'm just as sad as you are, Katie-Bean. But this is the only way I know of dealing with it."

I knew she was being honest. I heard her in her bedroom the

nights she stayed in, sobbing like her heart had been shattered to bits.

"It doesn't do you any good to mope," she continued softly. "You should spend more time with people. To distract you. Look at you," she said, putting her mascara down and pulling me toward her. She turned my head to face the mirror next to hers.

To see us together, you would never guess we were sisters. My long brown hair was lifeless; my skin, which thanks to my mother's genes never tans, was paler than usual.

And my blue-green eyes were so unlike my sister's sultry, heavy-lidded "bedroom eyes." "Almond eyes" my mom called mine, much to my chagrin. I would rather have an eye shape that evoked steamy encounters than one described by a nut.

"You're gorgeous," Georgia concluded. My sister ... my only fan.

"Yeah, tell that to the crowd of boys lined up outside the door," I said with a grimace, pulling away from her.

"Well, you're not going to find a boyfriend by spending all your time alone. And if you don't stop hanging out in museums and cinemas, you're going to start looking like one of those nineteenth-century women in your books who were always dying of consumption or dropsy or whatever." She turned to me. "Listen. I won't bug you about going out with me if you will grant me one wish."

"Just call me Fairy Godmother," I said, trying to grin.

"Take your frickin' books and go outside and sit at a café. In the sunlight. Or the moonlight, I don't care which. Just get outdoors and suck some good pollution-ridden air into those wasted, consumptive, nineteenth-century lungs of yours. Surround yourself with people, for God's sake."

"But I *do* see people," I began.

"Leonardo da Vinci and Quentin Tarantino don't count," she interrupted.

I shut up.

Georgia stood and laced the strap to her tiny, chic handbag over her arm. "It's not *you* who is dead," she said. "Mom and Dad are. And *they* would want you to live."

TWO

"WHERE ARE YOU GOING?" MAMIE ASKED, STICK-ing her head out of the kitchen as I unlocked the front door.

"Georgia said my lungs were in need of Paris pollution," I responded, slinging my bag across my shoulder.

"She's right," she said, coming to stand in front of me. Her forehead barely reached my chin, but her perfect posture and regulation three-inch heels made her seem much taller. Only a couple of years from seventy, Mamie's youthful appearance sub-tracted at least a decade from her age.

When she was an art student, she had met my grandfather, a successful antiques dealer who fawned over her like she was one of his priceless ancient statues. Now she spent her days restoring old paintings in her glass-roofed studio on the top floor of their apartment building.

"Allez, file!" she said, standing before me in all her compactly

packaged glory. "Get going. This town could use a little Katya to brighten it up."

I gave my grandmother a kiss on her soft, rose-scented cheek and, grabbing my set of keys off the hall table, made my way through the heavy wooden doors and down the spiral marble staircase, to the street below.

Paris is divided into twenty neighborhoods, or arrondissements, and each one is called by its number. Ours, the seventh, is an old, wealthy neighborhood. If you wanted to live in the trendiest part of Paris, you would not move to the seventh. But since my grandparents live within walking distance of the boulevard Saint-Germain, which is packed with cafés and shops, and only a fifteen-minute wander to the river Seine's edge, I was certainly not complaining.

I stepped out the door into the bright sunlight and skirted past the park in front of my grandparents' building. It is filled with ancient trees and scattered with green wooden park benches, giving the impression, for the couple of seconds it takes to pass it, that Paris is a small town instead of France's capital city.

Walking down the rue du Bac, I passed a handful of way-too-expensive clothes, interior decor, and antiques stores. I didn't even pause as I walked past Papy's café: the one he had taken us to since we were babies, where we sat and drank mint-flavored water while Papy chatted with anything that moved. Sitting next to a group of his friends, or even across the terrace from

Papy himself, was the last thing I wanted. I was forced to find my own café.

I had been weighing the idea of two other local spots. The first was on a corner, with a dark interior and a row of tables wrapped around the building on the sidewalk. It was probably quieter than my other option. But when I stepped inside I saw a line of old men sitting silently on their stools along the bar counter with glasses of red wine in front of them. Their heads slowly pivoted to check out the newcomer, and when they saw me they looked as shocked as if I were wearing a giant chicken costume. *They might as well have an "Old Men Only" sign on the door*, I thought, and hurried on to my second option: a bustling café a few blocks farther down the *rue*.

Because of its glass facade, the Café Sainte-Lucie's sun-lit interior felt spacious. Its sunny outdoor terrace held a good twenty-five tables, which were usually full. As I made my way toward an empty table in the far corner, I knew this was my café. I already felt like I belonged here. I stuck my book bag under the table and sat down with my back to the building, securing a view of the entire terrace as well as the street and sidewalk beyond.

Once seated, I called to the waiter that I wanted a lemonade, and then pulled out a paperback copy of *The Age of Innocence*, which I had chosen from the summer reading list for the school I'd be starting in September. Enveloped by the smell of strong coffee wafting up from all sides, I drifted off into my book's distant universe.

"Another lemonade?" The French voice came floating through the streets of nineteenth-century New York in my mind's eye, jerking me rudely back to the Parisian café. My waiter stood beside me, holding his round tray stiffly above his shoulder and looking every bit like a constipated grasshopper.

"Oh, of course. Um . . . I think I'll take a tea, actually," I said, realizing that his intrusion meant I had been reading for about an hour. There is an unspoken rule in French cafés that a person can sit at their table all day if they want, as long as they order one drink per hour. It's kind of like renting a table.

I halfheartedly glanced around before looking back down at the page, but did a double take when I noticed someone staring at me from across the terrace. And the world around me froze when our eyes met.

I had the strangest feeling that I knew the guy. I'd felt that way with strangers before, where it seemed like I'd spent hours, weeks, even years with the person. But in my experience, it had always been a one-way phenomenon: The other person didn't even notice me.

This was not the case now. I could swear he felt the same.

From the way his gaze held steady, I knew he had been staring at me for a while. He was breathtaking, with longish black hair waving up and back from a broad forehead. His olive skin made me guess that he either spent a lot of time outside or came from somewhere more southern and sunbaked than Paris. And the eyes that stared back into my own were as blue as the sea, lined with thick black lashes. My heart lurched within my chest, and it felt like someone had squeezed all the air out of my lungs. In spite of myself, I couldn't break our gaze.

A couple of seconds passed, and then he turned back to his two friends, who were laughing rowdily. The three of them were young and beautiful and glowing with the kind of charisma that justified the fact that every woman in the place was under their spell. If they noticed it, they didn't let on.

Sitting next to the first boy was a strikingly handsome guy, built like a boulder, with short, cropped hair and dark chocolate skin. As I watched him, he turned and flashed me a knowing smile, as if he understood how I couldn't resist checking him out. Shaken out of my voyeuristic trance, my eyes darted down to my book for a few seconds, and by the time I dared peer back up he had looked away.

Next to him, facing away from me, was a wiry-built boy with slightly sunburned skin, sideburns, and curly brown hair, animatedly telling a story that sent the other two into peals of laughter.

I studied the one who had first caught my attention. Although he was probably a couple of years older than me, I guessed he wasn't yet twenty. He leaned back in his chair in that suave Frenchman manner. But something slightly cold and hard about the set of his face suggested that the easygoing pose was only a facade. It wasn't that he looked cruel. It was more that he seemed . . . dangerous.

Although he intrigued me, I consciously erased the black-haired boy's face from my mind, convinced that perfect looks plus danger probably equaled bad news. I picked up my book and turned my attention back to the more reliable charms of

Newland Archer. But I couldn't help myself from taking another peek when the waiter returned with my tea. Annoyingly, I wasn't able to get back into the rhythm of my book.

When his table stood up a half hour later, it caught my attention. You could feel concentrated feminine tension in the air as the three guys walked past the terrace. As if a team of Armani underwear models had walked straight up to the café and, in unison, ripped off all their clothes.

The elderly woman next to me leaned in to her coffee companion and said, "It's suddenly feeling unseasonably hot, don't you agree?" Her lady friend giggled in agreement, fanning herself with the plastic-coated menu and ogling the boys. I shook my head in disgust—there was no way those guys couldn't feel the dozens of eyes shooting darts of lust into their backs as they walked away.

Suddenly, proving my theory, the black-haired one glanced back at me and, confirming that I was watching him, smiled smugly. Feeling the blood rush to my cheeks, I hid my face in my book so he wouldn't have the satisfaction of seeing me blush.

I tried to read the words on the page for a few minutes before giving up. My concentration broken, I paid for my drinks, and leaving a tip on the table, I made my way back to the rue du Bac.

Can't get enough of the DIE FOR ME series?

Don't miss these digital original novellas
set in the world of the Die For Me trilogy!

Available as ebooks only.

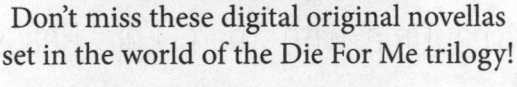

JOIN THE

Epic Reads

COMMUNITY

THE ULTIMATE YA DESTINATION

◀ **DISCOVER** ▶
your next favorite read

◀ **MEET** ▶
new authors to love

◀ **WIN** ▶
free books

◀ **SHARE** ▶
infographics, playlists, quizzes, and more

◀ **WATCH** ▶
the latest videos

◀ **TUNE IN** ▶
to Tea Time with Team Epic Reads

Find us at **www.epicreads.com** and @epicreads